Dismissed Dead

Dismissed Dead

ROD BRAMMER

To Harry ~ June
my friends.

Rod Brammer. 20th Sept 09

I'm Jane's toy boy
E&T wally.

First published 2009 by Elliott and Thompson Limited

27 John Street, London WC1N 2BX

www.eandtbooks.com

ISBN 978-1-9040-2772-0

A CIP catalogue record for this book is available from
the British Library.

Printed in the UK by J F Print

Typeset in Sabon

Whoever lives true life, will love true love.
'I learnt to love that England.'

ELIZABETH B. BROWNING

One

WHEN A SON is born into a middle-class family, the father, replete with pride and the desire to do the right thing, will straightaway get the boy's name down for Eton, Winchester or Harrow, in the hope his son will be grateful for this far-sighted indulgence. Happier though, is the son whose background is in land and sport, and has been for countless generations, and whose father leaves immediately for the gunshop to buy a 'best' gun for the squalling, wrinkled creature just issued from his mother's womb. His next duty would be to put his son's name on the waiting list for a chance to be selected, in the distant future of course, to have a rod on the River Test.

Keith Finlay was from such a family and on this particular day was fishing at Testwood. It was February and the wind was blowing from the east, bringing with it scuddy sleet showers and frozen rain. Finlay knew the chances of catching a salmon were remote, but not impossible and anyway, it was his last day of leave and he wanted to fish. The river now had stopped running at the top of the tide and the pool beneath his feet was about eight feet deep, clear enough for him to see the lure coming around in a gentle arc, deep and slow as conditions dictated. He flicked the lure out again, hoping for that momentary flash of a moving fish before it chased and grabbed the lure, but nothing happened. He stopped fishing and sought through his pockets to find his cigarettes, lit one with wet, frozen hands and, feeling the smoke coursing through his lungs, leant against the bridge. He was content.

There was a brief glimpse of a pallid sun, enough to marginally change the light. He dropped his cigarette and cast the lure again, knowing that the slightest change in light might make a fish take, but it wasn't to be. The light closed and he lit another cigarette. His hands were white and wrinkled with the cold, and he felt the first drop of frozen water dribble down between his thermal vest and the skin of his back. He was very cold, but he had been colder, and resolved to go on for just a few more casts. He heard the sound of an approaching Land Rover, which splashed on to the bridge and came to rest next to him.

'Anything there, nipper?' the driver asked, already knowing the answer.

'Hello, Uncle Jack. Nothing. I fished all the way down twice ... Didn't see a movement,' Finlay answered.

'Some Admiral chap telephoned for you just now, wants you to ring him back at once – that was about twenty minutes ago. Do you want me to take you to the house?' Jack asked.

'No ... if you go back, tell him you couldn't find me. I'll wander back when I've had a few more casts,' Finlay said.

'He did say it was urgent,' Jack added. 'Anyway, you must be frozen ... you'd perhaps better come.'

'No, bugger him. I'll come when I'm ready, Uncle Jack. He pretends everything is urgent just to see people jump about when he starts up. He probably wants nothing more than my expenses claim form.' Finlay smiled.

Uncle Jack laughed as he started the engine. 'OK, on your head be it. I thought Admirals were important.'

'Only in their own minds, Uncle Jack, only in their own

minds,' Finlay said, and flicked the lure across the river, bringing it around slowly, watching the flashing brass deep in the water. He fished on for another half an hour, moved nothing and was about to call it a day when the family Armstrong splashed on to the bridge, driven by Auntie Niney.

'Darling, do come in out of the weather,' Niney said, winding down the window. 'You'll catch your death. I've a flask of coffee here. Come and at least have a warm in the car, there's a dear.' Finlay could only see her head; the rest of her was muffled in a large cashmere shawl.

He made his way to the car and clipped his rod to the roof carrier and sat beside his aunt.

'Here you are. Have this. There's some brandy in it. You must be absolutely shrammed,' she said, feeling his face for any warmth.

'That's better!' Finlay said, handing her back the empty cup.

'Another?' Niney asked, filling the cup before he could answer. She took a long swallow herself before handing him the cup again. 'Your Admiral rang again, getting in a state about something, silly old sod. What does he think, you sit indoors all day waiting for him to telephone?'

'Better go and find out what he wants. Probably not important. War hasn't been declared or anything boring like that?' Finlay smiled.

'Not that I know of. Anyway that young Gordon-Smith girl is waiting on your return, so I suppose we'd better get back,' she said, starting the car.

'How long has she been waiting? I didn't ask her to come, Auntie … I do wish she wouldn't.' Finlay sighed.

'She's a nice girl, Kee, very suitable, I'd have thought,' Niney observed. She reversed the car off the bridge and headed back towards the house.

'Please, Auntie, don't keep fixing me up. I'm not ready for

suitable girls and I don't really fancy her,' Finlay said, trying to be patient. 'Anyway, I like Janet. We're sort of comfortable together.'

Janet Ward was Finlay's long-term girlfriend; they had known each other for a dozen years or more. She was an extremely pretty, vivacious girl, with a mass of copper curls, green eyes and freckles, who rented the family's stable block, filling it with horses and her tinkling laughter. Finlay adored her.

'You are comfortable together, Kee, because Janet is always game for a quickie in the hay with you! Darling, I do wish you would try a little harder. Jenny was a long time ago. You must get over her and start behaving like a normal young chap,' Niney persisted.

'It isn't Jenny, Auntie, I promise. I don't have much free time from my job and what I do have I want to spend at home with you, fishing.' Finlay knew what he had just said was not wholly truthful. Jenny was somebody who still held him fast, even though she had been gone eight years or more.

They went indoors to a beautifully warm kitchen. The Aga, turned up full, kept the kitchen and the passageway to the hall very warm. The fireplaces at each end of the hall were a blaze of logs and filled the air with the gentle smell of wood smoke.

'Felicity, why didn't you say you were coming? I didn't know you were here,' Finlay said to the pretty girl sitting at the kitchen table, nursing a cup of tea.

'I was just passing. I thought perhaps to drop in on the off chance,' Felicity said quietly.

To Finlay, Felicity Gordon-Smith seemed like a Barbie doll. She had what other women must have thought a perfect figure, on which she draped the most perfect clothes. She had been to an exclusive finishing school, spoke English in a tone of perfect modulation, and she was, Finlay supposed, eminently 'suitable' in the eyes of any mother or aunt. Though

Finlay also suspected that were he to put his hand into her pretty Barbie doll knickers, he would find a perfectly shaped piece of plastic.

She came from the north of the county, and had met Finlay at a riparian owners' meeting. Her family owned quite a long stretch of the Test above Stockbridge and farmed monoculture barley on the downs. She had somehow attached herself to Finlay ever since and, much to Janet's annoyance, seemed now to be always underfoot, in a perfectly bland way.

'I'm sorry but I have to make a call,' Finlay said to everyone and no one. He dialled the number and waited.

'Admiral Winter, please,' Finlay said. 'It's Finlay here.'

'Putting you through, sir,' the voice on the other end said very coolly.

'Finlay! Where the bloody hell have you been? I've been trying to get you for nearly two bloody hours,' Winter roared.

'I was fishing, Sir,' Finlay answered equably.

'You spend too much time fishing! I want you up here!' Winter shouted.

'Immediately, Sir?' Finlay asked.

'In the morning, you bloody fool, of course. Eight o'clock sharp. Two days planning then you'll be away... so be here!'

'Yes, Sir,' Finlay said. He put the phone down.

To Niney and Felicity the one-sided conversation had sounded as Finlay had wanted it to. 'I'm sorry, Felicity, I have to go immediately. See you next time I'm home perhaps.'

Finlay left the room and went upstairs to his bedroom and lay down, his hands behind his head, waiting to hear Felicity's car leaving, which it did within ten minutes with much revving and wheelspin. He heard Niney's footsteps coming up the stairs.

'Do you want something to eat, Kee, before you go?' she called, before arriving in his bedroom.

'I'm not going tonight, Auntie. I have to go off early in the morning.' He smiled, not moving from his position on the bed.

She came and sat beside him. 'That was naughty, Kee. You just wanted rid of Felicity! She does so dote on you.'

'Well, I wish she wouldn't! She's a pleasant enough sort, but please, Auntie, don't keep importing her. I'm not the least bit interested!' Finlay said with some emphasis.

'Darling, I do wish you would make an effort to start thinking about settling down with a suitable young lady,' Niney sighed. 'Jenny is not coming back ...'

'It's not about Jenny, Auntie. I've no intention of "settling down" as you call it, not for a good while yet. I like my job. It really makes a difference. What could be more important than looking after England's interests? I feel privileged doing what I do ... One day someone will come along that I will love as much as Jenny. Auntie, can you not see? Nelson put England before everything and that's what I feel I should do.'

'And he died for it!' Niney said, getting up and going to the window. She looked out at the gathering gloom outside.

'He knew he had done his duty... and I must surely do mine, Auntie. Please try to see that,' Finlay said.

'Well, hurry up and get it done, for goodness' sake. Else you'll finish up on the shelf a crabby old bachelor,' Niney said, leaving the room.

Two

NEXT MORNING THE drive to London seemed interminable. It was still insidiously cold, with the same sleety showers Finlay had fished in the day before. There wasn't much traffic when he left at 5.15, mainly lorries throwing up half-frozen spray, covering his windscreen with oily dirt which the wipers and washers could hardly shift.

At 7.30 he parked on Horse Guards and went into the offices. He showed his identity to the MOD policeman on duty, who, this morning, made a great show of searching him very thoroughly. The policeman knew Finlay well. 'Sorry about this, sir, but we've got some bigwigs arriving for a meeting at eight.'

Since moving into the building four years ago, when the Recce Group was first formed, things had improved somewhat. The place was clean, for a start, and most important of all was a new canteen, which was where Finlay now headed.

'Bacon and eggs please, Brenda, a large pot of tea and some bread and butter,' Finlay said to the girl behind the spotless serving area. She flashed him a smile.

'Got up late?' she asked. 'No time for breakfast?' She always flirted openly with Finlay, who paid her lavish compliments about her cooking skills, which ensured that she always tried to please him, and in summer she always found some reason to bend over him, showing him her more than ample bust. He sat eating quietly, looking at a copy of the previous day's *Sunday Telegraph*, and rather forgot about the time. It was just past eight when he tapped on Admiral Winter's door, before walking straight in.

Winter sat at the head of the planning table. 'You're late, Finlay!'

'Yes, Sir,' Finlay said, glancing at his watch. 'Ninety-two seconds, Sir. It won't happen again, Sir.'

'Sit down there and I'll make some introductions ... This gentleman is Lieutenant Finlay, the one chosen to effect what we have decided. And Finlay, on my left is General Brook, then we have Colonel Tomkins, you know Captain James, and the gentleman next to you is Mr Smith.'

Finlay smiled at the man. 'Are you of the Smiths from Dorset, Mr Smith, or those from Northampton?'

Smith tried hard but failed to stop himself laughing.

'Enough of that, Finlay!' the Admiral barked. 'We've no time for your bloody nonsense!'

General Brook looked unamused, Tomkins found something very interesting in the paperwork in front of him and Captain James smiled until quelled with a glance from Winter.

'What we are here to discuss this morning is Operation Kingstone,' the Admiral began. 'To begin with – '

'Excuse me, Sir,' Finlay interrupted, 'is that Kingston down the road or the one in Jamaica?' Finlay sounded bright and sharp. Captain James rose quickly and turned from the table, covering his laughter by making a big show of blowing his nose. General Brook threw his pen on the pad in front of himself and made impatient snorting noises. Winter stared hard at Finlay over his glasses, his blue eyes glittering dangerously.

'To begin with,' Winter went on, 'unless we pull this off, the whole of our tank squadrons are going to be very vulnerable. We want you, Finlay, to go into the Zone, via Berlin, and bring something out. That is the nub of it and it looks simple enough to me.'

'Everything looks simple from Horse Guards,' Finlay mumbled.

'What did you say, Finlay?' snapped Winter.

'I said, Sir, that there's a lot of border guards,' Finlay answered.

General Brook leant over and whispered something to Admiral Winter. Winter seemed dismissive of what he was saying.

'How many times have you crossed into the Zone, Finlay?' Winter asked.

'Seven or eight times, Sir. Doesn't get any easier though. It's getting out that always seems to pose the problems. Especially, of course, if they know we are there. What am I to bring out?' Finlay asked.

'In the folder in front of you, Finlay, are the details of the man you have to meet: an East German scientist who has invented a bullet, a bullet which carries its own propellant. More to the point, this bullet – in effect a tiny rocket – will, it seems, penetrate our latest tank armour with ease. It can be fired from the shoulder, from another tank or even from aircraft. It's so damn good we've been told that we have to have one, to see how to counter it. Professor Brennan will hand us one over in exchange for freedom in the West.'

'Sir,' Finlay began. General Brook sighed and again threw his pen down angrily. Finlay ignored his stuffy petulance. 'Professor generally means not a young man, also somebody not generally used to being terribly fit. It's difficult enough for somebody like myself. How do I get a middle-aged man out of the Zone?'

Admiral Winter shuffled his paperwork about and drew heavily on his pipe. 'It's just the bullet we want out, Finlay,' he said.

No one around the table would meet his eye except Mr Smith, who looked Finlay squarely in the face. Without turning away from Smith, Finlay said, 'You want me to kill Professor Brennan, Sir?'

Winter looked uncomfortable. Even in his job overt treachery was difficult for him, and to ask someone to enact his treachery was harder still. 'Yes, that's it,' he said simply.

'Will you have a problem with that?' Smith asked, still staring at Finlay.

'Yes ... I think I probably shall,' Finlay answered easily.

'But you will, won't you... I mean, kill him?' Smith asked.

'If that's what my Admiral requires of me,' Finlay said, again easily, but with an edge of diffidence.

'Just get the bullet back here, Finlay!' Winter ordered. 'You know what has to be done, so don't start getting some sort of conscience about it ... or are you losing your nerve?'

'I know what has to be done, Sir. Am I going in alone?' Finlay asked.

'No, not this time. Canavan will be your back-up. His job will be to protect you. Under any circumstances we must have this bullet. I cannot emphasise that enough,' Winter said crossly.

'Then I'll get it,' Finlay said, standing up. 'If everything I need to know is in here,' he said, picking up the folder, 'I shall go and get on with it. Thank you, gentlemen, and good morning.'

Finlay made his way downstairs to the Wardroom and rang the steward's bell to order some tea. He lounged back in one of the old leather chairs and began to read and start his own briefing. The folder contained, among other things, a large photograph of Professor Brennan. He studied it closely, trying to see what kind of a man he was. He was not young, and Finlay judged him to be around sixty when the photograph was taken. 'And God knows when that was,' he thought. 'And there you are, all keyed up to spend your last years in the decadent West ... you poor old bastard.'

Smith had appeared beside him, unannounced. 'Will you kill him?' he asked quietly.

Finlay looked up at him. 'Would you like some tea, *Smith*?' Again, the disdain was pronounced with the name.

Smith pretended not to notice. 'Yes, I would like some tea, but I'd also like you to answer my question.' He made it sound like an order.

'Well now, Mr Smith, that poses me with a problem. I don't have to answer your questions, you not being a member of the armed forces,' Finlay said, his voice almost saccharine.

'But I am from the Foreign Office, Finlay ...' Smith began.

'Wasn't that the place where Burgess and Maclean came from? The Foreign Office is where most of our international problems spring from, because it's staffed by the spineless dregs of minor public schools... hardly a recommendation.' Finlay smiled at him.

Smith smiled back. 'Your self-confidence borders on the arrogant, Finlay. You know who I am, don't you? And at what level I work?'

Finlay walked over to the bell that summoned the steward. 'Ah, steward, could you get Spencer please. There's a chap here who doesn't seem to know who he is. I don't imagine him to be dangerously doolally, but he came into the Wardroom without permission.'

The steward looked a little awkward but said, 'Yes, sir.'

A moment later, Spencer, head of security, appeared. 'Sir?' he enquired of Finlay.

'Throw this chap out please, Spencer. He's here without permission and seems lost,' Finlay said, pouring himself some tea.

'Can't really do that, sir, he's the boss of MI6,' Spencer said blandly.

'All the more reason to throw him out, I'd have thought. This is a Wardroom, not a tea room for pencil-pushing pansies. Get him out!' Finlay ordered shortly.

'You'll have to go, sir,' Spencer said to Smith, taking his arm and guiding him to the door.

Smith halted his progress by the door. He seemed almost amused. 'I shall not forget this day, Finlay!'

'Probably not, Mr Smith. Humiliation does rather hang in the mind,' Finlay replied easily.

FINLAY CARRIED ON with his planning, studying the best way in and out of East Germany, without making any notes. It was towards midday when the steward came to inform him that Admiral Winter had requested that they have lunch together. Finlay packed up the papers he was so deeply engrossed in, took them back to his own office and put them under lock and key. Winter inviting him to lunch would normally mean a pleasant interlude in the day, chatting about the things that mattered most to them – field sports – but he thought perhaps he was going to be hauled over the coals because of the way he had dealt with Smith.

Winter's chauffeur dropped them at White's.

'In a way, Finlay,' the Admiral said as they walked in together, 'I'm doing you an honour. Later in life you'll always be able to say, "I've had lunch at Whites."'

'Yes, Sir, many times now. My grandfather's been a member here for years. The food isn't as good as Boodles though, don't you know,' Finlay said quietly.

The Admiral grunted, 'I didn't know that.'

They sat and Winter ordered himself a single malt and Finlay a gin and water.

'Why do you always find it necessary to put people's backs up?' Winter asked in a resigned way. 'You know Rupert Smith is the head of MI6, and an important part of our organisation. He's well in advance of your station. If he asks you something, please comply.'

'Ask is one thing, Sir – order, quite another. Before I had him ejected from the Wardroom, I did check that he was a civilian and as such he has no right whatever to order me to do anything. Moreover, and I'm sorry to have to say this, Sir, even if you ordered me to take his orders, I still would not. That would be a slippery slope for me,' Finlay said.

'Tell me why, Finlay,' Winter said.

'Because you and I are commissioned officers, Sir, and under Queen's Regs we do not have to obey orders from civilians no matter who they are. The precedent was set in 1785 by Lord Nelson himself, when he would not take orders from Captain John Moutray. His alleged captaincy was not by commission, he was a civilian. The Admiralty upheld what Nelson had said and done... I think the incident happened in the Leeward Islands,' Finlay said, very sure of his ground. 'If I take orders from Mr Smith, I may be putting my position as a naval officer in jeopardy.'

'Oh nonsense, Finlay,' Winter said easily.

'The other thing, Sir, is that when we started out this was the Navy. Now we have a general and the FO involved and I, for one, do not like it because the FO is leaky, and Army people have the wrong mindset for what we do.'

'You really believe that, Finlay?' Winter asked.

'I do, Sir,' Finlay answered.

'Would you consider helping to select the applicants,

Finlay? We have put forty-five through the training now and I have to agree that the Army and RAF applicants are somehow different. Hard to put your finger on though,' Winter said.

'You picked the first fourteen, Sir. Our group is successful.Go back to the criteria you were looking for then,' Finlay suggested, flattered by the store the Admiral set by him. 'I'd be interested to know the reason why the applicants wanted to join. It seems to me some of the new recruits are glory hunters. If that psychiatrist Doctor Williams has any function at all, surely he should be able to weed them out.'

'You're right,' said Winter, nodding thoughtfully. 'Anything else?'

'Yes, Sir. I think we should get copies of each cadet application to Dartmouth and start the selection from there. Have someone there who knows what we want and get termly reports on the cadets,' Finlay said.

'And Sandhurst?' Winter asked, his eyes smiling.

'Yes, of course, Sir, else we might be cutting ourselves off from good blokes, but we grab the Army people before they get too brainwashed. Get them before they go to their regiments.'

'How many?' Winter asked.

'No more than sixty on the books, then it doesn't get unwieldy. A group that size needs no more than four senior officers to manage ... and those senior officers are Navy or Royals,' Finlay said. 'If we get too big, then we become just another part of the armed forces. There will, of course, be quite a bit of natural wastage – blokes wanting to get married, injuries, deaths and mental breakdowns, but if we just take the absolute cream and keep our eyes on those who all but made the grade, we can keep numbers up that way. Continual training on new technology and fitness must be made room for, so regular trips to "The Farm" for everyone ... even the senior officers.'

'What you've just said, Finlay, more or less mirrors what I have put in my last report to the CDS. It's to that office that I find myself reporting now, which in truth I am very pleased about. The more we can keep the politicians out of it the better. I find myself wholly mistrustful of any Labour government. One can never really be sure whose side they are on,' Winter said almost sadly.

'Perhaps you shouldn't be saying such things to me, Sir,' Finlay said gently. 'But I know exactly what you mean.'

'Well, let's get some lunch, young man. You have things to prepare when you get back. I'll have you on the selection board. I like your ordered mind.' Winter smiled.

FINLAY HAD LIVED long enough and travelled enough to know that every nation had a character of its own. To some of his contemporaries this was another of 'Finlay's generalisations', but Finlay had never been infected with the liberal thinking of the middle class or ever suffered from self-doubt. In his own mind, he knew he was right, always.

He was studying the sewage system of Berlin, a city so recently and comprehensively destroyed and now rebuilt. He imagined some American general arriving in Berlin after its fall and saying, 'OK, let's rebuild it, from the sewers upwards. Get it done!' They got things done.

Having buried thousands of its young men from Normandy to the Rhine and beyond, America gave succour to the crushed Germans in a spirit of altruism and stunning organisation. It was the American character as Finlay saw it.

Studying the layout and flows of a city's sewerage system was hardly edifying, but he knew he had to understand it fully if he was going into the Russian sector. The main problem he knew straight away was rain. This would turn the normally slow-flowing underground streams into suddenly raging torrents of noisome effluvia, and he didn't want to drown in watered-down German shit.

He looked closely at the wall the East Germans had installed at their border, with concrete pipes running through it. The file said they were a metre in diameter and on the day these particular photographs were taken the pipes were running at about halfway up their height. Festooned around them were stalactites of paper and excrement, and he suddenly wished he had not eaten quite such a large lunch. He knew that at best he was going to have to wade chest deep through the tunnels to get to the area of East Berlin he needed to be in. At worst he was going to have to swim. The thought appalled him.

Late in the afternoon a girl from the office brought him the forward weather forecast for Germany, and more importantly a signal from Canavan, already in West Berlin, stating that he'd had a quick look at the tunnel and provided there was no rain, they should get through into East Berlin. Finlay went back to the weather forecast, without much enthusiasm. It stated the wind would back around to the west. There would be light showers and an increase in temperature.

'Shot in the dark,' he thought. 'Certainly wouldn't put money on it. The meteorologists only ever get a fifty-per-cent accurate forecast for the next twenty-four hours. How they imagine they can predict the next month smacks of wishful thinking.'

Finlay worked on until the rush-hour traffic began to thin. He locked the papers away and wandered across the corridor to let Winter know he was going home.

'I'll be in fairly early in the morning, Sir,' he said. 'I'm up to speed on what has to happen and how, so I'll go home and enjoy my aunt's cooking.'

Winter made a noise in his throat and waved him away.

It was still blisteringly cold, but the sleet and rain had stopped. He drove slowly with the traffic, giving himself time to think about the forthcoming job. He hoped, for once, the weather forecast was right.

Two hours later he dropped down into Romsey and into thick fog. The town seemed deserted. The only human he saw was the fish and chip shop owner, reading a newspaper on the garishly lit counter, no doubt wondering about the wisdom of opening that particular evening. The car splashed its way along the top lane. The overhanging trees shone silver in the headlights, stark and mournful, waiting for the spring.

Finlay smiled to himself as he saw the yard lights flare on, knowing Niney had heard his car.

'Hello, my love,' she said, kissing him. 'I thought the fog would make you late, but you're right on time. Would you like a drink of anything?'

Finlay looked at his aunt. 'How did you know I was coming home? I nearly didn't because I have to go back in the morning and then drive down to Newbury. I'm off tomorrow, and leaving from Greenham Common.'

'Isn't that American now?' Niney asked, putting a bowl of soup down in front of him. 'Where are you off to?'

'Berlin. Should only be gone a week or ten days this time. Terribly secret. I have to fly from military base to military base ... Christ, this soup is good!'

'Dangerous?' she asked, with her back to Finlay.

'No, not really. Just pop into East Berlin and bring something back out. Should be easy,' Finlay said lightly.

'You're telling lies.' His aunt sang the sentence to the tune of 'Someone's Rocking My Dreamboat'. She sat down opposite him. 'Darling, I want you to give up this job and go back to sea. I know you think what you do is important, and I know it makes a difference... but will you promise me, when you

17

come back from this trip you'll transfer back to a ship?' Niney studied him. 'You've done your duty ...'

'I thought you liked me being at home a lot. If I go back to sea I could be away for ages,' Finlay said. 'If what I do worries you, Auntie, then I'll chuck it. When I come back I'll speak to the Admiral. In truth I've had enough anyway. I get fed up with going to London and when I'm away I get so homesick for here, for you and your cooking.'

'And the bloody river. It's the river that drags you back. I know you go to Saddlers Mill before you come back to me, you sod.' She smiled. 'Is that a promise then?'

'Yes. I'll make this the last trip, then come home. I'm sure I can think of a way to earn a crust. Where is everybody anyway?' Finlay asked.

'River meeting up at Stockbridge. Another piss-up!' Niney said.

'I'll put my mind to how I can earn a living, Auntie. Who knows, I may even settle down and get wed,' Finlay laughed.

'Huh! Let's start with small beginnings, shall we?' Niney said, not wholly convinced.

They ate dinner and discussed the varieties of spring barley being sown that year and whether or not to try some of the new malting strains.

'What time have you to go in the morning, darling?' Niney asked.

'About six, then I'll miss most of the traffic. There's no need for you to get up, Auntie... lay abed,' Finlay said.

In the event, Niney was in the kitchen when he came down ready to leave the next morning. She busied herself getting him toast, dressed in a silky dressing gown, her hair hanging loose around her shoulders. At forty-two she was still the most beautiful woman Finlay had ever seen. He got up from the table and hugged her tightly. 'I love you, beautiful Auntie,' he said.

She seemed surprised by this sudden show of affection. Such interludes had been rare since Jenny's leaving. She kissed the point of his nose, as a mother would. 'You just come back to me in one piece, please,' she whispered.

LATER, IN HIS office, Finlay went over the drawings of the sewerage system again. Satisfied, he repacked his briefing folder, which contained a passport and driving licence made out in the name of Gerald Shaw, an oil production engineer. There were two bundles of German money, one for the East and one for the West, and two thousand US dollars – the whole amount attached to a slip of paper awaiting his signature to confirm that he had actually received it. There was also the inevitable chitty for his side arm, stating: '.357 magnum Colt Python for issuing.'

'Good God,' thought Finlay. 'I'm not taking a cannon with me. The Yanks will charge me excess baggage!'

The briefing details stated Brennan would arrive in East Berlin, ostensibly to visit his ailing brother, on 4 March. On the 5th, Finlay was to go to the brother's place in Rudolfstrasse and collect the bullet, crossing back into West Berlin by any route chosen. Once in West Berlin, Finlay was to leave the bullet in one of the 'safe houses' and come home via Sweden. No civil airlines were to be used and no direct route home. 'And when you pass "Go" you can collect two hundred pounds,' mused Finlay.

There was also the chitty for the dentist to have the obligatory lethal pill fitted. All this, on paper, really was just as simple as the Admiral had said. After all, Finlay had been into the Zone before, and sometimes joked he'd had a season ticket for the tramcars in East Berlin.

Finlay destroyed the chitty and from his inside pocket drew out several blank ones he'd stolen some time previously from

Supply's Office. Then, in Commander Supply's spidery hand, he wrote, 'side arm of recipient's choice', and signed it with an excellent forgery of the Commander's signature before returning it to the folder.

'Oh well,' thought Finlay. 'There's two or three weeks in Berlin to work out the details. Doubtless things will have to be changed considerably by then.'

Finlay's time in the Service had taught him that plans were often changed before the commencement, usually on account of a change of heart by the politicians, whom Finlay despised above all others, whatever their leanings.

He sighed, cursed the still sleet-filled wind and decided to go over to Supply at Storey's Gate. He left the building by the front entrance, handing his entrance pass to the security guard.

'I'm off, Spence,' he said. 'See you soon, no doubt.'

Spencer took the pass, stamped it and filed it in the day-card index. 'Anywhere nice, sir?' he asked, without looking at Finlay.

'Yes, Spence, I'm off to the sun and warm beaches for a couple of months. See you when I get back,' Finlay lied easily, and thought of a wet, cold Berlin in February.

By the time he had walked round to supply, he was soaked. He entered the building's foyer and handed the woman at reception his identity card to receive, in return, the inevitable time-stamped entrance pass.

'Where you gotta go, luv?' she asked through a mouthful of doughnut.

'Supply first, then the dentist,' replied Finlay. She glanced up at him. Everyone knew what 'going to the dentist' meant.

'Bit young for this job, ain't you, luv? I'm glad my boy's got a nice steady job on the railway, that's all I can say. Anyway, I'll ring down and let them know you're coming. OK, luv?'

Finlay's first collection point was the clothes shop. His

selection of clothing was already packed in a cheap foreign suitcase of indeterminate make. Every stitch of clothing had been pre-selected for him, all made of Japanese textiles, all labels removed. The shoes, made in Poland, fitted well, were sturdy and likely to stay the course. Finlay looked at them as he repacked them and grinned to himself. 'Make a good shoemaker cry, they would,' he thought.

The next stop was with Bert, the armourer, who looked at his chitty and laughed loudly. 'You forge the Commander's signature better every time you do it, Keith. Soon be able to sign yourself out enough to retire on! What do you want?'

'The Hammerli P240 in .38 please, Bert, five mags and a box of the slowest soft nose you've got.' Bert was a favourite of Finlay's.

'I've got some real stoppers I've been making up for a P240. I think you'll love them!' Bert the perfectionist had loaded a batch of bullets with a slow powder and what could only be termed the softest of heads.

Finlay studied them. 'Beautiful, Bert, just beautiful. Nothing worse than having somebody charge down on you and your bullets going through him so fast he doesn't believe he's been shot.'

'Shall we go to the range, sir? I've set up a Hammerli ready. Best I could do without you being here.'

Finlay laughed. 'You knew I'd alter the chitty?'

They moved off to the range, and, on arrival, Bert passed the chosen side arm to Finlay. Finlay weighed it in his hand, admiring the balance as Bert ran out the targets.

'There you are, Keith. I've shot about a hundred rounds through, tightened it up and added a bit of weight at the back. Load her up and see what you think.'

Finlay pushed in a magazine, aimed and fired five shots at the first target in rapid succession, then, moving across the range, fired slowly and deliberately at a second target, placing three shots within a one-inch group.

Bert ran the targets back and whistled softly. He handed them to Finlay. The first target was shredded left of the bull by half an inch; the second had its bull missing and two holes ran into each other beside it.

'What do you think, Bert?' asked Finlay, anxious for the armourer's opinion.

'I've seen you do better. Let me take some weight off the trigger,' he said, rapidly pulling the pistol to pieces.

A few strokes with a file and the gun was reassembled.

'Try her now, and aim slowly. None of the John Wayne crap. Shoot as though you mean it.'

This time Finlay shot at one target – eight shots, slowly and deliberately – when the target was run back in, there were just three holes in it, all over the bull.

Bert whistled again. 'Anybody else, Keith, and I would have said they'd only hit the target three times. The gun suits you. How do you want to carry it?'

He sounded to Finlay like a bespoke tailor, which, in his own way, he was. He tailored the weapon to the user. 'Round the back, please, Bert, in a plastic holder. Those leather ones stick sometimes.'

Finlay signed the book stating he had been issued with the gun. 'Try and bring it back this trip, sir. The guvnor is fed up with you losing them all.'

Finlay laughed and shook hands with the armourer. 'I'll try, Bert, but you know how it is.'

And that was Supply over with and just the dentist to visit. This, Finlay did next, and he came away with a small lump under the left side of his tongue, made by the lethal pill stitched into his gum. Finlay wondered if he would ever have the courage to use it or, more to the point, if he would ever be in the kind of trouble that would require him to use it.

He left for Greenham in one of the pool cars. What might have seemed a snap decision by someone on high was generally the result of months, if not years, of painstaking work, to bring an operation to this stage.

At the end of it all came the pay-off; in this case, some sort of rocket-propelled, heavy-calibre bullet which could penetrate the Army's new armour plating, which itself had taken some British professor an age to perfect.

Three

THE RAF GREENHAM Common base at Newbury had been taken over by the American Air Force some time after the Second World War. It was used in a logistical support role for the rest of their bases in Great Britain and had no great claim to fame except at one time, when it had been used during the Berlin Airlift. The irony did not escape Finlay as he drove up to the main entrance and presented his passport to the young American on the gate.

Chameleon-like, Finlay had slipped into the skin of his new identity, so that when the American asked him who his appointment was with, addressing him as 'Mr Shaw', Finlay could answer immediately. 'Captain Mirando, please.'

The American waved him through. 'Park in the visitors' car park, buddy, then go through the big green doors directly in front of you.'

Finlay did as he was bid, then sprinted through the rain to the building and once inside shook the rain from himself like a wet spaniel.

In the reception area Finlay was confronted by a girl he would have described as being 'typical chocolate-box American', all curls and white teeth.

'Can I help you?' she asked, smiling. Finlay, fascinated by the rise and fall of the words 'Strategic Air' embroidered over her left breast, brought himself back quickly from his thoughts.

'Sorry. Yes, er, Captain Mirando, please. My name is Shaw.'

The girl, still smiling, replied, 'Yes, Mr Shaw. The Captain is expecting you. If you'll come with me, I'll take you along to his office.'

James Mirando was sitting on his desk, filling his pipe, when Finlay was ushered into his office.

'Mr Shaw, Jim,' announced the receptionist.

Mirando shook hands with Finlay, pumping his arm violently. 'Good to know you, Shaw,' he beamed with typical American effusiveness. 'You've got to be in a big hurry. Nobody uses us as transport these days, but you're more than welcome. I don't know what your game is, but I can guess, so we've given you all the help we can. I've got some coveralls and one of our uniforms ready for you.'

He produced the garments with the same flourish a conjurer uses when producing a rabbit from a hat. He had obviously had time to think about his English visitor and was determined to be part of the mystery surrounding him. 'When you arrive in Berlin you'll look just like one of us. Our Embassy called us up this morning and told us to help all we could.'

Finlay, warming somewhat to the American's friendliness, answered as non-comittally as possible. 'Well, Captain Mirando, we are still both on the side of the angels, I believe.'

Finlay, unlike most of his service contemporaries, had always had a sneaking regard for the American services. He found their organisational skills superb, their logistics matchless, and there always seemed to be so many of them. They had never had to suffer defence cuts, and if something had to be done they did it speedily and well.

Mirando clapped Finlay on the back. 'Anything else you need, Shaw, just ask and it's yours. We like to think– '

Before he could finish, an aircrew sergeant walked in without knocking and said, 'Say, Jim, what's this about us taking some Limey over with us tonight?'

Captain Mirando noticed Finlay's surprise at the lack of formality and looked a little uncomfortable. To save him any further embarrassment, Finlay answered the man quickly. 'Yes, that's correct, Sergeant, it's me, so avoid the bumps in the road because I hate flying.'

The Sergeant, quite unabashed, looked at Finlay with some disdain and replied, 'OK, bud. We get airborne at a quarter after six, if that's OK with you?' And, turning to leave, he glanced at his Captain and said, 'Jim, be seeing you.' Then he left.

Captain Mirando lifted both hands to heaven in a gesture of helplessness. 'I know what you're thinking, Shaw, but that's the way we do things and it works!'

Finlay remembered the dictum of an old Commander friend: 'The Yanks cannot actually fight as such, they don't know how. They just flood the combat area with men and machines to such an extent they cannot lose.'

Finlay laughed. 'Don't worry about it, Captain. My regard for your services and country makes me a dedicated Yankophile, if there is such a thing. You also make wonderful ice cream.'

At ease once again, effusiveness rose to the surface. 'Tell you what, Shaw, you Brits have a funny way about you, but you're all right. Let's get you something to eat and have a bit of a chin wag. We don't get many Brits here and the locals don't mix that easy.'

Finlay thought about the Berkshire set he knew around Newbury and decided that the Captain was probably right. They didn't mix readily with anybody from the next county, so what they made of their American guests he just dreaded to think.

Sitting in the canteen drinking coffee, Mirando was unable to contain his curiosity any longer. 'May I ask what you're going to Berlin for, Shaw?'

'Not really, Captain,' replied Finlay. 'It's not that exciting. Has something to do with our cavalry regiments. Logistics, placement … that sort of thing.' Finlay tried to sound as dismissive as possible.

'I've got the picture, Shaw. Best of luck with it, anyway.'

They stayed talking in the canteen until it was time for Finlay to leave. Mirando insisted on ferrying him out to the aircraft in a huge American car, which seemed to float over the runway. The plane itself looked immense and the weight of its wings gave the craft a very sinister appearance, as they sagged downwards, such was their size.

As they drew up, the Sergeant they had seen earlier met them. Finlay shook hands with Mirando and thanked him for his help. He began the long ascent into the heart of the aeroplane.

Seating Finlay in a small, barely cushioned seat among a myriad of packing cases, the Sergeant told him, 'Coffee will be along as soon as we get the old crate airborne.' His description did nothing to settle Finlay's already taut stomach.

'It's no good,' he thought. 'I hate planes.'

Four

THE FLIGHT TO Berlin was uneventful. The aircrew came in
turns to him, bringing him coffee and biscuits. They teased
him somewhat about his fear of flying and one of the pilots
made the huge aircraft perform some gentle gyrations for
Finlay's benefit. It confirmed his belief that only a certain type
of person flew aircraft, and the one thing they had in common
was that they were all quite mad.

It was with more than some relief, therefore, that Finlay felt
the plane begin its long descent into Berlin, and having landed
and finally taxied to a halt, Finlay was charitable enough to
think to himself that the flight had been, while not enjoyable,
not wholly without its lighter moments. And he recalled the
occasion the redoubtable Sergeant had emptied the contents
of the dry lavatory system earthwards into East Germany as
they flew the air corridor to the old capital.

'A present from the capitalist West to the comrades down
below!' he had shouted as he emptied the bucket. 'We always
empty here, Shaw,' he laughed afterwards. 'One day I
dropped the bucket. They probably thought it was a new
secret weapon!'

As they descended from the aircraft and hurried to the
military section of the airport buildings, Finlay reflected
ruefully that from now on he was in enemy territory.

There seemed almost weekly to be some kind of incident as one side fought the other in the silent deadly games of the Cold War. While the cunning and cruelty of the espionage services wreaked havoc with each other, the Berliners went about their daily lives and, at night, the glitter and gaiety of the city hid in its shadows the never-ending game of chance, played out by East and West. A game that kept the Hot War at bay.

Bidding the aircrew a brief farewell, Finlay looked for the nearest lavatory to remove his coveralls. He emerged from the cubicle dressed as an American Air Force corporal and made his way quickly to the civilian administration block.

He had been on the base many times before when he had done a training stint in Berlin early in his service. The thought worried him that he might well meet somebody he knew, or worse, someone from the other side who knew him. Anything, anything at all, that made him familiar with anyone was a risk he had to avoid.

Part of his itinerary was to collect a hire car and once in the administration block he approached the desk, pretending to be in a great hurry.

Finlay announced himself as Shaw and asked whether his car was ready – it had been pre-booked. A girl gave him a set of keys and asked him to sign the insurance and release forms, which he did with an unintelligible squiggle.

'Will you be keeping the car long, Mr Shaw?' she asked brightly.

'No, I shall only need it for a day. Being sent to Holland tomorrow,' he lied.

The girl showed him to his car, the inevitable Mercedes, and once she'd handed over the keys, shook his hand in best training-manual manner. Finlay turned to the Mercedes and opened the door. The airbase traffic was fairly heavy passing the administration block and, glancing back, Finlay watched the girl flag down a taxi, which left towards the main exit.

When the taxi was out of sight, Finlay threw the ignition keys on to the front seat of the car, closed the door again and walked back into the service area of the base, where he had a good view of the traffic flowing by.

Cars, lorries, jeeps and airbase buses were crawling past him, bringing one shift of workers into the base and another out. Finlay soon saw exactly what he was looking for: a jeep well loaded with young airmen singing and shouting their way out of the base. He danced through the traffic waving and, as the driver saw him and slowed, shouted in his best New England accent, 'Got room for a small one in there?'

A chorus of, 'Sure, OK, bud, right on, man!' followed. Finlay left the base, singing a bawdy song about a girl from New Orleans whose torso proportions apparently rivalled the size and mobility of an elephant's rear end.

'Where you from, pal?' one of the Americans asked him, shouting against the noise of the others.

'New England,' Finlay shouted back, breaking off from the song.

'Knew a girl from there once,' came back the response. 'About as cold as the New England winter,' he added.

'Yeah,' replied Finlay. 'That's why I left.'

The American laughed, flung his arm around Finlay and continued singing loudly. As the jeep slowed at some traffic lights, Finlay disentangled himself from his new-found friend and shouted, 'Catch you later, man. Got to find a hotel down this way!'

'Get your arse down the Golden Gate this evening, buddy. Don't be late, pal, or all the best girls will be taken.'

'Sure thing!' Finlay answered, his New England accent sounding more false by the second.

The traffic was fairly heavy. Finlay made a pretence of looking in shop windows and, making sure that he hadn't been followed, waved down a taxi.

'South Station, please,' he said to the driver in German.

He slumped into the back seat and pretended to doze. He could see the traffic pattern in the driver's rear-view mirror through his half-closed eyes and started noting the type and how closely they followed. 'The trouble is,' he thought, 'these German cars are all the same – BMW, Mercedes and Volkswagen Beetles.'

Three cars back was a BMW and five cars back a Mercedes with a front side light gone. If he was being pursued, it would be cars in these positions doing the following. As they drew near the station, the traffic became more dense and the taxi's progress was slow. Finlay knocked on the glass partition and, handing the driver a ten mark note, motioned him to pull over.

Finlay was out of the taxi before it had properly stopped and into a side street. Walking quickly westward, he went through the first underpass he came to and, emerging on the opposite side of the street, waved down another taxi and climbed in.

He gave the driver the name of a church in the British sector and, prompting him with a fifty mark note, requested that they get there with all speed. Finlay always described Berlin taxi drivers as driving with 'controlled enthusiasm', and this one was no exception.

The taxi covered six miles to the destination in about ten minutes, which, considering the density of traffic, was a very expert show of driving. Alighting in the dark church square, Finlay handed the driver the fifty mark note with enthusiastic thanks.

As he drove away, Finlay noted that the area was deserted, save one old man walking a black and white terrier.

Finlay walked out of the square towards where he knew the safe house to be. The Service had several of these in Berlin, generally on short leases, so that they changed frequently. Finlay's briefing folder had contained the most up-to-date lists of houses and, more importantly, that in which he was to meet his back-up, Patrick James Canavan.

In this case the safe house was a flat in a small block of about ten, rather more upmarket than the Service generally afforded.

Finlay entered the front doors, walked straight through the building and out of the rear entrance. He waited in the shadows for a couple of minutes then returned around the building to the front entrance and re-entered.

There was nobody in sight, so he judged it safe to ascend the stairway and soon found himself outside the designated door. From beneath the door, Finlay could see a strip of light and, shielding himself behind the side wall, he tapped lightly.

'Come in, Keith, and stop poncing about outside like some bloody fairy!' The voice from within was obviously Irish and was thick with drink.

Finlay entered and saw Canavan flat on his back on a large sofa, glass in hand. Canavan grinned. 'Good to see you, youngster. I'd get up and shake your hand and give you a drink, but Jesus knows, I don't think I'm able, for you see, young sir, I'm well pissed!'

He looked Finlay up and down through half-closed eyes. 'What the hell are you doing in that pansy boy outfit?' he asked.

Finlay exploded with laughter. 'Pat, you mad bastard!' he said. 'Is this the way you welcome your old comrade? Get up, you tired sod. Welcome me properly and pour me a drink.'

The Irishman stood shakily, swayed across the room and clasped Finlay's hand. He gazed down at Finlay, shorter by a good twelve inches, placed his other hand heavily on Finlay's shoulder and said through a cloud of whiskey fumes, 'Why, you lovely little sawn-off bastard, it's great to see you. Jesus knows, I've prayed for you and doubtless I'll be doing so again. Get unpacked and I'll get you your drink.'

Major Patrick James Canavan, drunk as he was, was something to behold. Six foot six of bulky Irish charm, with a shock of coal black hair that five years in the Recce Group and several more with the Defence Intelligence Staff had not yet streaked with grey at an age of nearly forty. He exuded fitness and strength, which years of hard drinking and womanising had hardly dented.

He turned unsteadily back to Finlay, holding up his forefinger. 'The Herberts know you're here, by the way. Your hire car at the airbase went up in a puff of smoke – saw it on the news.' Canavan said it as though he attached but little importance to it. 'Some airmen gave it a nudge from behind and poof, away it went!' He made an upward sweep of both hands, describing in mime the car exploding. Whiskey flew from his glass up the wall and over the carpet. 'Shit!' he muttered. 'I'd sooner see a church burn than waste a good malt, so I would. Anyway, they know you're here. Your bloody Foreign Office has more leaks than Murphy's petrol tank, so it does!'

Finlay laughed again at Canavan's performance. 'The dolly bird on the car hire desk gave me the keys and fled rather too quickly. Didn't fancy the car after that! We can have her picked up later perhaps.'

Only after some laughter did they both acknowledge the gravity of the situation.

'Bloody marvellous, isn't it?' said Finlay. 'Haven't been here for two years and already the Herbs are on to me! Oh well, I'd better get on to London in the morning and pull myself out.

Going into the Zone always scares me shitless and if Ivan and his gang are expecting me we'd not stand a chance in hell of getting out again.'

Canavan's drunkenness was replaced by something like normality. 'Oh, forget it, Keith. Don't take it personally. They've probably got somebody posted on Westminster Bridge and every time any one of us oiks turns up for briefing they go on yellow alert,' he responded. 'Let's get out of Berlin, push on up to Denmark for a few days, sample some of the crumpet up there, then come back via the French sector by car when we're ready. We'll have the bastards running all over the place!'

'Sounds good. I wonder if the station here has a spare car for us. Suddenly I don't fancy hiring one! Why Denmark though, Pat?' Finlay asked.

'Because they'll think you're heading back to your normal haunts. But we don't want a station car. We can pinch one here, then nobody knows where we are – much the safest. We can go out our own way, do the job our own way and perhaps get out alive and well. If we don't let London know anything, we can do the job, disappear completely and it's over to Ireland for a couple of weeks' fishing! We can stay at my home, last place they'd look. Keep them all guessing!'

The logic of it appealed to Finlay. If there was a leak, it was much the best thing to lie low, both before and after the job. 'Pat, you'll get us both arrested for thieving cars one day, but OK.'

There was a knock on the flat door. Canavan steadied up by divine intervention, or so Finlay thought as he motioned to him with an up and down movement of his hand. Finlay drew his gun and moved behind the door, and Canavan followed suit, placing his back against the wall on the door's right.

He nodded to Finlay, who jerked the door handle down and opened it in one movement. Canavan's huge hand shot out and grabbed the person standing there by the jacket and hurled him into the room. Finlay shut the door and turned to see Canavan sitting astride a man's back on the floor, his gun firmly jammed into the quaking man's ear.

'And who might you be, duckie?' he growled, pushing harder with his gun.

'Morgan… station duty officer… I've come to warn you,' the prostrate, winded Morgan gasped. 'They know you're here.'

Canavan pushed harder on his gun, 'Don't you know standing orders, you stupid little bastard? No one from station to approach the safe house. You've probably brought half their watcher section down on us now! Christ Almighty, I've half a mind to knock your stupid head in!'

Canavan's temper suddenly left him as he turned to look helplessly at Finlay. 'What bloody hope is there for this poxy outfit, if they insist on employing idiots like this?' Canavan rose away from Morgan, but kept his gun aimed at his head. 'Oh get up man, for Christ's sake. Are you hurt?'

'No, I don't think so,' Morgan replied meekly. 'But I'm afraid I've wet myself.'

The dark patch on his trouser front attested to this. Canavan and Finlay looked at each other, speechless for a moment, and then simultaneously burst into loud laughter.

'I'm afraid I'm rather new to this,' put in Morgan, still very meekly. This only caused more laughter from the other two and through this Finlay choked out, 'You're not likely to get old at it either, Morgan, going on this evening's performance. We've probably got half of the KGB and GRU downstairs, the CIA following them up and the Politzei trying to sort out the traffic jam they're causing!'

'Oh dear, I'm frightfully sorry. I thought I was acting properly but I seem to have made something of a gaff,' replied Morgan.

Canavan shrugged his massive shoulders in an exaggerated show of despair. '"A gaff," he says, a bloody gaff! You've put two operatives at risk, not to mention yourself, blown a safe house, pissed on the carpet, and you reckon you've made a gaff!'

He turned to Finlay. 'Let's you and I get out of here, Keith, and let this silly sod go back to wherever he came from.' Looking back at Morgan, he spat out, 'On your way out, you can explain to the watchers outside about your gaff and feel lucky if they don't put a bullet through one of your kneecaps just for a laugh!'

Finlay had started to collect up his travelling bag. 'Find a way out over the roof, Pat,' he said, and turning to Morgan, 'Let London know this place is blown. You'll probably be recalled but that's your own fault. Tell them we'll be in touch. Make sure you do it, Morgan. If somebody else uses this place and gets taken out, it'll be down to you!'

Morgan nodded. 'God, I'm sorry. Do you really think they will be watching for me? They won't try any rough stuff, will they? I mean, the opposition?'

Finlay shrugged. 'You can never tell. They know where the Berlin station is no matter how often it's moved. They always put watchers on anybody coming or going from the place. No, Morgan, you're safe enough. It's me they're after – old scores to settle. On your way now and let London know what's happened.'

Canavan had found his way to the roof and returned for Finlay. He was muttering something about the quality of recruits the Service was drawing these days – something about men's work not being suited to bloody university types. 'Do you know that bloody numbskull could only have been about twenty-five. Nothing but a babe!'

'I'm only twenty-six!' replied Finlay with some venom.

'Ah, so you might be, Keith, but you're older than my bloody grandfather.'

From the shelter of the roof, they saw Morgan get into his car and drive away, followed at around fifteen second intervals by no less than four cars.

'Exit the Herberts, followed by the Jerries, followed by the Yanks, followed by our man looking after Morgan,' quipped Finlay. 'I wonder whether there are still some down there or if they are on their way up! Let's shift, Pat, and pinch that car!'

They crossed several rooftops before climbing down into the street via a ventilation shaft on the side of a building.

Once in the street, they split up, Canavan leading the way by about a hundred yards. Finlay walked slowly along a row of parked cars, deciding which one to take. He settled on a Mercedes which looked fairly new, and with a flat piece of metal on his key ring, he had the door open and within thirty seconds was starting down the street towards Canavan. As he climbed in, Finlay accelerated towards the city centre.

'Half a tank of petrol, Pat,' Finlay said, indicating the fuel gauge. 'We can run back into the city, change cars in the American sector and then head up to Flensburg. Anybody tailing us?'

'Not that I can see,' said Canavan. 'Take a couple of rights to make sure.'

Finlay took the next turning right, right again and thrashed the car up a side street. Right again and they were following the vehicle that had previously been behind them.

'Family caravan,' said Canavan, looking at the vehicle. 'Let's get the hell out of it, Keith.' He lit two cigarettes and handed one to Finlay, then settled back into his seat as Finlay headed the car for the east/west autobahn and back to West Germany proper.

The talk turned to fishing as they motored northwards, of

past fishing days. They also laid the plans for their return to Ireland once they had this job out of the way.

'Do you know, Keith, I'm really looking forward to the sea-trout fishing this year. Let's both get to Ireland for the August fishing. We'll make it a date.'

And they left for Flensburg and Denmark.

Five

IN ROOM 17 of the Old Admiralty Building, Admiral Winter had gathered together some of his heads of section to discuss the foundering Operation Kingstone. Also present were the Undersecretary for the Ministry of Defence and Mr Smith, representing MI6 and the Foreign and Commonwealth Office.

Admiral Winter had briefed the Undersecretary on the possibility of Kingstone going badly wrong, either because of a leak within the department or the Soviets being more vigilant than usual.

'The fact is,' said the Admiral, 'Finlay has been blown. His hire car had a bomb attached to it. The station duty officer in Berlin panicked and went to the safe house and was followed by just about every agency in Berlin!'

The Undersecretary stopped him. 'In that case, Admiral, I am certain you should abort this one. In fact, we shall insist!'

The Undersecretary was worried. The embarrassment of an incident which might fall on himself before a scheduled meeting with his Soviet opposite number at some diplomatic junket he was due to attend in the very near future, was too much.

The Admiral looked weary. 'I would have pulled them out at once, but I'm afraid we've lost contact with them. They seem to have vanished!'

The Undersecretary turned grey. 'Vanished?' he choked.

'They haven't been taken? I mean, for God's sake, what's this going to do to the forthcoming talks?'

He began protecting his own position. 'I want it minuted that I have never agreed to this operation!' He leant across the table and gathered up his papers. 'Keep me informed at all times, Winter. I want no covering up!' With that, he scuttled out of the room like a frightened rabbit.

Admiral Winter shrugged his shoulders and glanced around the table at his team, grunting furiously. 'Bloody politicians, spineless buggers!' He lit his pipe, puffed and pulled loudly, sending showers of sparks over his papers. 'Let's go on, shall we?'

Before he started, he shook his papers free of tobacco ash. 'Right! At this stage I'm not much worried, but unless we hear something within the next twenty-four hours we had better institute some action and enquiries. We may even have to contact the Germans. But since they're our allies, they may be a little put out about us sending the type of operatives we have done!'

He pulled noisily on his pipe again before continuing. 'Both Finlay and Canavan are very resourceful but very much inclined to go it their own way, even possibly aborting the operation themselves. On the other hand, I have known them both to act in a manner which has shown me just how damned irresponsible they can be. I have known them to jeopardise both their own lives and those of other people – not to mention property – just to sneak off to go fishing!' His voice had risen to a shout, almost as though Finlay and Canavan were standing in front of him, receiving the dressing-down he felt they deserved through not making contact. The word 'fishing' was accompanied by a loud crash as he smote the table in front of him and the head of the South American desk looked up quizzically.

'Did you say "fishing", John?'

The Admiral looked at him sharply, trying to detect some irony in the question. 'Yes, I did say fishing! Do you remember when that damned satellite of the Russians came down in Finland? Finlay was damned nearly on the spot, involved in another job. So what does he do? He finds the damn thing, pulls it to pieces, sorts out the bit that is needed and walks away as calm as you like, breaking off communication quite deliberately.'

'He got it back, John – that's surely what counts,' Smith interjected, trying to hide his amusement.

'It would have been easier if we'd known what was happening, Rupert! The Finns were close to ejecting our Ambassador, the Russians were demanding the parts of their machine back, while Finlay was away fishing for ten days.'

'I don't think I should worry too much about Finlay, John,' Smith replied. 'He's a survivor, a natural-born rebel, and he gets the job done.'

THERE ARE SOME cities in the world which, regardless of the season, are a delight, and Copenhagen is one of them. Finlay had made many friends there, most of them members of the intelligence community. Finlay had to be circumspect as to whom he contacted. They stayed in hotels for their six-day stay, but never more than one night in each. On the sixth evening they decided they now ought to return to the task in hand.

Canavan broached the subject. 'Are we moving back to Germany, Keith?' The opening gambit was really more of a statement than a question.

'I think we should, Pat. We've been here too long already. Let's find somewhere south of Hamburg to hole up for a while. From there we can buy the rest of the equipment we need and then move down to Hanover.'

Finlay always relied on complete spontaneity of movement, the theory being that if he had no precise plan in mind there could follow no pattern. Therefore, there was nothing from which anybody else could form a pattern.

'Is it wise to do the crossing actually in Berlin?' Canavan asked. 'We have time to go cross-country into their side of the city.'

'I don't know, Pat. Set out logically, the situation is that the Herberts knew we were coming. By leaving Berlin, they must think, logically, that we've either called off what we were there for or that we've gone for a different entry point. Me, I'm for a straight "over the wall" job, pick up chummy and his bullet and out the way we came or through Czechoslovakia.'

Canavan had not missed the implication. 'You want to bring the Professor out as well, Keith? He's getting on a bit for that sort of thing. Anyway, the boss said just the bullet, so maybe they don't really want him in the West.'

Finlay picked up the Hammerli from the table. 'The boss hasn't got his finger on the trigger, has he? Anyway, we'll have to see what he looks like; with our luck, he's probably in a wheelchair. I just can't kill the poor old sod!'

Canavan, much more the practical one of the pair, sighed deeply at what he saw as Finlay's lack of commitment to his duty. 'Oh, for Christ's sake, Keith, grow up! Just because he looks a nice guy in his photograph doesn't mean a thing. He was probably a Nazi in the last lot! They've no sense of honour, these bloody Krauts, you know. They'll follow anybody who promises them greater glory for the Fatherland. Suppose you had invented a bullet which would bugger a Russian tank, would you let the Russians have it?'

'Of course not,' Finlay snorted.

'Then why feel bad about taking out this old bugger? He's only after an easy life in the West to end his days. No, sod it,

Keith, it's not worth the risk. Let's take the bullet, waste the Professor and get out. You've been ordered by London, so salve your overweaning conscience with that.'

Finlay would not be drawn by the sting in the remark. 'Let's play that bit by ear, Pat. We might be walking straight into a trap anyway and beyond that there may not even be a bullet.'

Canavan gave a very non-committal grunt in reply. Finlay knew he wanted no part in bringing Professor Brennan to the West. He also knew that he had no right to ask Canavan to help him.

After Hamburg, the intervening days were spent in a variety of middle-of-the-road hotels between Hanover and Frankfurt, and so it was on the first day of March that they finally crossed back into Berlin via the French sector.

The Professor's departure either way had not been mentioned since Copenhagen. With Canavan playing devil's advocate, they arranged their routes and timing down to the minute and laid their plans for two alternative routes out.

Their entry would be via the main sewers, using the 'student terminal', a route hacked out by well-meaning student idealists in the sixties. It had run deeply into the Eastern sector of the city but discovery had not been long in coming and the East German authorities had sealed and flooded it so that the route was now considered unusable.

The East Germans, however, with an eye to economy, still allowed the West to process their sewage for them. The natural drainage was from East to West and Finlay had joked that where sewage flowed, they should surely be able to go as well. The sealed point and the flooding beyond were negotiable in Finlay's mind. There had to be fairly large gaps in the ceiling to allow the normal rain water through. 'An inch of rain on the city streets is an awful lot of water to get rid of,' he thought. 'There has to be a way through.'

Getting out again from the East, with or without Brennan, would either be via the sewer again, swimming with the flow, or by heading south and then west to a crossing point within the bounds of a newly planted government forest project, which would be well guarded, but would offer excellent cover to within half a mile of 'the strip', the actual wired and mined border.

'Do we check with London first, Keith, to make sure Brennan has not altered his itinerary?' Canavan asked in such a way as to make it clear that he himself thought they should not.

'No, we'll go tomorrow as planned and send a postcard before we leave. By the time the Admiral gets it we should be back out.'

'Sending a postcard' meant just that in reality, for such things were common practice. A seemingly innocuous message was sent to the home of a section chief on a postcard showing a local view, thus giving him a definite location of the sender.

Canavan seemed completely nerveless over the whole affair, alternately reading paperbacks and wanting to talk fishing. Finlay, on the other hand, could not affect such nonchalance and spent his time going over the details again and again and smoking too many cigarettes.

Canavan watched him pacing the hotel room floor, studying for what seemed like the hundredth time the street map of East Berlin. Finally, he could stand it no longer. 'Will you, for Christ's sake, sit down and rest, Keith? You're pacing up and down like a caged lion!'

Finlay grinned. 'Sorry, Pat, I'm always like this before going into the Zone. I shall be sorry tomorrow if we have a long swim. I'll be tired out!'

Canavan, trying to lighten the atmosphere, turned it to a joke. 'I'll not be pulling you along as well, will I?'

And so they passed the night, Canavan sleeping on the sofa

and Finlay going over, yet again, the details of their trip. The problem of Professor Brennan was one he had to face. He hated the idea of just shooting him, and probably his ailing brother also, in cold blood.

Finlay looked at his companion, now deeply asleep, and wondered what made him the person he was. Canavan opened one eye and looked back, his instinct of survival so strong that he could feel somebody looking at him, even in sleep.

'What now? For Christ's sake, settle down and stop robbing a man of his sleep. Sure, I wouldn't have your nervous system. You'll die of a heart attack before you're forty!'

'I'm sorry, Pat. I just can't settle. I suppose if we were criminals I'd be a dead loss.'

Canavan sat up. 'What do you mean, "if"? For Christ's sake, Keith, come out from that wall of respectability you hide behind. You *are* a criminal! Forget the Queen and Country bit, laddie. London has a file on you listing every criminal fibre in your body. Why do you think you got sorted for this work, anyway? Well, I'll tell you! You are one of the most cold-blooded bastards I've ever met. You're a danger to humanity itself – but, given the right motivation and brainwashing, voilà! What have we got? The patriot, the true blue Englishman, tea at four on the patio and all that crap! Like me, Finlay, you're a bloody thug – worse than me, in fact, because you've got brains!'

Finlay was amazed at this outburst. 'You tell me what drives you then, Pat, if it's not love of your country?'

Canavan now spoke softly, not so excited. 'My country is Ireland, remember? I accept that I do this job because I'm a soldier. If they ever kick me out I'll join the IRA or the Ulster Volunteers – either side, wouldn't make any odds to me, just as long as I could fight something or somebody. Shall I make some tea?'

Canavan flicked the kettle into action as he continued. 'I'll make your tea for you, watch your back, fight with you, laugh with you, wipe your English arse for you, even die for you, because I love you like a brother. Just don't ask me to think too deeply about the morality of it all. Life in this game can be very short, so enjoy what you have left of it. And now, since I'm fully awake, read off the checklist of what we need to take again.'

'Right,' said Finlay. 'Here we go. Rope, smoke grenades, magnesium bombs, magazines and bullets, two torches, wire cutters, lock kit, jemmy, large hammer, plastic detonators, poly bags and two of the new one-time dry suits.'

Finlay unpacked one of the one-time dry suits and held it up. Made of very thin latex rubber with heavier rubber cuffs, ankles and neck band, Supply had claimed they were completely waterproof, the whole garment fitting over normal clothes. The problem with them was that as yet they had only been produced in one size, the idea being that the normal stretch of the material made up any differences.

Finlay pronounced them to be a super idea, just right for putting over your dinner jacket if you had to swim to your dinner date. 'But for somebody your size, Pat, it probably means a slow form of castration if you run or swim in it. Me, I shall float off down the river like a bloody deflated Michelin man.'

The appraisal of the gear and the repacking had put the seal of reality on their mission. They now looked forward to the off, both feeling that it would be 'all right on the night'.

With the dawn, the industrious Germans and their city began to rumble into life.

They lingered over their breakfast in the hotel dining room, Canavan eating what Finlay called 'foreign rubbish', while he ate his way through a mountain of fluffy scrambled eggs and crisply grilled bacon.

'When we get out, Keith, we can leg it for Belgium, hop on a plane to Amsterdam and away to Belfast. Easy enough to get into Ireland from there, then we can get a car to my home and lay up for a couple of weeks. Should be some salmon in the river by then.' He stubbed out his cigarette. 'Shall we make a move? I'll let the manager know to make up our bills for this afternoon. You could get a couple of hundred cigarettes before you go up.'

Once back in their room, Finlay flopped heavily on to his bed. 'I'll set my watch for three, Pat. I'd better get some sleep.'

'Soon be going now. Sleep on, me boy, you'll not get much tonight.'

FINLAY JOLTED UPRIGHT to the sound of his alarm. 'Are we going to get this show on the road, Irishman?' he shouted at Canavan.

After ablutions they packed their cases and, as they left the room, Finlay looked back. 'Nothing left behind?' he queried.

'No, Keith, let's get gone!' Canavan slapped Finlay on the shoulder and cleared the stairs to the first landing with one leap. 'Come on, get your arse in gear,' he said as Finlay caught him up. 'Let's earn our salaries!'

They paid their bills and asked the hotel reception to call a taxi. The receptionist paused, telephone in hand. 'Taxi to where, sir?' she asked.

'Berlin Station West, darling,' Canavan said easily. 'We have to go back to Hanover.'

And so they started Operation Kingstone, Canavan exuberant, anxious to get on with it, like a spaniel on a shooting morning, Finlay quiet and thoughtful, his mouth dry and metallic, his stomach muscles tense with apprehension.

Six

FINLAY AND CANAVAN entered the railway station together, bought one-way tickets for Hanover and entered the station buffet. Here they split up, Canavan sitting by the door watching the milling rush-hour crowds, while Finlay positioned himself at the back of the buffet, where he could watch those who came in and out. They occasionally glanced at each other, registering nothing, but acting the part of bored middle-class Germans waiting for their respective trains.

After an hour had passed, Canavan signalled Finlay with the merest suggestion of a flick of his eyebrow. Finlay looked at his watch, picked up his suitcase and left the buffet. He made his way slowly over to the lavatory and once inside, shut himself in a cubicle, where he quickly changed clothes and repacked his suitcase. When he left the cubicle to wash his hands he looked like any other German artisan moving about the station. He glanced in the washroom mirror. 'Not bad,' he thought.

He stowed his suitcase in a left luggage locker, put the key in a large manila envelope and pushed it into a postbox. He walked past the buffet without looking in, bought himself a car magazine and settled on a station bench to read. Half an hour later, Canavan walked past him, dressed in shabby clothes and carrying a rucksack. Finlay watched over his magazine as Canavan left the station, his huge frame easy to spot in the crowd.

Finlay was looking for anybody who might be keeping track of Canavan. He could rely on his instincts to pick out a watcher. He waited ten minutes before following Canavan out of the station building and into the concealment of the rush-hour crowds. He moved quickly eastward, walking fast as though hurrying home, and kept up the pace for a good hour.

By now he had left the crowds behind him and as he moved into a poorer part of the city, few people walked in the same direction. He halted occasionally to check he was not being pursued, made a detour around a building site and arrived back on the original route he was following. Waiting by a corrugated iron fence surrounding the building site, he sank back into the shadows. His watch showed 6.45. He waited for what felt like an age and looked at his watch again: 6.57.

For all his great size, Canavan always seemed to move about silently and with consummate ease. 'Anybody about?' he breathed.

'No, I'm sure we're clear. Let's make a move, Pat.'

'OK,' replied Canavan. 'Easy though. We're about half a mile from where we go down.' He looked up at the sky, imploring, 'Christ, don't let it rain.'

The sewer entrance they had chosen was in an ill-lit side street, one of the few still cobbled in West Berlin. To make sure they were not being followed they waited under the wall of a small factory, fifty yards from the manhole cover. Further up the street, a streetlamp showed white, and it started to rain, the raindrops zipping through the pale light like tiny, falling stars.

The two men looked up at the sky. Finlay sucked his teeth in typical sailor fashion and looked at Canavan, who, as if in answer, said softly, 'We've still got to try, Keith.'

The street was empty as they walked over to the manhole and the rain began to splash from an overhead gutter. Removing the cover, Canavan motioned with his head. 'Down you go, squire, back where you belong!' Canavan followed Finlay down, pulling the cover back over as best he could behind them.

The tunnel in which they now found themselves really stank. The smell caught at the back of Finlay's throat and made him gag. At the bottom of the ladder, a single raised walkway ran above and alongside a flowing stream of rainwater and sewage, illuminated at long intervals by lights sunk into the walls. Under the first such light, Canavan halted and reached for the map.

'Right then, Keith, along this way for half a mile, second right, third left and that should bring us under the border and the sealed-off exit. I'll lead off, you stay close.'

Finlay looked at the stream below them. It had risen and was now flowing deeper and more swiftly, its colour darkening from the stirred up filth. 'It's rising, Pat,' he observed. 'Must be raining harder up top.'

They became conscious of the sound of rushing water, which increased to a loud rumble the closer they came to its source. When they saw the sealed exit, with its two huge gushing pipes shooting out horizontal jets of dark liquid, Canavan breathed, 'I don't think we can shoot those rapids! The pipes are big enough to fit through, but the current's too strong.'

They were standing close together, looking down at the torrent, inhaling through necessity the thick, acrid smell.

'Look, you push me as far as possible, Pat. Once I get right through, there's sure to be a gap between the surface and the roof the other side so I can grab some air – or at least I hope there is! If the handrail along the walkway continues on the other side, I can dive down and attach a rope, let it run back through to you, and Bob's your uncle, we're on our way!'

'And what if there is no gap between the roof and the water? What then?' asked Canavan.

'Well, then I shall be back down that pipe a damn sight quicker than I went up it! And we'll have to wait until such time as the level drops a bit. If I can get the rope back through to you, I shall come back out anyway. With that current, I doubt I shall have much option. Let's get those suits on and give it a try.'

They both struggled into the rubber dry suits, laughed at the spectacle they made and climbed down into the flow of liquid. The going underfoot was very slippery and, as the water reached Finlay's waist, the pressure was almost sufficient to sweep him away.

Reaching the pipes, Finlay motioned Canavan to hand him the coiled rope. Slipping it over his shoulders, he shouted in Canavan's ear, 'Pick me up and I'll try to reach the end and pull my way through. Give me about forty-five seconds. If I'm not through then, let go of me so I can pop back.'

Canavan lifted Finlay and they paused while he drew in deep breaths, expanding his lungs to take in as much of the stinking air as possible.

'Next time, Pat!' shouted Finlay.

He drew in a last deep breath and thrust himself at the tunnel. His head, shoulders and trunk disappeared into the jet. Finlay felt Canavan pushing from behind as he blindly reached for the far end of the pipe, which may or may not have been there. Suddenly, his fingers felt the rim; he gripped and pulled and progressed gradually upwards, the torrent of liquid pressing him back down with unmitigating force.

In what felt like hours but could only have been seconds, Finlay pushed himself against the current and through the far end of the pipe and, by using the sealing wall as purchase, kicked himself upwards to what he desperately hoped was air above him. He broke the surface of the water and gasped noisily, sucking in the dank air in total blackness, then raised his arms above his head – but he could not feel the roof above him. Swimming to his left, he found the tunnel wall and searched for a handhold to rest himself. There was none, so he allowed the current to let him drift back to the wall and clung there, spread-eagled, until his breathing returned to near normal.

There wasn't an iota of light and Finlay had to rely on the pull of the current to give him any sense of bearing. If the East Germans had left the handrail intact along the walkway before sealing the tunnel and allowing it to fill, this is what Finlay had to find. If it was there, he judged it to be about ten feet beneath the surface. He swam forward for ten strong strokes and dived downwards, feeling for the pipework of the handrail.

He was about to give up on his first dive when his hand, pulling backwards, struck it heavily. He rolled over and kicked for the surface, allowing himself to drift back against the wall. He rested again before dragging the rope from his shoulders and, grasping the clip end, let it uncoil and fall away into the current, teasing it straight and hoping that the current had pushed it through the pipe to the waiting Canavan.

Swimming forward again, he dived down until he again collided with the submerged rail and, giving the rope two turns around it and jamming the clip over the free end, he surfaced once more and drifted back to the wall.

His breathing was now becoming difficult, as the air in the tunnel lacked much of the oxygen which was, of course, more freely available on the other side of the pipe. He rested a while, forcing himself to take deep breaths, sucking into his lungs what little oxygen he could.

He guessed that about ten minutes had passed before he swam upstream again, this time keeping more to his right, until he thought he must be in the centre of the flow. He dived down and allowed the current to take him back towards the pipes. Shielding his face and head with his arms, he felt himself carried rapidly down and forward.

He crashed heavily against the wall before being pulled into the pipe feet first, and, straightening his legs, he rocketed through towards Canavan, who broke his fall as he shot past.

Grabbing him by the hair, Canavan hauled him out of the current and helped him to stand upright. Finlay promptly started coughing and retching, vomiting freely as Canavan again took hold and lifted him on to the walkway. Finlay lay there, gasping in the sweeter air between sicking up some of the liquid he had inevitably swallowed when thrust through the pipe. Canavan, kneeling beside him, wiped his face with a hand towel produced from his holdall.

'Christ, Pat, that's pretty grim the other side,' he said, sitting up. 'I hope all those jabs we get work.' He turned away to be sick again. 'There's a good space of air up near the roof – couldn't touch the ceiling from the surface. I got the rope tied to the handrail the other side, about ten feet down I think ...'

Canavan was wiping Finlay's face clean. 'Will you shut your mouth, you damn fool Englishman! Thought I'd lost you that time, for sure. You were gone some twenty minutes before the rope came through. I thought you were trapped and drowned.' He lit two cigarettes and put one in Finlay's mouth. 'Sit and rest. We've got time in hand and I'll lighten this holdall as much as possible,' he said, unpacking it. 'Has the dry suit worked?'

Finlay wriggled around and moved his arms up and down. 'Doesn't feel like any came in, but it's a hell of a job to dive in. Kept popping up like a cork!'

Finlay rested while Canavan abandoned anything from the holdall he judged they would not need. Finlay grinned. 'Keep the cigarettes dry, Pat, and your lighter. When you see the other side, you won't believe it. It's black as a cow's guts and about as smelly.'

Another twenty minutes passed before Canavan rose. 'I'll go first and take the bag. When I'm through you'll know by the rope.' He bent down and helped Finlay to his feet. 'This is it then, youngster. From here on in we're on the wrong side of the wall. I'll watch your back!'

They entered the stream together and made their way over to the pipes. Canavan caught at the rope streaming in the current and hauled it taut in his hands. He turned, gave the thumbs-up sign to Finlay and began pulling himself through the rush of water. His bulk almost checked the wall of water and his feet remained in Finlay's view for what seemed an eternity.

Finlay could feel the movement of his companion through the rope. He looked at his watch. Canavan had now been submerged for nearly two minutes. There were two definite jerks on the rope and then nothing. Finlay took up the slack slowly until the rope was taut. Nothing.

Either Canavan was through and on the surface or he was drowned. Finlay had the greatest difficulty entering the tunnel without the lift from Canavan behind him. The water pulled and tugged at him, forcing his head down on to the rough bottom of the pipe, but once through and aside from the current, he rose rapidly to the surface. He broke through nearer to the side wall than his previous attempt and bumped his head hard against the brick work.

'Pat, you all right?' he gasped. 'You here?'

'No,' came the laconic reply. 'I'm not here, I'm anywhere but here! Christ Almighty, this is like a nightmare!'

They swam towards each other until their hands touched. 'OK, Keith? Christ this water's cold. We'll swim for ten and rest for two. Stay close within touch range. By the map, we've got about half a mile before we turn off right, then it should become shallower and we can walk. Let's get over to the other wall so I can feel when the turning comes.'

They swam off, Finlay on his back, high out of the water and held up by his suit, Canavan breast-stroking and trying to keep the tunnel wall within touch. It was completely dark, the blackness total. The first ten minutes passed quickly and they couldn't judge how far they had come. They did not speak, but both breathed easily. Again they set off and again after ten minutes, they halted and rested. 'OK, kid?' breathed Canavan.

'You?' answered Finlay.

'Three more goes, I reckon, and we should find it.'

They set off again, ten minutes swimming, two minutes rest, ten swimming, two minutes rest.

'Jesus, it had better be soon, Keith, I'm running out of puff.' Canavan was now breathing heavily, his plastic suit obviously proving of less use to him than Finlay's.

'Give me your bag, Pat. I'm OK still. You concentrate on the turning.' Finlay reached out in the darkness towards Canavan's voice. Their hands touched and held while Canavan struggled to remove the canvas bag from round his neck. He passed it back to Finlay, who put the strap over his head, then rolled over on his back and rested the bag on his chest.

On they went. They were about four minutes into the next stage when Canavan snorted, 'It's here! Turn right!'

They swam on. 'Don't stop, Keith. Keep going or I shall cramp up!'

'I can feel a draught, Pat!' They were both now near to panic. Finlay's arms felt heavy and his strokes were becoming shorter. 'Keep on, Pat! Hang on!'

'Well, we can't go back, that's for sure.' The words came in long gasps from Canavan. They struggled on a minute more.

'I can touch, Keith, just!' Canavan swam on for a few strokes and stood up. The water came up to his waist. 'I'm standing, Keith! Where are you?'

'Here. It's all right, I think we've won!'

They rested, Canavan holding Finlay's arm. 'We should find a ladder up on the left-hand side about a hundred yards from where we first touched.'

They were both breathing badly and the foul air had not helped their swim. Finlay could hear the blood pumping through his ears. They pushed on, walking slowly and feeling for the ladder which they both knew had better be fairly close. Neither man was very far from complete collapse.

The first of what they judged to a hundred yards passed and they had not found the ladder. They pressed on.

'It's getting deeper, Pat. Do you think we've missed it? We'll be swimming again shortly.'

As if in answer, there was a dull thump and Canavan swore. 'Jesus Christ, I've got it! Up this and we are in the fresh air!'

Above them, they could see a tiny pinprick of light, almost like a single star in the blackness. Finlay heard Canavan pull himself on to the ladder and the spot of light was obliterated as the Irishman's footfalls clunked heavily on the metal rungs. There was the sound of Canavan's grunting efforts before Finlay heard the scrape of metal upon metal, and light briefly entered the sewer before Canavan descended again.

'All clear in the street, but I can't lift the cover and balance at the same time. Come up behind me and hold me against the ladder while I lift it off.'

Finlay followed Canavan up the ladder, aching to be in the fresh air again. When they reached the top, Finlay grasped the ladder and held Canavan's balance while the Irishman attacked the cover. Again there was the scrape of metal against metal, and a gust of pure, fresh air hit them like a sledgehammer.

'Got the bugger, Keith.' Turning to speak, Canavan bent slightly, broke Finlay's grip and catapulted him backwards down into the sewer. Finlay fell into the putrid water with a heavy splash, and emerged through the slime coughing, spluttering and cursing his companion. 'For Christ's sake, haven't I swallowed enough of this bloody muck for one night?'

He reascended the ladder to where Canavan was standing, only to find him paralytic. He was laughing quietly, his whole body shaking. 'Sorry Keith – couldn't help it,' he cried between his convulsions.

An approaching car brought them to their senses but, once past, they could not help laughing again, partly in relief and partly at the ludicrous position in which they found themselves.

'Charlie Chaplin couldn't do better than this, Pat. For God's sake, let's get out of here before another car comes!' Finlay started pushing Canavan up. 'Get out of it, you crazy sod. I've spent enough time down here!'

Canavan eased himself out, followed immediately by Finlay. They were in a cobbled street, dimly lit. The rain made the cobbles shine and the air smelt wonderful. Taking cover in an alley, they stripped off their rubber suits, rolled them tightly and stowed them in the holdall.

'These suits are superb, Pat. I've only got wet feet,' remarked Finlay. 'Are you dry?'

'Sure I'm dry, but I think the damned thing has gelded me! And I'm frozen to the bone. I hope this Professor has a bathroom, cos my God, you stink!'

The relief they felt having covered the first leg of their journey was immense. 'By my reckoning, Keith, we've got about a quarter of a mile to walk. From now on, we speak German. If we are stopped, let me do the talking, but you be ready with that man-stopper of yours. First hint of trouble, you start shooting, Keith, and run like hell towards the south. Let's move and look like two tired Krauts coming off the late shift.'

They reached the Professor's address within a quarter of an hour, meeting only one person on the way. Canavan bid him a tired 'good night', to which the German responded equably in the same vein and passed by without a glance.

The address turned out to be a drab block of flats in a drab street, a marked contrast to the streets of West Berlin, which were garish and alive with the forced gaiety of a city surrounded by menace, isolated in a vacuum of what might be borrowed time.

Finlay motioned Canavan to wait as he entered the doorway and ascended the concrete stairs. He knocked on the door of the flat and moved back, taking cover behind a pillar. He felt for his pistol as the door opened three inches and an elderly face appeared. 'Ja?' it enquired.

'Professor Brennan?'

'Ja?'

'We've come to take you out,' said Finlay.

Seven

PROFESSOR BRENNAN STOOD facing Finlay and Canavan across a sparsely furnished room. Without taking his eyes off him, Finlay motioned with his gun. 'Check the other rooms, Pat. I'll watch him.'

Brennan stood in a state of obvious tension. 'Do you speak English, Professor?' Finlay asked, motioning again with his gun for the old man to take a seat.

'Not good, but perhaps enough for our needs,' he replied, too nervous to sit, but when Canavan walked back into the room, he gave the old man a quick body search and pushed him into a chair.

'He's clean, Keith, and so is this place. What's next?'

Finlay shoved his gun into his waistband, trying to smile. He said to the Professor, 'We both need a bath. While Pat here is cleaning up, you and I must talk.'

Some of the tension had gone and Finlay's instinct told him that they had not walked into a trap, so he was now prepared to take Brennan at face value, at least for the moment.

'I will prepare you some food as we talk. You will excuse my English. There are some things you should know. I am not coming back with you and you cannot leave here until tomorrow night.'

Curtly, Finlay responded, 'Why not? I want to be out of

here tonight and back in the West before it gets light. The longer we stay here, the greater our risk. Have you got what we came for?'

The Professor looked alarmed at Finlay's tone. 'My friend, I am not coming with you. My brother has died and has to be buried. Tomorrow there is a big military parade, nearly a holiday. The city will be crowded and you will be able to get out more easily. That is the reason I gave London for giving them a special day to arrive and leave.'

Canavan, still very cautious, said, 'If we have to stay here until tomorrow night, you realise that you will be unable to leave the flat during that time either?'

Brennan sighed. 'I understand that you still think this may be a trap, but I have no intention of going anywhere.' He moved to a cupboard and opened the door.

Instantly Finlay was beside him, his gun drawn. It was a very frightened Brennan who backed away, blanching.

'What are you looking for?' asked Finlay, moving aside the packets of foodstuffs in the cupboard with his gun.

'What you came for, in the red biscuit tin.'

Finlay picked up the tin and placed it on the table. 'You open it, Professor, and do it slowly.'

'Of course I will open it,' said Brennan, smiling wanly. 'You do not yet trust me, my friends.'

Finlay, nerves still a little brittle, said, 'No, we do not, and pretty soon you're going to catch on that we are not your friends! So be a good chap and open the box.'

From the red biscuit tin, Brennan produced what Finlay and Canavan had come for: a long silver-coloured bullet about eight inches in length and one and a half inches in calibre. As Brennan handed it to him, Finlay guessed it weighed about a pound.

'This is what you came for, I believe,' said the Professor.

'You don't need me. I am surprised you really expected to take me back with you – but now that I am no longer going, you are no doubt relieved. Tomorrow, I will take you out of the city by car to wherever you want to cross the border. Because of my position this will be easy. I cannot force you to trust me, but my children are in the West, so I had hoped to see them again before I die. What I have given you was to be my passport.'

Finlay looked at Canavan. 'Get your bath, Pat. I think he's on the level.' And to Brennan he said, 'What about that food, Professor? I'm ready to eat anything!'

Soon there was the sound of running water and steam began to issue from the open bathroom door.

'Your friend is very careful,' said Brennan.

'Yes, that's his job, to get me out,' replied Finlay. 'What do you get out of this, Professor Brennan, now that you're not coming over? It's all been a waste of time for you, surely?'

Brennan shrugged. 'I did want to come with you, you know. But I had to keep my end of the bargain anyway once you were on your way. Perhaps, someday, there will be another chance.'

Finlay was perplexed by the way the old man had given up. 'But if there's not, what then? Look, Professor, is money any good to you? I have about fifteen thousand West German marks. Can you buy your way out?'

Brennan smiled. 'Money is no use to me, young man. There is nothing to buy and you cannot trust anybody enough to bribe them. No, you take the bullet. It is my gift to the West, where my children now live, children I will not see again. They escaped this prison, thank God. Here, they are just the same as the Nazis – some of them were Nazis. I spent twenty years under the Nazis and too many years under these people.

I will be glad to die. My only sadness is my children and their children.' He sighed again. 'I will prepare some food for your careful friend, and when you have cleaned yourself, I will have some ready for you.'

The Professor turned his back on Finlay and went into the small kitchenette.

'Poor old sod,' thought Finlay. 'Back home he'd probably be living somewhere in Surrey with a fat golden retriever and belong to the local gardening club.'

He followed Brennan into the kitchen. 'Tell you what, Professor, if and when we get this bullet out, perhaps I can get London to allow me to come back for you, or perhaps get you invited on a trade mission. You'd like England.'

The old man smiled. 'You are very kind, but do not let us deceive ourselves. Your employers would never let you come back here just for me.'

Finlay argued, 'But surely you must still be very valuable. Is this bullet all your own work?'

Finlay was trying hard to assuage his conscience. Just a few days ago he had been quite prepared, under orders, to kill Brennan. Looking at him now, the Professor might have been anybody's grandfather, and he was so without hope for his own future.

'I'd come back for you, old chap,' said Finlay, putting his hand on Brennan's shoulder.

'Perhaps,' was all the Professor answered.

Canavan appeared at the door. 'Now that smells good, Professor: bullet-maker and you can cook as well. I feel like a new man, Keith!'

'You smell somewhat better, Pat! Hope you haven't used all the hot water.'

When Finlay had bathed and eaten he withdrew into the bedroom with Canavan to discuss their next move.

Canavan, still doubtful about Brennan, began the conversation. 'Well, Keith, you're in charge of this one. What do we do with him? I think we should kill him – that way is the safest. This could still be a set-up, you know! Come on, brains, what do we do with him? To me he looks a shifty old bugger, too smooth by half!'

Finlay thought for a moment, weighing up the risks of leaving Brennan behind alive. 'No, Pat, we won't kill him, not here anyway. If he's on the up and up, we can get out of Berlin with his help. My instinct says that for now he lives, and I always take note of my instinct. I've been here before and I've come home before. No, I'll not kill him yet.'

Canavan expelled his breath loudly. 'You and your gut feelings, Keith. I suppose you're right. OK, so we let him help us, then what?'

'We'll have to play it by ear, Pat. We'll know if he's on the cross, then I'll be the first to take him out.'

Canavan remained unconvinced. 'I still say we should kill him. Your softness will get you into trouble one day!'

Finlay looked at Canavan and saw what he did not like in himself: the cold-blooded weighing of the worth of a man's life. When he had joined the Service, such things had troubled him a little, and even after all the violence and treachery the job had entailed, he had not yet inured himself to it.

Finlay paced the room. 'OK then, Pat. I'll insist he comes back with us.' In his mind, Finlay knew this was a non-starter.

'Oh, for Christ's sake, Keith, you've seen the way he creeps about. If we run into trouble at the wire, he'll hold us back and we'll all be taken!'

'All right, all right! I know what has to be done. We'll use him to get out and then, in the finest tradition of our Service, once we've used him, I'll kill him.' Finlay sat heavily on the bed. 'Where's the bloody map? Come on, Pat, let's think about our way back.'

They rejoined the Professor. Canavan, with forced bonhomie, said, 'OK, Prof., any more coffee about?'

'Yes,' replied the old man.

Finlay suspected by the sheepish expression on his face that the Professor knew what they had been talking about. He spread the large map out on the floor. 'OK,' he said. 'This is the way I think we should go.'

Together, the three men went over the route to the crossing point, noting where the watch towers were located, the likely dead ground and so forth, on their approach to the wire.

Finlay measured the distance with the top joint of his thumb and traced his finger over the map. 'That's the nearest guard house with the tower on the left of it. If they have no patrols out, it will take them at least ten minutes to react and get to this point where we cross. If the ditch marked here runs up this close to the wire, it is sure to have electric eyes and tripwires. It's the eyes that are the problem as we cannot bank on seeing them, so we won't know if we can reach this point here, three hundred yards from the wire, undetected.

'However, if this is a young spruce plantation, as the map says, we can get through that, up this line we take to be a ditch, and there we are! Two or three hundred yards from the wire – home run only!'

Canavan nodded, traced his finger along the map and stopped at the end of the woodland. 'Along to this hummock or hole, whatever it is, you go in to the wire and cut, while I watch your back, then it's just the dogs!' He grinned at Finlay, loving the thought of crossing the strip.

There was a great deal of competition within the Service for who could claim the greatest number of crossings of the strip. Finlay had eight to his credit; for Canavan, this would be his tenth.

'The strip' was the fifty yards of actual border for its whole length fenced by strands of barbed wire to a height of about fifteen feet. Most of the area beyond the minefield was ploughed and harrowed to a beach-like fineness to show any footmarks of those who had passed the first two deterrents. In some places, instead of mines, there were dogs, Dobermans, loose-running and trained to attack anything that moved.

'Hope to Christ it's mines, Keith. We'll have all the hours of darkness to cope with them, but if it's those bloody great woofers, we'll have to shoot our way over. It'll be like the gunfight at the O.K. Corral!'

Finlay laughed. 'I've got thirty-two bullets and there aren't going to be that many dogs. Anyway, dogs like me!'

'Those bastards won't!' laughed Canavan. 'Have you seen the sort they've got? Every one of them like the Hound of the Baskervilles, bred with double rows of steel teeth and shoulders like prize fighters. Evil sods, I can tell you! Won't be any use saying, "Here, doggie, doggie!"'

Finlay laughed at Canavan's exaggeration. 'There isn't any dog alive, Pat, that a .38 bullet won't stop, no matter where it hits him, and when they see their mates being chopped over, they'll soon get the message. Anyway, a few dog bites are better than getting your arse blown off by a mine!'

'Well,' answered Canavan, 'if you think you can reload that pea-shooter of yours with one of those great hairy bastards hanging on to your leg, then well and good. Give me mines any time; those I can cope with!'

'Good,' said Finlay, with an air of finality. 'If it's mines, you can go first! I wonder if the old boy is making some more coffee.'

Brennan reappeared from the kitchen. 'Have you decided what to do with me?' His frankness was a little disarming.

'Yes, Prof. You run us out of the city to our crossing point, say goodbye and we'll part company. If you get caught out, we'll be long gone anyway.'

Finlay looked at Canavan. 'Better get some rest, Pat. I'll keep dog until six, then you till twelve, then we'll check the route again. I think we should leave about four tomorrow afternoon, Professor, which means we'll be travelling through rush-hour traffic. That should get us where we want to be by six in the evening, when it's properly dark. Any thoughts, Professor?'

'It would seem right to me, young man, but I have never crossed the border so I cannot really help, even though I would like to. If tomorrow there is not time to say goodbye I wish you now God's speed. And I hope some day that I will make the crossing myself.'

Canavan left them. It was 1.30 in the morning and Finlay yawned deeply. 'This time tomorrow,' he thought, 'we'll be well on our way home.' He thought about Canavan's proposal for a quick disappearing act and getting some fishing done in Ireland. He stretched and yawned again. 'Yes, Pat. Good idea. We'll go to Ireland.'

'What are you dreaming of, young man?' asked Brennan.

'Fishing, Professor. You know, the rod and line sort.' He made casting motions with his hands. 'You ever go fishing?'

Brennan shook his head. 'Not since I was a boy. There was not much chance under the National Socialists. It was not "productive" enough, so it was not encouraged and I never learnt it properly. You are lucky to have been born English, for you can always have your freedom to do as you wish. Your country has not suffered like ours, mainly through our own madness, and now we live in a prison. You still have your democracy, traditions and your confidence that your way is the right one. You must be proud of this, no?'

Finlay thought for a moment. 'Do you know, Professor, I think the average Englishman takes it all for granted most of the time. Only when it's threatened do we appreciate it. I often wonder what would have happened if the Germans had invaded us. I suppose some would have carried on the fight, even up to the present. They would have started out as "Freedom Fighters", but would by now have become terrorists – much like the Palestinians are today. One generation passes and the original reasons for the fighting are lost. Anyway, history is always written by the victor.'

So they passed what remained of the night, discussing topics as far apart as National Socialism, the Rolling Stones and ballistics. At six, Finlay woke Canavan and rolled into bed himself. 'Easy on him, Pat, he isn't such a bad guy. He's an interesting old cove when you get talking to him.'

Canavan, still half asleep and stiff from the previous night's excursions, said, 'I'll wake you with lunch, youngster. I wonder if the old man's got a chess set.'

The smell of cooking woke Finlay sometime later. He got up and wandered sleepily into the living area of the flat. Brennan and Canavan were in the kitchen, standing by the cooker, deep in animated conversation.

Canavan turned. 'Oh, you woke then, Keith. Lunch will be just a little while. Kurt here is quite a cook – beat the hell out of me at chess too!'

Finlay smiled at Canavan's change of attitude towards the Professor and said, 'And that's with no sleep and he's twice your age. Makes you wonder how they lost the war, doesn't it?'

Canavan and Brennan both laughed. 'Ah,' said Canavan. 'You bloody English! Kurt and I have something worked out for your lot. I'm going to join the IRA and kick you lot out of Ulster, then Kurt and his buddies are going to build a bloody great rocket, attach it to England, and put the bloody lot of you into permanent orbit. The English think they're God's chosen people, so we'll just put you up a bit closer to him and you can ask him about it yourselves!'

'Balls!' was all Finlay could think of to say to that.

The three men ate a lunch of bacon, cabbage and potatoes and drank more coffee, then Finlay and Canavan went over their route again. They unloaded Canavan's bag and discarded what they did not need. For border crossings of this sort, lightness of load was essential and their equipment was cut down to rope, smoke grenades, magnesium bombs, one torch, spare magazines for their side arms and the wire cutters.

'Is that it then, Pat?' asked Finlay. 'Doesn't look much to take on the mighty Russian Bear, does it?'

'You'd better hope we don't have to!' joked Canavan. 'Else we'll get a good mauling!'

It was almost time to leave.

Eight

BRENNAN, AS GOOD as his word, drove Finlay and Canavan out of the city. The traffic, by Western standards, was fairly light, and Brennan, driving over the cobbled streets, had both his passengers sitting on the edge of their seats. The small Skoda left a lot to be desired in the way of suspension.

'Jesus, Kurt,' growled Canavan. 'Change your mind and come over with us. You'd get a BMW from your brothers in the West. And for God's sake, slow down. If you hit something, we'll all be sunk!'

The old man laughed. 'When I was young, my father had a Mercedes, and that was a car! Here, you have to please the Party even to own one of these. I am lucky. I have this for my work. Do not complain, my friends, we will get you to Volpke.'

Volpke, a small rural village some eight miles from the border, was their chosen crossing point. It was heavily guarded, because on paper it looked the easiest place to get close to the wire, but Finlay and Canavan knew that it was those borders with a surfeit of guards which were the easiest to cross. Numbers bred carelessness.

'With a fair wind, Keith, in twelve hours from now we can be safely tucked up in bed after a long hot bath and a few drinks to send us off to sleep!'

'I'd like to think so, Pat, but let's get across before we talk comforts.'

Canavan, undaunted about the coming crossing, laughed at Finlay's fears. 'Anybody who flits between Russia and Finland like you has nothing to worry about. Those buggers up there are real professionals!'

They drove on in virtual silence for the next hour and a half. There were very few cars on the road and, despite the bad road surface, they made good time. About thirty miles from Volpke, they picked up a following car, which hung back half a mile and remained the same distance behind them for several miles.

Finlay turned to Canavan. 'Now that looks like a follower, Pat.' He was unworried by it, as they were always dealing with such things. 'Slow down, Professor,' he ordered. 'Do exactly as I say. When I say stop, you stop as quickly as this thing will allow you. I'll bail out and Pat will tell you how to proceed then.'

Brennan slowed the car and Finlay prepared to jump out. Then, inexplicably, the following car accelerated quickly, catching them in seconds. Finlay and Canavan both drew their guns but the car pulled past rapidly and became just two glowing red lights in the distance. Finlay stayed put.

'Police?' asked Canavan.

Finlay's mouth was dry. 'I don't think so. Whoever they were, they probably don't realise just how close they came to getting killed.'

Tension gone again, they drove on in silence. It began to rain steadily.

'Someone's on our side,' Finlay remarked. 'Looks like being a rough night.'

They drove on. The rain fell harder and the little car rocked and swayed in the increasing wind as it splashed its way over the last few miles.

Another twenty minutes of driving got them to within six miles of Volpke.

'Not far now, Pat. Stop about a kilometre short of the village, Professor. We'll skirt around it on foot,' said Finlay.

Tension quickly built again. Finlay closed his eyes tightly to prepare himself for the darkness once out of the car.

Brennan slowed down and pulled off the road. 'Will this do, young man?' He did not look at Finlay, but stared straight ahead, a muscle in his face twitching slightly.

'Yes, Professor, I think so,' Finlay answered quietly. He looked at the old man and put his hand on Brennan's arm.

'Drive carefully on the way back, Professor, and thank you for everything. Perhaps we'll meet again.'

Canavan got out of the car and picked up his bag. He reached through the driver's window and took Brennan's hand.

'Next time, Kurt, I'll beat you at chess!'

Canavan and Finlay stood in the road and watched the rear lights of Brennan's car disappear back towards Berlin.

'I thought you were going to kill him,' Canavan said simply.

'Yes,' replied Finlay. And after a long silence he said, 'I was, wasn't I?'

They moved away from the road and struck off westward. It began to rain harder than ever – cold, heavy rain that beat through their inadequate clothes in the wind.

'Damn it,' cursed Finlay. 'This is much too heavy to last! What we want is a steady downpour and a force six!'

Once their eyes were completely acclimatised to the darkness, Canavan set a good pace, swinging forward across fields towards the West. A narrow gravel-covered road caused them to halt their progress, at which point they split up and checked up and down to see if it was in any way patrolled.

Once they had satisfied themselves that this was not the

case, they pressed on. They passed a small isolated farmhouse about two fields distant, from which glowed a yellow light from a ground floor window. A barbed wire fence squealed in protest when Canavan inadvertently walked into it and a dog barked half-heartedly from the farm.

After an hour's march, they rested briefly in a small spinney they had noted on the map. The wind roared through the tops of the ash trees, rattling the branches and throwing small twigs down to the ground.

Canavan pointed south-west and said quietly, 'Over there, about two fields away, should be the start of the spruce plantations. If it was clearer, we might see the glow from the border lights by now.'

They pushed on quickly, the wind and rain covering their approach, but both knew that this close to the border patrols might be anywhere. At last they reached the spruce plantation and, walking quietly along its outskirts, found the ditch they had seen on the map. They were not disappointed by its size, about four feet deep, the first six inches of which were filled with spruce needles. They lay down just inside the plantation. Finlay checked his watch. It was a quarter to nine. He moved closer to Canavan.

'There won't be any "eyes" in this lot, Pat,' he said. 'No doubt there are plenty of tripwires though. The bullet is in my right-hand pocket. If I get hit, take it and go on.'

'Not unless you're dead, I won't!' Canavan answered. 'Sod the bullet.'

Finlay knew it was no use arguing with Canavan. Once before when they were in a tight spot in the Yemen, Canavan had risked his own life and the mission to go back for Finlay, who had been outflanked and surrounded by their pursuers.

'I'll take point now if you like, Pat,' said Finlay, moving to the ditch. He slid down into the bottom and, making sure

Canavan was with him, proceeded on hands and knees, gently probing the air in front of him with slow up and down movements of his hand, feeling for tripwires which he felt sure were in front of them somewhere.

Progress was of necessity very slow and it had taken them almost two hours to cross most of the plantation. They were about twenty yards from open ground, still in the ditch, when Finlay found the first of them, touching it with his hand on the upstroke.

Without speaking, he rose slowly feeling the air about him, looking for another wire at head height. Nothing. He placed himself astride the one he had found, motioned to Canavan and pointed down between his feet. Canavan nodded and, remaining in a crouched position, crossed the wire. Finlay, back on his hands and knees, moved forward a yard and found another. Again they negotiated the wire.

They found two more before they reached the end of the ditch and the open ground beyond. Across the open ground, closer than the map had indicated, was the strip. The wire fences were all dimly illuminated by lights strung out on poles.

Finlay touched Canavan's arm and they moved off left, crawling slowly down the outside of the plantation. After about seventy yards they found the small depression in the ground that had showed on the map. They both sank down into it and looked across the two hundred yards or so of flat ground between themselves and the wire.

The wind lashed the rain across the open space in front of them, swinging the lights on the fence. Finlay took the wire cutters from the bag and motioned to Canavan that he was going over to the fence. For a moment, Canavan's teeth showed whitely in the dark. He was smiling. He squeezed Finlay's shoulder.

It was at that moment that a roe deer, which must have been within five yards of them, broke cover and bounded out into the open ground. There followed a loud bang as a flare shot skyward, triggered by the deer colliding with a tripwire, and a machine gun actuated by the same mechanism swept an arc of bullets across the open ground and back again.

The deer was swept off its feet as the flare burst above them and drifted on its parachute swiftly in the wind. Finlay and Canavan were instantly bathed in white light and another bang sounded as a second flare soared upwards.

'They must have them on timers, Pat. Damn their bloody thoroughness. Let's get back into the wood a bit. They may not look further than that deer, not on a night like this!' Finlay said, hoping he was right.

As they got back under the shadows of the small trees, they could feel the fresh needles under their hands, chopped off by the bullets from the machine gun.

'Second time we've been in the shit this week, Keith,' remarked Canavan, without much humour in his voice.

'Time the Herberts and watch where they avoid tripwires. I hope to God they find that deer.' Finlay was surprised by his own calmness, despite the predicament they were in.

Eight minutes later, they heard the first sound of voices, coming from their right. From where they lay, Finlay and Canavan could see soldiers approaching. They had spread out in a line between the spruce trees and the fence and were systematically searching the sparse ground covering. Finlay could count eight silhouettes when they were about 150 yards away.

'No dogs,' breathed Canavan. 'We might just pull this off, m'boy!'

As they drew level to where the two men lay, there was a shout. One of the soldiers had found the deer and their line closed around its body in a huddle. One of the silhouettes, obviously in charge, sent two of the soldiers towards the fence to check for signs of anybody having attempted to cross.

One of them made exaggerated high stepping movements about five yards short of the fence and this, Finlay judged, was another tripwire. The two soldiers returned to the group, satisfied that no attempt had been made to break the barrier.

Finlay and Canavan lay breathing easily, almost amused at the little drama being played out in front of them. However, when two more soldiers were detached from the group and made straight towards the place where they lay, both men tried unconsciously to flatten themselves still further into the wet earth beneath them.

Finlay and Canavan could hear them talking, cursing the rain as they approached. 'Christ,' thought Finlay. 'They're going to walk right on to us!'

They lay still, their faces hidden. From where he was lying, Finlay saw one of the soldiers stop about six feet in front of Canavan. He turned and seemed to look directly at Finlay, then moved away again and shouted, 'Nichts Hier!' He headed back to the group assembled around the deer.

Finlay heard Canavan breath out and he could feel his own heart still hammering against his ribs. A shout from the group told the two returning soldiers to wait where they were and the others would return with the dogs, just to make sure. The main body of soldiers moved off quickly back the way they had come, while the other two drifted closer together, about thirty yards from where Finlay and Canavan remained in hiding.

Looking at his watch, Finlay allowed six minutes to pass, then he gently eased himself into a sitting position and drew his gun. Drawing up his knees and using them as rests for his elbows, he looked down along the barrel. He shot twice.

Temporarily blinded by the muzzle flash, he cried, 'Both down, Pat!'

Canavan was already on his feet, running towards the two inert soldiers, whom he stripped of sub-machine guns and magazines.

'Cut the wire, Keith,' said Canavan, throwing him a machine gun. 'And sort the mines with that. I'll cover should they get back. For Christ's sake, hurry though, or we're done for this time!'

From the Western side of the wire they could see lights approaching fast. 'Who the bloody hell is that?' yelled Finlay, running towards the fence. 'They must think they're the bloody Cavalry!'

Jumping over the tripwire, Finlay arrived at the fence. 'Monsieur, nous sommes Anglais,' he shouted across at the vehicle opposite.

A very English voice shouted back, 'So are we, mate, Royal Green Jackets – you're opposite the British sector. Who are you, for God's sake?'

Finlay was sitting down, stripping the lace from one of his shoes. 'SAS. I'm going to throw something over. Cut the wire your side and chop a path with your machine guns.' He tied his shoelace around the bullet and, whirling it around his head, threw it over the gap. He heard it hit something metal the other side. 'Whatever happens tonight, you get that back to the Admiralty immediately!'

The Green Jackets were hacking the wire. Finlay, cutting at his side, shouted to the Green Jackets opposite, 'There are two of us …'

At this point, automatic fire came from behind Finlay. The soldiers had returned and Canavan had opened fire on them.

'We'll give you covering fire!' shouted the Green Jacket, and several of them scrambled out of a scout car.

'Stop!' shouted Finlay. 'Under no circumstances whatever will you return their fire!'

'But...' began the Green Jacket.

'Under no circumstances, got it? Take that thing I threw over and withdraw immediately. Go on, man, get out, or you'll start something we can't have!'

The East Germans were sending up flares every few seconds, which were caught by the wind and whipped away downwind. Finlay started running back towards Canavan and immediately lost the shoe from which he had removed the lace. He picked it up and pushed it into his shirt. He remembered the tripwire in time, jumped it and at once came under fire from somewhere on his left.

The earth around him exploded and danced under the bullet's impact as shards of broken stones stung and cut his legs. He lay there, covering his head with both hands, until the fire shifted back to Canavan. Finlay was up again, running towards the muzzle flashes of Canavan's gun.

Canavan was retreating back towards the trees. His heavy, accurate fire had stopped their assailants' advance temporarily. A vehicle, which sounded to Finlay like a half-track, was racing down the fence, bent on backing the East German's efforts.

Finlay and Canavan fell into a depression in the ground at the same time and the half-track opened fire with a heavy machine gun directly pointing at where they lay, its bullets hurling turf and clods of earth upwards.

'Hang on, Pat, let me fix this shoe or I'll never be able to run!' He stripped the lace from his other shoe, snapped it in two and relaced them. Canavan opened up with the German sub-machine gun on a group of soldiers trying to outflank them. His fire was met with return from the half-track.

Finlay, now lying on the bank beside Canavan, picked his

targets slowly and knocked them down with the Hammerli. 'That was an English patrol on the other side, Pat. I threw them the bullet.' He laughed briefly. 'They were all for joining in!'

Another burst from the half-track covered them both in earth.

'Let's get back down that ditch, Pat!'

Canavan made no answer. Finlay glanced at him still lying there, then grabbed at him. 'Pat!'

Canavan slid down the bank and rolled heavily on to his side. In the light of the flares, Finlay could see that the front of his head had been blown away. The blood ran in watery streaks down his face before the rain had time to wash it away.

Finlay choked and gasped. 'Pat! Pat! I'm sorry, mate.' He knelt beside Canavan, oblivious of the renewed firing, and closed his friend's eyes. His own misted with tears. He felt beaten.

He looked up and saw two soldiers not twenty yards away, moving towards him in a crouching run. Finlay, upright as though on a range, sighted the first and shot him down, then again, and the second man collapsed backwards with the impact of the next bullet.

Finlay's grief had turned to boiling anger. Five soldiers approaching from the left were the next to occupy Finlay. He shot once and saw one of them spin round and collapse as the others dropped and opened up with machine guns.

The bank above Finlay flew to pieces under the weight of fire and Finlay knew he had to move. He grappled in Canavan's bag for smoke grenades, which he threw across in front of him. Wreathed in smoke blowing downwind over him, he sprang over the bank into the young spruce trees and started running for his life.

Behind him, the fire was still momentarily directed at the

place where Canavan lay and then into the trees on his right. The wind, rain and gunfire covered the sound of his crashing retreat and for three or four hundred yards Finlay ran as he had never run before.

Turning left, his breath now coming in sobs, he ran northwards through the young trees. He stopped a moment and listened. The pursuit and firing still came from his right, but at some distance now.

He came to the end of the spruce plantation and in front of him, some two hundred yards away, was more cover. He knew if he could reach that and keep moving he may have a chance. He began running, the sound of pursuit moving away from him.

Finlay was running his fastest when the bullet hit him six inches above the left knee. It shattered his thigh bone and passed out the other side of his leg and continued on into the night, its work done. Finlay cartwheeled over and landed flat on his back, winded.

He lay inert for a few seconds, wondering what had happened, before his instinct for survival dragged him to his feet again. He staggered for about two steps and fell.

Again he struggled upright, only to be clubbed down by an East German soldier. He saw the blow coming and tried to ride it, but it was too late. The rifle butt crashed into his mouth and Finlay felt himself whirling away into blackness.

FINLAY'S BRAIN STRUGGLED back to consciousness unwillingly. He had hoped he was dead. He was aware of something warm splashing on his face. The liquid stung his eyes as it seeped under his eyelids and it tasted bitter around his mouth. He opened his eyes to see a soldier urinating on his face and tried to move, but four others were standing, one each on his wrists and ankles.

Another soldier took the place of the one above his head and the foul-tasting liquid splashed down on him again. Another, seeing him awake, kicked Finlay heavily in the ribs and kept kicking until his ribs gave way.

Finlay knew he was about to die and, with great effort, forced his tongue backwards under his gum, searching for the pill that had been stitched there. It had gone and in its place was a roughly cut hole. His captors had found it and removed it while he was unconscious.

Finlay knew despair then. To be alive and captured the wrong side of the strip was the recurring nightmare of all his Service colleagues.

A voice above him barked orders and only the two soldiers standing on his wrists remained. One man, obviously an officer, was shouting down at him, cursing him and kicking him in his bullet-shattered thigh. He cursed Finlay about the losses in men he had suffered and kicked him again.

He then drew a small pistol and waved it in Finlay's face, shouting something Finlay could not understand. He marched around Finlay's inert body, stood between his legs and aimed the pistol at his head. Finlay closed his eyes and waited, only to receive another kick, this time in the temple.

The officer with the pistol took deliberate aim and shot Finlay through his right leg, just below the knee. Finlay felt the bullet as a heavy blow and his newly wounded leg jumped in uncontrolled spasms. Once again, the kicking started and Finlay lapsed into black unconsciousness, a blessed relief from the pain which was by then consuming him.

Nine

ADMIRAL WINTER LOOKED out over St James's Park, his
shoulders hunched and his hands thrust deeply into his
pockets. He was surrounded by a thick cloud of tobacco
smoke as he puffed fitfully on his pipe. Behind him in the
room sat most of the section heads of the Joint Defence
Intelligence Staff, two very senior civil servants and Mr Smith,
from the Foreign and Commonwealth Office. On the table,
standing upright, was the anti-tank bullet, having recently
arrived from Berlin via RAF Lyneham.

Without turning, Admiral Winter voiced his thoughts.
'I wonder how long it will be before the Soviets announce
something.'

Nobody ventured an opinion.

Mr Smith rose from the table and joined the Admiral at the
window. 'It was eight days before they released any
information on the survivors from the B27, eight days of
waiting that time, even after the Norwegians picked up
wreckage from the Barents Sea. They are in the right this time,
so I don't suppose they will be long about kicking up a fuss.'

The Admiral glanced at his watch. 'The Minister will be
here in about ten minutes wanting to know the ins and outs of
a duck's arse, probably only to make sure no mud sticks to
him. Bloody politicians!'

'The Green Jacket officer, was he sure Finlay made it back to the trees?' asked Smith for about the third time that morning.

'Yes. As far as they could ascertain it was Finlay who was last on his feet throwing smoke grenades. They said it was the same chap who threw the bullet over. He was short, definitely English and he told them to get the bullet back to the Admiralty. Canavan was tall and Irish and referred to this place as "the office", but to Finlay it was always "The Admiralty".

'There's no mistake, it was Finlay who got it over and who was last on his feet. The smoke he put down obscured his retreat to the Green Jackets as well as to the Soviets, but they reported continued firing even after the smoke had cleared.'

A telephone rang and one of the civil servants reported, 'The Minister is on his way up, Sir.'

The Admiral answered with a non-committal grunt but didn't move from his position at the window.

'If Canavan were wounded, what then?' asked Smith.

The Admiral thought for a moment. 'Finlay would not let him be taken alive, nor would Canavan desert Finlay and leave him alone. No, as I see it, Canavan was killed when they began their firefight. Finlay got back into cover and was most likely killed or wounded thereafter.'

'There may be a chance he is still alive, possibly still on the run, then?' ventured Smith.

The Minister arrived, slamming the door behind him, and crashed his briefcase on to the table. Admiral Winter remained looking out of the window.

'Well, John, what a mess this is. I was never keen on this damned operation; I knew it would go wrong! Haven't you anybody but incompetents working for you these days? Good God, there was almost a full-blown border incident involving British troops. If the officer in charge of the border patrol didn't have the good sense to withdraw, it could have been very nasty! The embarrassment this is going to cause the Government both at home and with the Russians will be monumental! What have you to say?'

Admiral Winter turned, glowering, and walked slowly down the table towards the Minster.

'Firstly,' he barked, 'my men are not incompetents; secondly, it was my man who ordered the army patrol to withdraw; thirdly, it's part of my job to embarrass the Russians; fourthly, instead of bewailing an operation that has gone wrong, you should be preparing a statement ready for the media should this story break.

'The BBC have reported flares and heavy firing on that section of the border and the *Daily Express* has been ferreting about. Now, why don't you earn your keep and keep a lid on this as far as possible instead of crying over spilt milk!' Admiral Winter emphasised the last part of his statement by poking his forefinger at the Minister's face.

The telephone rang again. One of the civil servants picked it up, listened and handed it to Winter. He listened for a moment, muttered, then replaced the receiver and sighed heavily. 'The Russians have announced that they have shot dead two agents from the West and will be making the strongest possible protest to the Government concerned.' He walked back to the window. 'It means, gentlemen, that they do not know where they came from or else by now their Ambassador would be knocking on the front door of the Foreign Office!'

The Minister looked distinctly relieved. 'We shall deny they were ours, of course, should we be asked. What a relief to know they were killed!' He coughed uncomfortably. 'Well, you know what I mean. Damn bad show about losing good men like that, John. I take it you will be informing next of kin and that sort of thing.' He picked up his briefcase. 'I'll leave you to tie up the loose ends then. Good morning, gentlemen.'

He left the room quickly, obviously glad to think the matter was closed. Winter, white-faced with rage, spat out, 'Bastard! Spineless louse!'

Smith put his hand on Winter's arm. 'Steady, John. I've never known a politician with any more backbone than that one's got – it goes with the job. What about next of kin? Do you want me to get that bit done?'

'No. Thanks all the same,' replied Winter. 'I'll get the Belfast office to go and see Canavan's father. I'll motor down to Hampshire to see Finlay's people myself. I shall go this evening,' he said, gathering up some papers.

'Do you know them very well, John?' queried Smith.

The Admiral looked at Smith for a moment. 'Yes, I do as a matter of fact. They're neighbours, almost.'

Winter marched to the door and left without saying another word.

Smith gazed after him and said to the retreating footsteps, 'You poor old bugger, John, you poor old bugger.' He then picked up the bullet, put it in his briefcase, nodded a goodbye to the others and followed Winter from the room.

NINEY WAS MARKING a field map with the progress, or lack of, of the spring sowing and preparing dinner at the same time, and she swore lustily when she heard a strange car arrive in the yard. Getting up and looking from the kitchen window into the gloom of a February evening she noted the large black Rolls Royce and recognised it as the Winters' car from across the valley. 'No, please God, no,' she said to herself.

She met Winter at the front door. 'Well?' she said sharply. 'What do you want?'

'Could we go inside please, Mrs Terry?' Winter said quietly. Niney preceded him into the kitchen. 'Well?' she said.

'I have some very bad news, Mrs Terry. Perhaps you had better sit down,' Winter said.

'Where is he?' she said icily. 'What has happened to him?'

'The operation went wrong. We know Keith's partner was killed and I'm afraid the Russians are saying they have shot your nephew,' Winter said softly.

'No ... no ... no, they haven't. I would know if he was dead!' she said fiercely. 'I would be able to tell ... I would know in here!' she said, putting her hand on her heart. She went to the telephone. 'Carl, find James and Jack for me... yes please, at once, and tell them to come home immediately.'

Niney picked up the brandy and two glasses and poured herself a large measure. 'You get your own!' she said to Winter, pushing the bottle to him.

'Mrs Terry – ' Winter began to speak.

'You just get him back here, John Winter, or you won't live to get your pension!' Niney said, her reserve now breaking. She began to shake.

'Do you want me to tell his parents?' Winter asked. 'I could get someone to do that at least.'

'And tell them what... "sorry about this, Mrs Finlay, but I'm afraid the Russians have shot your son"?' Niney slurred. 'Will you tell Jenny as well? Who's to do that, for Christ's sake? She's in Toronto?'

'I didn't know they were still in touch,' Winter said.

'You stupid man! They are not still in touch. If Jenny had had her way he would never have gone into the Navy. It broke her heart and his... Anyway, what's it to do with you? Here's his grandfather now. You can explain to him what has happened to his grandson!' She picked up the brandy and her glass and went into the hall.

Uncle Jack came in to find her there. Niney was drunk and very angry. 'I can tell you now, Jack, Kee is alive... I know he is... I shall go to the Russian Embassy and beg them to let us have him back.'

After Winter had gone, Finlay's grandfather joined the others in the hall. 'I didn't know he was doing that type of thing,' he said. He looked grey and old.

'He promised me before he went he was giving up the Service altogether ... why oh why didn't we listen to Jenny,' Niney sobbed. 'But I can tell you now, James, he's not dead, I would know, I promise you. I will never believe that until it is proved ... I can feel he is alive.'

Finlay's grandfather and Jack looked at each other sadly. 'Come on, darling,' Jack said. 'Perhaps you would be best lying down.'

'I shall be all right! We have to find out how we can get him home,' Niney said as emphatically as the brandy allowed.

'Niney my love, the Russians have shot him. He's not coming home,' Finlay's grandfather said.

Niney dropped to the floor as if poleaxed.

ADMIRAL WINTER ARRIVED early in Horse Guards the next morning. He had one more duty to perform, one which made him very sad, one he wished he didn't have to do.

He went to the personnel file and withdrew the one marked as Finlay's. Lighting his pipe he put the file on his desk, unwilling at first to open it. Then, steeling himself, he began to read. It was Finlay's service life laid bare. As he read an occasional slow smile crossed his face, then sometimes a frown. He finished the file and wiped his eyes, then wrote: 'A short brilliant career.' Then the words: 'Dismissed Dead.'

He shut the file carefully. Sighing heavily, he put it in an internal envelope ready to send to the MOD.

FINLAY WOKE SUDDENLY, not slowly through the mists of sight and mind, but from coma to complete wakefulness in a second.

He was lying in a bed between clean, crisp sheets, in a small room illuminated with subdued blue lighting. In both arms were drip feeds and his left leg, stiff with plaster of Paris, was strung up and held with traction weights. His right leg he felt swathed in bandages and both ached abominably. His jaw and face throbbed, his mouth was wired shut and there was a tube inserted into his right nostril. Another tube ran from under the sheet to a bag attached to the bedside.

He tried to move and immediately groaned with a shattering pain in his side. He tried lifting his arms, but they were strapped down to the bed frame.

Finlay heard a chair scrape on the floor and a face appeared momentarily above him. She looked like a nurse. She was gone at once. A door opened and closed and Finlay listened to the footsteps growing fainter. He drifted back into a heavy sleep.

When he woke again, daylight flooded the room and the brightness made him screw his eyes up. He tried to move but the straps on his arms and the pain in his side held him fast. He was aware of someone else in the room and he tried lifting his head; again pain thrust him back. A female face appeared above him and a cool hand descended on his forehead.

She said something in Russian and disappeared again. 'Finlay,' he thought to himself. 'This time I think you are in real trouble.'

He thought about Canavan and an unutterable sadness engulfed him. It was impossible to think that he was really dead – the tall Irishman, so full of charm and lionhearted courage, was gone. He realised he was crying. Tears coursed down his face and chased across the sheet beneath him.

Finlay heard the sound of returning footsteps and voices. The door opened and the face of a middle-aged man appeared above him, smiling broadly. 'Finlay, my dear chap! So you've decided to stay with us after all. At times we thought you just did not want to live!' The face continued to smile happily. 'Now that you are awake, how do you feel?'

The effect on Finlay was absolutely stunning. The man spoke perfect English with perfect modulation and simply no trace of an accent. Finlay wondered whether he was back in the West.

His visitor continued, 'You're surprised that I know who you are, I see.' He produced a clipboard and thrust it into Finlay's line of vision, tapping it significantly. 'I know everything about you, Finlay!' Again he smiled and winked conspiratorially. 'Damn fine show you and Canavan put up at the border; pity we had to kill him and knock you about so much. Never mind though, the nurse here tells me you're mending beautifully and we'll soon have you up and about again!'

The English was flawless, even down to the inflection and use of idiomatic phrases, which only confused Finlay further. He was convinced he was dreaming; he couldn't believe what had happened.

The other man laughed. 'My dear chap, if you could only see your face - the surprise! What were you expecting, a great square-shouldered Russian with bad breath and an unintelligible accent?'

The man pulled up a chair and leant over Finlay. 'My name is Gregor. I'm your case officer and if you are wondering about my English, I learnt it in your own country at one of your universities and I've been back and forth ever since. Now, come along, Finlay, say something at least!'

Finlay looked blank.

'Now look, old chap, all this must be quite a shock to the jolly old system, I know, but we expect you to co-operate with us, and just to prove that we really do know something about you, I'll read some of the file we have on you.' He flipped back some of the papers on the clipboard, settled himself in the chair and started reading: 'You are Lieutenant Keith Finlay, born on the twelfth of December, nineteen hundred and forty-one. Your father is Captain Gordon Finlay, Royal Navy. Your mother is Kathleen Grace Finlay, maiden name Hill, and you live in the village of Nursling in the county of Hampshire.

'After a very bad start at grammar school, you were educated at Dartmouth Naval College and passed out in February 1958, having done extremely well. You served in various ships, on various stations, until your obvious talents were spotted and taken notice of. You then transferred to Admiral John Winter's new group, which was a very bad career move, wouldn't you say?

'You enjoy fishing and shooting. You smoke too many Senior Service cigarettes, speak French, German, some Norwegian and you drink pink gin. Shall I go on? You see, we really know you very well!'

'How do I like my eggs?' asked Finlay through his teeth.

Gregor laughed. 'Now, according to what we know of you, that's precisely the answer I should have expected!' He rested the clipboard on the bed. 'We are going to see an awful lot of each other, Keith, as you can imagine. I hope you will co-operate with me, that being the best course of action for somebody in your position. Now, is there anything I can get you?'

Finlay sighed. 'They have you, Finlay, bang to rights!' he thought bitterly. To the Russian he said, 'Do you think I could sit up a little please, Gregor? And I would love a drink of water.'

Gregor turned and spoke to the nurse, who answered him shyly. 'She says we can raise you slightly and you can have a very small drink of water.' His smile was fixed and very false. 'I do so hope you will co-operate with us, Keith. It will save so much time and unpleasantness and it will be much easier for you.' The implied threat was very obvious.

'What will you do with me?' asked Finlay. 'Put me on trial like you did with Wynne and then swap me for one of your men? Lots of press and propaganda value, is that what I am?'

Gregor shook his head. 'Oh no, nothing like that, Keith. You see, we've let it be known that you are dead. No, old chap, there are greater things in store for you.

'The choices are as follows: one, we pump you full of truth drug, get what we can from you and then shoot you; two, do the same but put you in a labour camp for the rest of your life; or three, and this is what we hope for and why we have treated you so well this far, is that you will see the hopelessness of your position and tell us what we want to know. By that, I mean everything you know – why you came here this time, every possible thing you know. Then, if you satisfy us that you have done your best, perhaps we can employ you in some training capacity. You must put from your mind, though, that you will ever return to England. Co-operate with us, put right the wrong you have done us, and who knows? You could end up by being quite happy and comfortable here. Now, what is your initial reaction to that?'

Finlay snorted. 'You've got more chance of getting struck by lightning, that's my initial reaction!'

Gregor remained affable. 'Well, it's early days yet, Keith. I am quite sure that you want to live!'

Finlay knew that to be true, at least.

Gregor sat for a moment, sifting through the papers on his clipboard. 'One moment, Keith, I must go and fetch some papers I have forgotten.' He got up and left the room, allowing Finlay time to reflect on his position and how he was to cope with his interrogation.

He knew from training films and sessions with MI5 roughly how this part of the interrogation would proceed. At first, the Russians would try to persuade him gently to part with information, giving incentives in the form of privileges or promises. The case officer would try and become his friend and get Finlay to rely on him, until such time that the Russians had judged they could obtain no more information through that means. Then, if they ran true to form, the heavy interrogation would begin. What form this would take was anybody's guess. Finlay knew that such torments as starvation and being kept from sleep he could probably cope with, but the sheer brutality of the Russian interrogation system was legend. He wondered how he would cope with it in his present state.

Thinking as objectively as possible under the circumstances, Finlay realised that he had to string out the soft interrogation as long as possible to allow himself to heal and thus be able to stand the heavy stuff, which he knew must come.

The only way to achieve this was by telling them something new and, in their eyes, valuable, fairly frequently. But how much to tell them he did not know.

What would satisfy them? And, above all, how was he to remember what he had said so that he would not be caught out in a lie?

They would probe his every weakness and avoid his strengths until they were certain he had told them all he knew about his Service; the chances of survival thereafter were slim at best.

The nurse returned, together with another, and they made him more comfortable, raising him slightly on pillows so that the rest of the room could be viewed. They gave him water from a spouted drinking bowl which one of them eased gently into his cheek.

The water tasted delicious and washed the fur from his tongue. The original nurse said something in Russian to her colleague and they both giggled.

They were still laughing when Gregor returned and, asking what the joke was, he laughed with them and said, 'They say you have good teeth, Keith, and wonder what you look like without swelling and bruises. I'll show them, shall I?'

He removed from his clipboard a large brown envelope and produced from it a wad of photographs. 'I'm sure these will interest you,' he said sardonically as he drew one from the pile, read something on the back and held it in front of Finlay. 'One of you leaving the ferry at Malmo last year.' He handed it to the nurses.

'Here's a better one of you, more recent. Last meeting at Salisbury races. I do like that one, very good light.' His tone was heavily mocking. He went on shuffling the photographs and produced some showing Finlay in Paris, Madrid, Oslo and Helsinki, but more disturbing were those taken of him in England. There was one of him drinking outside a pub at the entrance to Christchurch Harbour.

'You can see, Keith, we are very widespread and cover the ground well. We knew you would be careless one day and that we would have you here. But then, we have files on most of you. We know your battle order as well as you do, and the changes you sometimes make. We even help to make some of them!' He replaced the photographs in the envelope. 'Anyway, you have been quite a hit with your nurses. You will basically keep the same ones until you are fully well. Try to learn our language and enjoy their company.' He rose as if to leave. 'Rest now, and I will be back this afternoon.' He touched Finlay's shoulder. 'It's all a new situation, old man. Let's see if we can make the best of it.' He smiled and left the room.

'Jesus, what a snake,' mused Finlay, but he was wary of the sheer professionalism of the Russian. He looked across the room to where the two nurses were busying themselves with a trolley. 'Yes, you beauties,' he thought. 'No doubt you've got your orders as well!'

As though on cue, one of the nurses turned and smiled at him.

Ten

OVER THE NEXT three days, Finlay's conversations with Gregor were light and easy, seeming to cover the most innocuous subjects. From his own training, Finlay decided that the Russians were probing gently to satisfy themselves that the information they already had on Finlay was correct, and it disturbed Finlay to know that most of it was.

To achieve such a level of intimate knowledge of one field operative only made Finlay wonder to what extent the whole of his organisation had been penetrated. And, more importantly for the moment, it made him wonder how much he could safely tell them in order to satisfy them enough to let him live - if, in fact, that was their intention.

After careful thought, Finlay decided that his best immediate course of action was to confirm the truth of what the Russians already knew. He felt it would perhaps add veracity to later statements he knew he would have to make.

On the fourth morning, Gregor arrived as usual, full of his false affability. 'My goodness, Keith, you do look better this morning. Our nurses are really looking after you. A few nights of uninterrupted sleep has done wonders!'

Finlay groaned inwardly, but he said, 'Yes, I suppose you're right, Gregor. When does the real stuff begin? I'm not so stupid as not to know what your job is!'

The Russian patted Finlay's arm. 'Don't let it worry you, my friend. We are realists here in Russia. You could be some use to us. Co-operate and you stay alive; really give us some help and you could even become quite comfortable here.'

'I'm in Russia, then?' asked Finlay.

Gregor laughed briefly, a sort of schoolgirl giggle. 'Ah, so your brain is functioning as well, Keith. Yes, you are indeed in Russia, in Moscow in fact, or rather just outside. The precise location would mean very little to you, so it doesn't matter.'

Then, as though being prompted, he sat upright in his chair and cleared his throat. 'Now, Keith, perhaps we should get on. This afternoon we want to ask you some more direct questions; please answer them truthfully. It is obvious that you are not a fool, so you will know that some of this afternoon's questions are designed to catch you out, while others we really do not know the answers to. Let us start off in the right spirit and we can get the whole thing over and done with quickly. I'd like to go back to my masters and let it be known that already we have some degree of co-operation from you.'

'If it has become obvious that I'm not stupid,' answered Finlay, 'please don't treat me as though I were. Everything we say and do is being recorded and most likely filmed.' He motioned his head towards the x-ray viewer. 'And I expect the camera and microphones are behind that viewer over there.'

The Russian grinned. 'Absolutely correct, old chap! Should have known better, shouldn't we? I suppose we should have granted you the compliment of recognising you to be the complete professional. However, we must get on with the job in hand, so could we begin, do you think?'

'Not a chance, old chap,' answered Finlay, mocking the use of Gregor's English. 'You know I cannot answer your questions. Would you in my place?'

The Russian's tone changed slightly. It carried the hint of warning. 'And what do you judge your place to be? You are a spy, caught inside our borders. You have killed some of our soldiers and wounded others, but still we offer you a chance to redeem yourself. What have you done to deserve this treatment?' he asked, waving his arm around the room. 'Why not be sensible about it? Co-operate and you may yet live!'

By way of answering, the Russian reached down to his briefcase and pulled it onto his lap. He looked hard at Finlay and smiled coldly. 'I wasn't going to show you this, not until you were stronger anyway, but it might help to demonstrate just how hopeless your position is!' He produced a newspaper from his case with a flourish, folded it carefully and thrust it under Finlay's nose. 'Look at the Hatches, Matches and Despatches, as I believe they are called!'

Finlay automatically looked at the date on the top of the newspaper. It read, 'Daily Telegraph 22 March 1967' and further down the page, ringed with blue, 'Finlay, Keith. Beloved son of Gordon and Kathleen. Suddenly, abroad. No greater love.'

He managed somehow to ask, 'How old is this newspaper, Gregor?' His voice was no more than a strangled whisper.

'Sorry, old chap, can't tell you that,' answered the Russian shortly. 'Keep the paper if you wish, just to remind yourself! But you do see my point, don't you? Sorry as I am to hammer it home, you must realise you will not be going back to England, ever. The best you can hope for is to remain alive in Russia, and the "alive" part depends on your co-operation.'

'Do you think I could have my hands free, please?' Finlay asked quietly. 'After all, I shan't be going anywhere, shall I?'

The pathos and irony of the statement was entirely lost on

the Russian. 'Yes, of course, old chap!' He proceeded to untie the wrist straps which had hitherto held Finlay's arms fast to the bed frame.

'Are there any bargains I can strike, do you think, Gregor?' asked Finlay, rubbing his wrists and flexing his arms. 'If my Service thinks I'm dead, then there's no going back, as you say. Too much embarrassment all round.'

'Only the one already on offer; co-operate and you may live. What you have to do, Keith, is think yourself into a new situation - try at least - and see what co-operation brings.'

Finlay stared blankly at the wall opposite. 'What have I got to lose?' he thought bleakly. 'Think myself into a new situation.' He looked at the Russian directly. 'I will answer questions which do not directly endanger anyone from my Service. How does that suit you?'

The Russian smiled broadly. 'It will do for a start anyway, Keith. I knew you were a realist! Now, to begin with, how did you arrive in East Berlin?'

'Through the sewers, via the sealed tunnel opened up by the West German students,' answered Finlay. His response was rapid, showing his willingness to answer.

'Were you to abduct somebody, and, if so, who?' The Russian was writing rapidly.

'We were not told. People favourable to us were to meet us in a café and hand him over. He was supposed to be semi-conscious through drugs. Canavan was the muscle!' Finlay watched the Russian for a response, of which he made no outward sign.

'Who were the people you were to meet in the café? Give me their names.'

'No,' replied Finlay. 'They were doing it for money, I believe, not out of conviction.'

The Russian wrote something on his pad, then looked up at

Finlay, his pale eyes void of any emotion. 'Do you know the profession of the man you were supposed to abduct?'

'Army chap, I believe, not really sure. It's always felt the less we know the better, just in case something goes wrong.'

Each man watched the other closely, Gregor looking for too off-pat an answer, Finlay watching to see how far he was believed.

'How many times have you crossed our borders, Keith – illegally, I mean?'

Finlay, pretending vagueness, counted on his fingers and looked into the Russian's eyes steadily as he said, 'Eight times.'

The Russian raised his eyebrows and said coolly, 'So many? You have been a busy chap! How did you get down to Volpke and why did you choose to cross there?'

Ignoring the first part of the question, Finlay answered truthfully. 'We chose that part of the border because of the amount of cover up to the wire and also because any part of the border so heavily protected and patrolled must be the easiest place to cross. We thought the border guards would be fairly complacent, there being so many of them. We would have made it over but for a bloody deer running out in front of us and setting off the flares.'

'A modicum of truth makes it all sound real,' thought Finlay. He continued, 'We got our directions a little adrift. We thought we were opposite the French sector but, as you know, we were in fact opposite our own.'

'From what regiment were the British soldiers on the other side and what part did they play in this?'

'Royal Green Jackets,' answered Finlay promptly. 'They were doing what they always do in such circumstances, investigating the flares and gunfire. I asked them to cut the wire on their side and explode the mines with their heavy machine guns. However, as you know, the Germans came back too quickly for us and I ordered the Green Jackets to withdraw at once. I did not want any cross-border shooting with all the implications that would involve.'

The Russian wrote steadily for some minutes. 'That accords roughly with what was reported to us, but where was the man you were supposed to be abducting?'

Finlay laughed bitterly. 'The bastard didn't turn up in East Berlin where he was supposed to, so the whole thing was a complete waste of time, effort and lives anyway.'

The Russian sucked his pen noisily. 'A bit far-fetched, you know. Why didn't you wait in East Berlin until your supposed "army chap" was kidnapped?'

'To do that would have meant delay and our having to risk contacting London. You were already on to us anyway – the Avis car bombed, our man leading you to one of our safe houses.'

'Hmm, interesting,' responded Gregor. There was a long silence while the Russian made some notes and Finlay, though tiring, was trying to go over what he had already said.

'Carry on,' said the Russian and, when Finlay did not, he looked up. 'Well?'

'You're asking the questions, Gregor. Tell me what you want to know.'

That was their first check. Both knew the training manual rules on interrogation. The game was to make the one talk to find out exactly what the other knew and Finlay felt he had volunteered enough for the moment. He knew he had to remember, more or less verbatim, what he had said so he had to keep it simple. In addition, during the first session with the Russian case officer he had begun to realise his own poor mental and physical state.

Gregor stood up suddenly. 'That's enough for today, I think,

Keith. We'll see how strong you are tomorrow.' He packed his briefcase and moved towards the door. 'Don't forget now, anything you want, just ask and I'll see what can be done. See you tomorrow then, chin-chin.' And he was gone.

Finlay relaxed and closed his eyes. He knew the Russian to be an expert interrogator, with his alleged concern for Finlay, his mock warmth and bonhomie. But it was his flawless command of English that Finlay knew to be the most dangerous. Gregor could easily trap him into saying something outside of the parameters Finlay had already laid down in his own mind.

He forced his tired brain into constructive thought again. At the Service training school he had had many lectures on the art and craft of interrogation, both how to do it and how best to counter it.

He remembered them being very exhausting and also very painful when more robust training had been the order of the day. Finlay realised that at some stage in the not too distant future, the Russians would inflict a more physical kind of interrogation on him and he wondered how he would fare under some rough handling in his present state of health.

He picked up the Daily Telegraph and read again his own death notice. It upset him to think just how much his family would be suffering now. He flung the paper down with a heavy sigh, not sure whether it was genuine or for the benefit of the hidden camera.

Over the next few weeks, if he wanted any chance of living, never mind escape, he had to convince his captors that he was ready to change sides.

He made another effort to think positively, dragging his mind back to his days of training. 'I'm going to beat this bugger Gregor,' he mused. 'What I have to find out is just how much of the real truth I need to give them and just how friendly I have to be with this snake to be convincing.'

He tried moving his right leg, bent it double and flexed his foot and toes. The pain was immense and his calf muscle seemed almost to flinch. 'That should give me something to work on,' he thought. 'At least I've got one whole leg, I'll bloody well hop out of this place if needs be!'

Finlay slept. The forthcoming mental battle with his case officer was one he had at least to draw. To lose meant death one way or another.

Eleven

BEFORE THE NEXT session with the Russian case officer, Finlay had time to set out in his mind how he was going to cope with his debriefing. Over the next weeks and months, should the interrogation last that long, he had to convince his captors of the truth in what he was telling them.

He also knew that he himself had to remember exactly what he had told them, without recourse to notes, tapes or any of the aides the Russians had. The trick was to play along for long enough to find out exactly what they knew, and to stay alive long enough to become mobile again and try making a break for it.

One thing he was very determined about; if he was going to be shot it would not be before at least one attempt at escape.

There was, he knew, just one way to handle the situation and fool the Russians, and that was to really believe in his own story and lies. He needed to enter the mind of somebody other than himself. Acting would not be enough. The stakes were too high. If an actor is unconvincing or forgets his lines, he has just embarrassment to cope with, maybe the loss of his part in the play; if an agent plays his part badly or forgets his lines, loss of life may follow. The strain would be immense. Carried on for long enough, Finlay understood the dangers of his mind objectifying and becoming a jumbled mass of truth and half-truth, incoherent, with no set track to run on. Pushed to the limit, eventually the mind would implode. This was the way to madness.

With the morning came the two nurses, who bustled about tidying his room, clearly preparing it for an important visitor. After they had finished, they set about Finlay's bed and then started on him. All the while they chatted between themselves and Finlay listened intently, trying, from the tone and inflection within their speech, to acquire some understanding of what they were saying.

Finlay, having been washed and shaved, felt somewhat more human. He had taken the opportunity of such close contact with the two nurses to turn the episode into a bit of a game. They had laughed and giggled over washing him, and he in turn gave them what he hoped was a winning smile, but which, under the circumstances, he feared might look more like a leer, his wired-up jaw restricting his attempts.

Finlay tried speaking to them by pointing at himself and saying 'Keith' and then at them and adopting a questioning look. The elder of the two girls understood him quickly and, pointing to herself, over-pronounced the name 'Daria'. Then, pointing to her colleague she said a name which to Finlay sounded like 'Lucy'.

Finlay tried repeating their names: 'Daria and Lucy.' They both laughed at his pronunciations, holding on to each other and making more of the situation than was necessary. Their laughter was quickly cut short when a white-coated male, accompanied by two much older nurses, entered the room.

The man, obviously a doctor, spoke to the young nurses sharply and they left the room immediately, hanging their heads. The doctor turned to Finlay and began to examine him thoroughly. After checking his blood pressure, chest and those reflexes he was able to test, the doctor spoke to Finlay.

'You speak none Russian?' the doctor asked, looking pleased with his own attempts at the language. Finlay shook his head.

Meanwhile, the two nurses were removing the dressing from his right leg and, having done so, stood back for the doctor to examine it. Finlay could see dark bruising on the front of his leg where the last German's pistol bullet had entered, and when his leg was lifted, the exit point had a fairly healthy-looking scab.

The doctor nodded and said something to the nurses, who began redressing the leg. He next examined Finlay's face and jaw and, making cutting movements with his fingers, said to Finlay, 'Tomorrow.' This Finlay understood to mean that the wires holding his broken jaw in place were to be removed. The doctor nodded again, smiled and made ready to leave. 'Tomorrow,' he repeated as he left, the two elderly nurses following him.

Finlay cursed mentally. The visit from the doctor had further disorientated him, as the scab he had seen on his leg had given him an indication of how long he had been in the hospital, or at least how long ago the leg had been wounded. He thought perhaps between ten days and two weeks had passed.

If his jaw had been broken by the blow from the rifle butt – as he was fairly sure it had – ten days was hardly sufficient time for it to have healed enough to have the wiring removed.

But he was not so much worried about the jaw itself, as the length of the time he'd been there. 'I wonder,' he thought, 'Whether I've been pumped with Pentothal already and this charade with Gregor is just a way of checking what I might have said.'

Soon afterwards the two young nurses, Daria and Lucy, returned. Finlay thought, 'I'd better respond to one of them fairly quickly. If they let her stay after that, I'll know she's a plant and that they're expecting her to get information from me. If they remove her straight away, that would confirm that she's just a nurse and they don't intend my stay to be that comfortable after all.'

He felt like a drowning man as he studied the two nurses and cold-bloodedly chose the elder of the two, Daria, on whom to test his theory. 'After all,' he thought wryly, 'she is the better looking and I might as well spend what time is left to me in the company of someone beautiful rather than someone ugly!'

He found himself scrutinising her minutely, giving her a critical study, looking for any potential weakness or foible. She was tall, slim and dark, with something of the Asiatic about her, a throwback to the hordes of the conquering Khans, except her eyes which were almost a violet blue.

She caught Finlay staring at her and came over to him, smiling, asking in Russian if he wanted anything. Finlay, in sign language, requested a drink. She leant over him with a spouted drinking cup. Finlay steadied her hand with his own and far from objecting, she smiled directly into his eyes.

'You're making it look good, Daria,' he thought bitterly, smiling back. 'I suppose in Russia you lie back and think of Lenin.'

When he had drunk, he said 'Thank you' very clearly. Daria raised one of her arched eyebrows and replied, 'Thank you.'

She smiled again and wiped Finlay's face where the water had trickled down from the mug, making just a little too much of the operation.

'Yes, my little Commie bitch. If you're a nurse, so was my granny!' Finlay thought.

It comforted him a little to think that the Russians were going to try such an amateurish ploy. Finlay thought he could go along with it and turn Daria his way.

Twelve

OVER THE NEXT two weeks a routine was established between Finlay and his captors. The case officer, Gregor, would arrive after breakfast and stay until about four in the afternoon, questioning Finlay, probing deeply into the same things time after time.

The amount of food Finlay received was gradually reduced and as the food decreased so the intensity of the questioning increased. Finlay realised what they were doing and did his best to keep alert, but at the end of a particularly intense day of questioning his head began to swim with fatigue and his speech became slurred.

Gregor came back that evening and Finlay was woken up for further questioning. When he began to drift into sleep again, electric fans were switched on to keep him awake with their chilly wind.

Gregor patted Finlay's arm. 'We are really making progress, Keith, dear boy. I'm very pleased with our work.'

Finlay looked at his tormentor with ill-concealed hatred through his sleep-starved eyes. 'Are you a queer, Gregor?' he asked suddenly in a deliberately questioning stab, to try and ruffle the Russian. It had the desired effect.

'What do you mean "queer"?' the Russian retorted, flushing slightly to cover confusion or anger.

106

'Well,' replied Finlay, grabbing the initiative. 'Homosexual - you know, lust after small boys' bums or young men in tight trousers. I only ask because, as you know, a lot of our Foreign Office types are – they like to hang around us real men. I just wondered if it was the same in Russia, that's all.'

Finlay's deliberate crudity had obviously stung the Russian. Gregor unconsciously drew back further from him and his eyes showed the distaste he felt for Finlay.

'It's not the same in Russia, I can assure you.' Gregor's voice was not so affable, but he was regaining composure.

Finlay grinned wolfishly. 'I've taken quite a fancy to Nurse Daria, Gregor. Just wanted to make sure I wasn't treading on your toes, as it were. But then, with your persuasions, I wouldn't be, would I?'

The Russian forced himself to laugh. 'I'm glad you seem to have formed a friendship with Daria, but be careful, we are not fooled easily,' he warned.

Finlay could see the triumph in Gregor's eyes. He felt Finlay was weakening, needing some kind of relationship to carry him through his predicament. He became very matter of fact again.

'We must get some ground covered, Keith. Don't make me change your nurses just to concentrate your mind! Now, can you tell me who the leader of Section B in Leconfield House is?'

Finlay feigned surprise. 'You know about Leconfield House then? I'm sorry, I don't have much knowledge as I'm not attached to them. Our contact is very limited.'

'We know that!' he replied. 'We want to know more about that section chief, so tell me who he is.'

'How can I?' retorted Finlay. 'Nobody knows that sort of thing outside MI5. In my section we have no need to know, certainly not at my level, anyway.' Finlay didn't have to sound convincing, because in truth he didn't know the answer to the Russian's question.

'Well Keith, we'll pass over that for the present ...'

Finlay did not let him continue. 'It's no use saying you're going to pass over it, Gregor. I've said I don't know, and that's the truth of it! You're thinking I'm more important than I really am. I'm just a hired blunt instrument of the Government and if I didn't do this work I'd probably be some sort of criminal.'

The Russian looked at him coldly. 'But that's exactly what you are, a criminal! And unless you want to be treated like one, answer our questions!'

'How can I answer questions I don't know the answer to? Do you want me to make them up for you so you'd then catch me out and think that everything I have said is untrue?' Finlay sounded exasperated. He recalled that his training manual had explicitly told him to tell the exact truth when possible. It lent credibility to untruth and helped create confusion in the interrogator's mind.

'Don't upset yourself, my dear boy. Of course we don't want you to lie,' the Russian responded more warmly. 'Let's begin somewhere else. For example, tell me something about co-operation between Mossad and your Foreign Office.'

Again Finlay could answer truthfully. 'There is none. The Foreign Office is Arabist to a man. The Jews have never been forgiven for the way they bombed the King David Hotel. The last time they tried to operate in England they were sent packing. They co-operate with the CIA and FBI, not us.'

The Russian made a gesture of despair. 'You are talking nonsense and if you continue then I shall not be able to help you.' He got up to leave. Looking back to Finlay, he said, 'You can't win, Keith. You must answer truthfully at all times or something unpleasant will happen to you!'

Finlay sighed. 'I'm trying, but I think that you think I know more than I do.'

The Russian shrugged and left.

This was the last debriefing session that Finlay was able to go over and remember with any clarity. His head ached constantly now from trying to memorise all he had said over the past weeks. He clung desperately to his original story as to why he and Canavan had been in East Germany. He now fully believed the story himself and had to reach into the deepest recesses of his mind to find his true self.

Thirteen

THE DEBRIEFING SESSION continued for another week, following much the same pattern. Finlay was closely questioned on such things as coastal defences and submarine detection systems on the continental shelf around England's shores.

He told them all he could remember from the *Naval Review* and *Jane's Fighting Ships* – anything they could find out for themselves, in fact. By the end of each session he was barely coherent. His ears buzzed and his head swam constantly and after the sessions were finished he was not allowed to sleep for more than half an hour at any one time.

When Finlay thought his mind was finally coming apart at the seams, he was questioned for two days continuously, always the same two questions: 'Why did you go to East Berlin and who were you meeting there?'

Finlay stuck to his story. His mind didn't seem able to change it anyway. Faces floated in front of his own, screaming the questions at him. Ice bags were packed around him to keep him awake. After the two-day session, Gregor's face hovered over him. 'Alright Finlay, we believe you. Get some sleep now.'

Somewhere deep in Finlay's mind a moment of elation bubbled before he crashed into exhausted sleep. Finlay had believed Gregor's statement and he relaxed.

He had no idea how long he had been asleep for when suddenly he was shocked into wakefulness and a moment's panic. The door burst open with a crash that shook the room. He jerked up on to his elbows, fully awake, only to be deluged with icy water and then punched heavily in the face.

Three men grabbed him, pulling him from the soaking bed, then leaving him to slump partially on to the floor. His left leg, still attached to the traction weights, held him suspended upside down. He received several kicks in the face and head before the weights were cut free and his plastered leg crashed heavily down.

They picked him up under the arms, dragging him from the room and along a corridor, one of them continually kicking at his buttocks and legs and striking him across the back with a heavy cane.

The pain from Finlay's plastered leg threatened to engulf him completely but he knew that he had won a victory over Gregor. If he could but stand what he knew was coming next without changing his story, all would be well. He would, he knew, die without outward dignity, but at least his mind would remain his own.

He was dragged through another set of doors and thrust down on to a hard seat. His arms gripped either side, and a massive white light which almost seemed to consume his brain was thrust in front of his face.

An unseen questioner barked, 'Why did you come to East Berlin?'

Finlay answered, surprised at the clarity of his own voice. 'I've already told you!'

A strong hand grabbed his hair and dragged back his head. 'Who were the people you were meeting? Give us their names.'

Before Finlay could make any sort of response, he briefly

smelt cigarette smoke as a lit cigarette was thrust into his nostril. As he tried to breathe, the hot ash mixed with mucus and ran down his throat making him gag. A heavy blow in the stomach winded him and his shouts of pain and struggling became weaker. Finlay wanted to die.

He was stripped naked and beaten with a heavy cane about the body. Always the questions were repeated.

'Why did you come to East Berlin? Who were you meeting there?'

Finlay had gone beyond giving an answer. He tried to croak a response, but nothing came.

He felt himself being lifted and flung on to a hard platform. His head, wrists and legs were now held by straps and he could hear himself screaming as something cold was thrust roughly into his anus and something metallic gripped one of his testicles, something cold and sharp.

Finlay's dulled mind was momentarily jerked alive with the first of the electric shocks. The pain was indescribable, like nothing he had ever thought believable. He was screaming in agony when the platform was tipped and his head and shoulders were plunged into icy water. His struggles quickly became weaker and he felt himself fall into a black tunnel of nothing.

But his tormentors were professional. They took him to the very edge of life and then revived him, only to repeat the exercise, more briefly this time, as the light of Finlay's life was going out. Then they stopped, pushed a tube down his throat, sucked out the fluid and got him breathing again. Finlay could feel his face being slapped hard, but he ignored it. He did not want to be alive.

A voice was shouting in his ear, 'Why did you come to East Berlin?'

Finlay was trying to answer. 'I've already told you.'

Again his head and shoulders were lowered under the water,

only this time Finlay did not struggle. Instead he swallowed and breathed it in, trying to drown. The dark black tunnel of nothing rushed up and swallowed him...

He awoke lying on a stone floor. A light bulb, burning high over him, swam in lazy circles. He couldn't move. He lay there wondering why he was still alive. 'After all,' he thought, 'I did my best to die.'

He tried to move again, but nothing seemed to work properly. The light bulb spun on. He closed his eyes and sank back into the tunnel. When he awoke again he felt he was standing. In fact he was suspended by his wrists, his back against a wall, his feet just touching the floor.

Warm air flowed around him. His body was now warm, but just a sheet of pain.

'Why did you come to East Berlin?' a voice asked.

'I've already told you.' He was trying to speak but whether it came out clearly he could not know. Again, the electrodes were pushed into his body. Finlay's brain quivered in protest at what was to come. The shocks made stars explode in his head and drove his body rigid, seeming to blast his muscles into jelly.

Again the question, 'Why did you come to East Berlin?' There followed a period of electric shocks and, again, the light bulb swinging above him while he cringed on the stone floor beneath it.

He seemed now to be outside himself. Only when the electrodes were in place and exacting their price on his body did he become aware of anything and always the same two questions.

'Why did you come to East Berlin? Who were you meeting there?'

In desperation the Russian torturers increased the intensity of the shocks.

'Why did you come to East Berlin?' the voice asked.

'Why did you come to East Berlin?'

'Why did you come to East Berlin?'

Finlay fought against the pain. The black tunnel of unconsciousness would eventually engulf him. He struggled and struggled into wakefulness, and found himself back in his original room and bed.

The sunshine streamed into the room and the blind rattled cheerfully in the breeze which came gently through the open window, laden with the smell of spring. Someone had placed a bowl of fresh primroses on the table and their scent danced with the dust in the shafts of sunlight.

Finlay weakly moved his arm to touch them and, feeling the soft petals between his fingers, he lifted them to his face and began to cry silently.

His hands were shaking uncontrollably; he could not even remember who he was. Physically, he seemed to be bruised from head to toe, great acres of blue brown patches splattered all over him.

Nothing seemed to hurt very much beyond the darker patch on the outside of his left thigh. Finlay ran his fingers over the patch and he winced as his forefinger felt a scabby place. An itchy sharp pain touched him, so he left it alone.

'I've been in an accident,' he thought. 'I wonder what it was.'

Finlay's mind was blank, his memory gone. He tried to stretch a little but gave it up and settled into the pillow, wearing the absent smile of insanity.

Fourteen

FINLAY REMAINED IN a state of total amnesia for three days, recognising neither his Russian case officer nor the two nurses. When Daria saw his condition she wept openly, her salty tears falling on Finlay's face. It meant nothing to Finlay. 'I suppose she must know me,' he thought, but beyond that thought was nothing but shocked blackness.

When the protective shrouds of amnesia fell away on the third day and he lay in a stunned trance, his stomach crawled with fear of the torture being repeated and sweat trickled down his ribs endlessly. He was sane enough to question the reason for being kept alive, but not sane enough to construct any conclusion about it.

When Gregor arrived, Finlay ignored him for the first hour, his mind a mixed jumble of hatred for this man and a need to talk to him. He heard the Russian speaking to him, but could only make sense of passing phrases; his concentration span was nil.

He supposed he must have slept for some time because when he awoke the room was grey with the dusk of evening. His mind was sharp and clear and everything about him stood out sharply in the gloomy light. When he tried to move the pain in his groin made him gasp and with the pain came a hatred that made his bile rise with its intensity as he remembered the violation inflicted on his body.

The door swung open quietly and Gregor entered the room, proof, if needed, that he was now under constant surveillance. The Russian put on a superb show of absolute contrition, making excuses for his inability to protect Finlay from what had happened and claiming to have saved him from any further misuse.

The sincerity in his voice sounded almost genuine. He said, 'I told them that you were willing to come over, but they would not believe me until they had tried to make you tell them something different with their disgusting methods. I reasoned with them, pleaded with them, pleaded with them for days to give you up.'

Finlay made no answer, but listened intently, his face slightly averted as the Russian continued. 'After the first week I honestly believed they were going to continue until you died. Most people do die. To lose your valuable knowledge and expertise in some matters would have been a total waste.

'We had already agreed together, you and I, that you could never return to England, so why they had to inflict such bestiality on you for seventeen days I do not know. Sometimes I think Russia will never be totally civilised. How can we expect the world ...'

Finlay had stopped listening. What he had taken to have been a matter of hours had, in fact, been days. He glanced down at his naked body. 'Over two weeks gone,' he thought. 'No wonder I'm so bloody skinny.' He gently felt between his legs to assess the damage there. His testicles were grossly swollen. He wryly thought, 'I'm a bit like the proverbial rat catcher's dog, all ribs and balls.' While feigning sleep he worried lest he was no longer a complete man.

'... so that's what we have decided to do.' The Russian's words were getting back through him. Gregor touched

Finlay's shoulder. 'My dear boy, I don't believe you've heard a word I've said to you!'

Finlay eyed him coldly. 'Why don't you fuck off, you lousy Russian poofter. I co-operated, didn't I, and look what happened. You'll get nothing from me, no matter what you do, so why don't you have me shot and save yourself the trouble of trying. My co-operation brought me nothing but a broken body and probably impotence.'

'Keith, my dear boy, I've just been telling you, we are going to move you to a military convalescent home, get you better and give you a job to do. That's what you've won by your co-operation! As to your probable impotence, Daria will be going with you to nurse you back to health and I'm certain somewhere along the way you can check up on the second worry. I'm sure your fears will prove groundless!' He winked conspiratorially.

Finlay ignored the last remark. 'What work will I have to do?'

'With your diving experience, Keith, something along those lines to begin with. It will help you to get your strength back. When you see that you can be just as happy here as in England. I know you will want to tell us all you know. Keep on with the co-operation and things will work out splendidly. Daria will help you with the language and settling down. We don't want to waste your talents, do you see my point?'

Finlay agreed. 'I'm a long way from diving fitness. When will I be moved?' He did not think his apparent surrender completely fooled the Russian. 'I suppose if I'm to live I must do something. Gregor, am I allowed to know such things as the date and where I'm going?'

Gregor stood up. 'Of course you're going to live, and the date is Tuesday, 1 May. When you have won our trust, then you will know where you are. You will be moving towards the end of the week, Keith. And now I must leave you, as I have a parade to attend this evening.'

As he paused by the door he turned back and looked at Finlay. 'You have lots more information stored away, Keith, which we will want at sometime when you are well. The same rules must apply. Your continued life will always depend upon your co-operation.'

From then on things improved dramatically for Finlay. He even waxed enthusiastically about his forthcoming job. In truth, diving had always been a favourite pastime with Finlay. Food was now brought regularly, English cigarettes, books and practically everything he asked for.

Daria fussed over him attentively. Occasionally, Finlay caught her looking at him under her dark lashes, her violet eyes showing she was happy to be with him. Over the next two days she made every excuse to be close to him, touching him, holding him and, on one occasion, brushing her lips against his cheek. Try as he might, Finlay could not dislike her. She had only ever shown an outward compassion, even though, as Finlay knew, this was as she had probably been ordered to do.

His experiences of women had, to date, been somewhat limited, and he had never been able to understand his fellow officers' compulsion to leave the ship as soon as it was tied against the jetty and head for the nearest whorehouse. He supposed that tradition had demanded it of sailors and once he had joined them in a famous 'sporting house' in Plymouth. But he'd been disgusted with the raddled meat on offer and had made some vapid excuses and returned to the ship, worried somewhat about his own sexuality.

Finlay was convinced that Daria understood English. When he spoke to her in his own language, sometimes her eyes would flicker slightly or she would look away shyly. On one occasion, when she was sitting close to him on the bed, he had reached up and traced the arch of her dark eyebrow with his finger and said, 'You are very beautiful, Daria.' She turned away and Finlay thought that even if she didn't understand, the inflection in his speech had probably conveyed his meaning clearly.

On the day of their move away from Moscow, Daria arrived with a suitcase, exuding an almost pre-holiday enthusiasm. She was not in her normal uniform but was dressed in a cotton skirt and blouse. Her dark hair was let down from its rather severe style and fell in dark spirals to her shoulders.

Finlay smiled at her and held out his hand. 'You look like a Russian Princess, Daria!'

She stiffened slightly, her smile had momentarily frozen and Finlay knew she had understood.

When Gregor arrived, he was bright and his usual affable self. 'You'll both be off in about an hour, Keith. An ambulance will take you to the airport.' He rubbed his hands together in a gesture of pleasure.

'Aren't you coming with us, Gregor?' Finlay sounded disappointed, as in fact he was. One day Finlay hoped to exact his revenge on this dissembling snake by killing him. But he need not have worried; the Russian informed him that he would be joining them later and would 'fly down in about three weeks'.

'Down' to Finlay meant south.

In due time the ambulance arrived and once loaded they drove to the airport. Throughout the drive Daria had rested her hand on the side of the stretcher and Finlay had noted the time on her wristwatch; 9.15. Soon after take-off he had glanced at her watch again; 9.50. The sun was streaming through the starboard windows as they passed through the cloud cover and then the plane headed in what Finlay judged to be a south/south-easterly direction.

He feigned sleep but as he lay there he could not help reflecting on the distance now opening up between himself and Europe. Eventually he nodded off, but woke with a start when the ancient propeller plane struck some turbulence. He began to fight the safety straps holding him to the stretcher, until the girl appeared above him, cooed something at him and tenderly wiped the sweat from his face. Her hand was soft and smelt delicately of almond oil.

Finlay slept again and when he next woke, Daria gave him some iced water to drink. The plane had become hot and stuffy, but all the while she had remained seated on the edge of his stretcher, her hand protectively on his arm. She stayed there for the rest of the journey, gazing out of the window and occasionally smiling down at him.

As she wiped his face for the umpteenth time, he again caught sight of her watch. It was 4.20 and soon after this the engine note changed and the plane began its descent. They landed with a heavy bump, which made Daria jump up from her seat and check her charge.

Finlay was soon unloaded into the bright sunlight. The air was dry and hot and the tarmac radiated its heat through the stretcher. The heat was such that Finlay noted it mentally. Wherever they were, the noonday sun's rays must have struck almost straight down.

The stretcher was loaded into another ambulance and they were driven for about twenty minutes over smooth roads. Finlay reckoned by the traffic noises outside their vehicle that they had passed through a fairly major town by southern Russia's standards. The destination, when they finally arrived, proved to be a large complex of low modern buildings, mainly timber built, nestling in the lower folds of some fairly gentle hills.

Finlay could see from his stretcher other patients, either walking or being pushed in wheelchairs, some in dressing gowns or pyjamas, some just sitting in deckchairs enjoying the last of the sun. And he could unmistakably smell a large area of water, though not that of a sea.

He judged by the time that they had been flying that they were anywhere between 900 and 1500 miles south-east of Moscow. He bludgeoned his withered mind into activity, even screwing up his face with the effort. 'South-east of Moscow, low hills and a lot of water.' He added up the known facts as he dug deeper into his mind, cursing his tardiness during the geography lessons of his youth.

It came to him suddenly. The mental process of deduction fell into place. 'The Caspian Sea. That's where it is!' Finlay's mind churned over rapidly; he knew somewhere to the south of him lay Iran, almost an American protectorate. How far was it? How many days?

He began to hope again.

Fifteen

FINLAY AND DARIA were allocated a room with French windows opening out on to a large lawn which sloped down towards the water. The water ran away to the north, but what troubled Finlay was that he could see the east and west coastlines right up to the horizon. He knew that this would be impossible had they been the coastlines of the Caspian Sea.

'It's far too small. Where the hell is this place?' he asked himself. If it was the Caspian, or an inlet of that particular sea, then they must have been on the Russia/Iran border, if he remembered correctly the shape of the sea from maps he had seen.

'It can't possibly be,' he thought. 'They would never leave me so close to possible escape, unless they have something in mind which I have not foreseen.'

He studied the room some more, looking at the contrast between the snowy sheets and the heavy wool coverlets. Something within the pattern of the coverlets niggled at Finlay. He had seen that type of pattern before, he was sure, but where? Suddenly, it became important to remember; for he knew that the design was typical of a region...

He breathed the word 'Turkmenistan!' just as Daria walked

into the room. She looked at him sharply as he clutched the coverlet, walked quickly over to him, took the cover from his hand and placed a finger to her lips as she waved her hand around the room, shaking her head.

If Finlay had wanted any further proof that the girl was won over, this was it. Finlay now had a friend in the enemy's camp. He could foresee that she might become a problem, but just at that moment he needed all the help she could offer.

He took her hand and pulled her down beside him and, taking her face in his hands, said as softly as possible, 'Thank you', and kissed her softly.

Tears started in her eyes. She was troubled by what was happening. Finlay had broken her innate professionalism, which left her exposed. He knew the danger such exposure put her in, and the situation laid him open to his own conscience about the way he was using her.

That night, as they lay chastely in their separate beds, Finlay looked across at the sleeping girl. She lay breathing quietly, one bare arm outflung. He felt very sorry for her, knowing that in spite of her professionalism, her feelings were getting the better of her and that he had encouraged this for his own ends. For her it was a no-win situation. For him, his only thought was escape, and he was going to use whoever and whatever was available to achieve it.

Later in the night, Finlay woke screaming from the nightmares which now dogged his sleep. Daria rushed to his side and calmed him down again, wiping away the sweat which soaked him. She pushed open the French doors and returned to his bed, lying quietly beside him, her breath flickering on his face and, before long, she lapsed into sleep again.

He lay awake for the rest of the night, the girl asleep, her head resting in the crook of his arm. Her hair smelt clean and fresh but even when she stirred in her sleep and relaxed softly against him, he felt nothing stir within him.

As dawn broke and he lay staring out of the large windows towards the water lapping on the brown sand of the shoreline, it came to him that he was staring at the Aral Sea. A light breeze had carried in the scent of fresh water and the dark smell of rotting bankside vegetation. He pressed his tired brain to search out what he remembered of the geography of the region. 'East of the Caspian, north of Samarkand and Tashkent.' The nearest friends would be Pakistan or Afghanistan.

He closed his eyes, tried to conjure up in his mind a map of the area, but nothing came. He was very tired.

His last thought before drifting into sleep was, 'Afghanistan - they're pretty much on the side of the Russians anyway.' Then he slept.

They were woken sometime later by a loud knocking on the door. Daria stumbled sleepily across the room and opened it. She stood there talking for a while, seemingly arguing, but eventually she moved to one side and allowed a short and extremely elderly woman into the room.

Armed as she was with mops and dusters it was fairly obvious as to her trade and, without so much as a glance at Finlay, she began a perfunctory cleaning operation in the room. Daria gave a shrug of her bare creamy shoulders, raised her eyes to heaven in an attitude of prayer, then flounced like a petulant child into the bathroom.

The old woman looked at the two beds, Daria's hardly slept in and Finlay's a sweat-dampened, tangled heap. She clicked her tongue in disapproval, glared at Finlay and said something unintelligible. Finlay just grinned and shook his head.

She came closer and repeated the question. Again Finlay shook his head. By now she was standing over him and she reeked of Russia, a particular body smell that most of the older generation seemed to possess in that country. Finlay always thought of it as somewhere between English didicoy and wet dog. Furthermore, her foul-smelling breath made Finlay shudder.

'Oh, for Christ's sake, Granny, stand off a bit, will you! I don't understand a word you're saying and I've got a very weak stomach!' He smiled at the old lady as he gently pushed her away. She cackled loudly at the discomfort she caused by her nearness.

She carried on with her cleaning task, humming some obscure tune to her efforts with a duster. Occasionally she would stop her dusting and look dreamily at the ceiling, then break wind loudly and continue with her work. Finlay lay in bed and shook with laughter, causing the damaged parts of his anatomy to ache furiously.

The old lady guffawed to herself when she produced an exceptionally loud report, at which Daria appeared at the bathroom door. Her nose wrinkled in distaste as she walked to the windows and threw them open. She spoke sharply to the cleaner and, holding her face, began pushing her towards the door. Finlay was exhausted, tears streaming down his face. It was the first time in months that he had laughed.

Daria, having recovered some of her poise, made a motion with her watch that she was leaving for about half an hour. Finlay knew that this was to report on what she had learnt, if anything, and to let her masters know how they had spent their time.

Finlay lay back and started to doze, but the smell of the old woman came back to him and he woke with a start to find her standing over him. She placed a foul-smelling hand over Finlay's mouth and, holding a finger to her lips, motioned him to remain silent.

She took up his cigarette packet and began to study it minutely, removed a cigarette and motioned to Finlay to find her something with which to light it. Finlay took out one for himself and lit them both, then pushed the packet towards the old lady.

She put up a hand, what would have been the classic sign of peace had she been a Red Indian, and began rummaging through the books on the bedside table. She studied the back cover of each in turn, until apparently she found what she was looking for.

She thrust a paperback under Finlay's nose, pointing at a row of printed prices on the back cover. Finlay, so used to sign language now, knew exactly what she wanted when she pointed to the price marked in American dollars. He shook his head vigorously and pointed to the pound sterling sign.

He was surprised by what followed. The old lady bent her head and placed her forehead on Finlay's hand, then held it and kissed it gently. She looked at Finlay and, without another word, brushed his hair from his face as a mother would with her son, patted his hand and left the room, taking the paperback book with her.

Finlay, perplexed, thought, 'I wonder what that was all about? Probably got herself tumbled by an English sailor somewhere and has never forgotten it.' He went back to sleep, dismissing the incident from his mind.

That afternoon, with Daria's help, Finlay walked as far as the veranda outside the room and spent the afternoon watching her writing at the table next to him. He had not been as weak as he expected, but his head swam and there was continual buzzing in his ears. Having once been on his feet though, Finlay was anxious to get up strength again.

The food, when it came, was plain but good, and Finlay ate everything that was put before him, even picking up and eating that which Daria had left uneaten. She seemed pleased that he appeared to be feeling better and later, before she left again for what Finlay assumed were more orders, she kissed him quietly and softly and looked at him tenderly with her violet eyes.

Sixteen

Mr Smith, head of SIS, sat thumbing through the lists of overnight messages that had come into the building. It was 7.30 on a beautiful spring day, but Smith was feeling just a little peevish. His mouth was dry from smoking too many cigars already that day and his interview with the Prime Minister had gone rather badly.

'The trouble with politicians,' he thought acidly, 'is that they have no vision and rarely have an original thought of their own.' The interview had concerned a cut in funding for his particular branch of the security services and, furthermore, his loss had been the Foreign Service's gain, which galled him.

The messages he was reading through had come in by various means – normal wireless traffic from embassies around the world, ships, submarines, aircraft and telex.

Some had arrived from 'legal' agencies. Those rare ones from 'illegal' agencies were clipped together separately. The latter were from agents scattered around the world, the clandestine, shadowy people from the real world of espionage. He read them all meticulously, initialling some and writing notes on others before they were distributed to the various sections to which they appertained.

There was a discreet knock on the door. 'Come in,' he

called shortly. His working day had begun and his mood had not improved.

His secretary entered and, apologising for the interruption, said, 'This has just come down from the cipher room, sir. The duty officer thought you ought to see it straight away.'

Smith took the proffered envelope. 'Thank you, Jane. Could you get me a pot of tea, please?' He watched her leave the room before he opened the envelope. The decoded message read:

From Shoe. Tashkent.

English national in convalescent hospital in Muynak. Blond, blue-eyed, metre-fifty, 25–30. One of yours? Held KGB. Advise. Stop.

An added note from B Section stated: 'Shoe is a long-time sleeper. We have had no contact in two years. We had assumed death, either of him or his wireless.'

Smith picked up the telephone. 'Jane, forget the tea for a moment! Please get me Admiral Winter at Horse Guards urgently. If he's not there, find him and if necessary take all the help you need to do so.'

Smith replaced the receiver and picked up the wireless message. 'As I live and breathe,' he said out loud to himself. 'Finlay - he lives yet!'

His telephone rang and he snatched it up quickly. 'Ah, John, can you come over immediately – think I've got something for you! … Good, expect you in about ten minutes then.' He put down the receiver, pleased that for once it looked as though he had something for Winter's section.

He walked to the window and watched the Thames flowing past, the sun playing tag with the wake of a passing tugboat, making it shimmer and rainbow brilliantly. 'Now, how do we get him out and when?' he thought. He remained staring pensively out of the window until his secretary appeared again.

'Admiral Winter, sir,' she announced.

'John, lovely to see you! Take a seat. I think today is going to be a good one for you and, if I'm right, you can buy me lunch at the Club!'

Smith handed him the slip of wireless message pad and stood watching for Winter's reaction. For just a second the paper trembled in Winter's hand and he looked enquiringly at Smith.

'I would love above everything else to believe, like you, that this refers to Keith Finlay, but surely, Rupert, it's been too long?' The Admiral spoke softly, quite shocked and already half believing.

'That's him, John. I'd set my pension on it! Don't forget, he was the one who made it back to the trees. He was taken alive, I know it!'

Smith was more ebullient than Winter had ever seen him, but he grunted, 'Better to have been killed than taken alive by those bastards. He'll have been through it at their hands!'

Winter reread the message as though trying to find some other clue to confirm what he really wanted to believe. As though to prompt him, Smith asked, 'He wouldn't have gone over to them, John, would he?'

'Never!' answered Winter. 'But I'll bet he's putting on a bloody good act as though he has.' He rose from the chair suddenly, as if he had made up his mind now that Finlay was alive. 'Where the hell is Muynak?'

They both moved over to the large wall map and Smith, who had once been head of B Section, covering Russia, placed his forefinger immediately on it.

'There it is, John, on the southernmost shore of the Aral Sea.' He moved his finger over the map. 'There's Tashkent, Samarkand, and here's our nearest friend. Not that reliable as friends go, but I've some good men there.' His finger was resting on Pakistan.

Winter made no comment on the observation about Pakistan but said, 'Your man Shoe, who is he?'

'Before my time, John, but I know that his grandfather was a White officer during the revolution. The family, or what was left of it, had a pretty rough time under Stalin. Shoe came to us during the last war and offered his services, so we fixed him up with what he needed and he has been in spasmodic contact ever since. He has never sent us that much, but enough and always absolutely accurate. Now we have to decide what to do. Do I risk my "sleeper" to get Finlay out? Or if you think that's not on, and depending on what Finlay knows, do you want him killed?' Smith's stark professionalism shocked Winter.

'Bloody hell, no! Of course not! If it is Finlay,' Winter said, stabbing at the piece of wireless message pad, 'he will not have gone over, nor will he have told them too much, just enough to stay alive! No, let's get him out as soon as we can. It will leave the Reds with egg on their faces!' He thought for a moment. 'Though of course you're right, Rupert. Finlay does know altogether too much and given time they'd force it out of him, so the sooner we can move the better!'

Smith lit a cigar. 'That's what I wanted you to say, John. If we are going to move on this it should be soon. They may move him again. First thing will be to establish that it really is Finlay, but my guts tell me that now. I think I know how to approach this one, John.' He pulled slowly on his cigar. 'By the way, when does the salmon fishing finish on the Test?'

Admiral Winter started digging in his inside pocket for his diary. 'Last day of September, Rupert. I'll put you in my diary for a day.'

Smith grinned. 'Not for me, John. Can't stand the sport, much too barbaric for me. But I've just set myself the target of having Finlay home before then. I think he'd appreciate a day when we get him back!'

Seventeen

THE NEXT MORNING, when the fat old woman came to clean the room, she totally ignored Finlay and set about her task with more vigour than the day before. When Daria left she ignored the proffered cigarette which Finlay held out. It was as though she had not even seen it.

Finlay, still tired after a night spent wracked with nightmares, was perplexed. The old lady gathered up her cleaning gear and left without a word.

That day, Finlay walked unaided as far as the cedar on the lawn, some hundred yards from their room. Sure now that the girl was an ally, he determined to speak to her and let her know that he knew she understood his language. He had to find out exactly where he was and what she knew of the Russians' future plans for him.

As they rested beneath the tree, Finlay said, 'Daria ...' But she put her hand to his mouth to silence him. She leant forward towards him on the grass, exposing briefly her rounded breasts. Finlay could see the black end of a small microphone taped between them.

Finlay quickly continued, 'Daria, when will Gregor come?' He repeated the words, 'Gregor, when?'

She answered in Russian and held up her fingers.

'Nineteen days,' responded Finlay, nodding. She helped him

up, and Finlay walked the whole circumference of the lawn before returning to the room unaided.

With his gathering strength, Finlay's brain took on a new awareness. Things began to clarify in his addled mind. He took more note of his surroundings, observed that there were boats tied to a small jetty jutting out from the brown sand of the beach.

Behind the hospital, the low hill climbed away south towards what he judged to be Turkmenistan, away to the upland plains and folds in seemingly endless arid steppes, to the borders of Afghanistan.

With this new awareness came a new wariness. Finlay knew that he mustn't seem to heal too quickly or else the Russians might return him to Moscow and more interrogation, the thought of which made his stomach crawl with fear.

In England it would be late spring, with its wealth of greens and warm rain, and the water meadows at home would have taken on the almost emerald colour that marked their richness. The river would have fined down from its winter level and the keepers would be readying their tools for the first weed-cutting. To Finlay it all seemed so long ago since he had smelt the river; he became profoundly and desperately homesick for the country he so loved.

As the sun rose higher, the sky changed from its early morning azure blue to almost the colour of beaten copper. The early summer of Asia, with its arid dryness and hammer strokes of oppressive sunlight, drove all the patients into the coolness of their hospital rooms. Finlay was the first to retreat from it and by noon was to be found playing chess with Daria in the shadowy stillness behind the drawn blinds.

Finlay talked to her constantly, telling her about his life in the Navy and of the ships he had served on. He knew that she would report all this and that her masters would, no doubt, count the relaxation as significant progress. She pretended not to understand and answered in Russian and tried, with the aid of a Russian English dictionary, to make him explain what he was talking about.

She played her part of the charade with consummate skill and Finlay wondered bitterly how much she was acting. The lines of his judgement were getting blurred, he knew. At the same time he had only this girl to rely on, and with that reliance there came a warming to her.

He watched her in the afternoon, writing at her table, and tried to analyse his feelings towards her. When she looked up and smiled her warm smile, Finlay knew that, despite everything, he had begun to feel for her.

That night, as she lay next to him, calming the horrors of his mind that beset him, he felt for the first time the coolness of her form slaking the thirst of his own burning skin. And later, as she slept, he propped himself on one elbow and looked down on her sleeping face.

He stroked the cool firmness of her bare arm and as she woke she smiled up at him, the whiteness of her teeth reflected by the first of the dawn. He wanted her then, this enemy of his country, but he realised with horror that his impotence was not leaving him.

He stroked the firm outline of her breast and allowed his hand to wander to the coolness of her flanks, but there was nothing. He looked out at the widening dawn and said in a whisper to the girl, 'I'm sorry, so very sorry.'

He rose, walked to the window and gazed out, cursing inwardly the land and the people it had spawned who had so effectively ruined him.

The next morning she seemed over compassionate, treating him more like a child than a man, and when the old lady came to clean the room Daria left almost immediately. The woman again ignored him and Finlay just marked her down as being half crazed.

Feeling strong enough to cope alone, he showered quickly and, expecting the old lady to have completed her chores, returned to the main room with just a small towel around him. The old lady, still there, sucked in her breath and gasped in horror as she glanced towards him, seeing the evident ill-treatment he had received. She gathered up her dusters and fled the room.

'Silly old bat!' thought Finlay. 'Reached her age and afraid of a naked man!'

Finlay's captors had not missed his returning strength and that night there was a guard placed by the French windows. Finlay watched his silhouette through the blind and heard the unmistakable sound of a dog scratching itself. He cursed his carelessness in letting them notice so easily and resolved to feign some kind of relapse in the near future.

The night passed in the usual way. Finlay, now almost afraid of sleep for the horror it brought, lay awake into the small hours. Once he rose and paced the room, then he knocked on the French windows and went outside and joined the guard. He did not bother to speak to him, and when the dog growled at Finlay, he curtly said, 'Shut up and lie down!' - which the dog promptly did.

He lit two cigarettes and handed one to the guard, who took it gratefully. He was a fairly rotund, middle-aged man, who Finlay thought should be at home in bed with his wife.

The guard studied Finlay, squatting on his haunches, staring at the night sky, and no doubt wondered why he was not in bed with the lovely young nurse who looked after him.

In the morning, feeling tired and pretty ill-willed, Finlay refused to get up and snapped at Daria when she began to insist. 'Clear off, sling your hook!' he told her, and Daria appeared genuinely shocked and hurt by the turn of events and fled to the bathroom to cover her feelings.

Within minutes the old cleaning lady had arrived, which just seemed to exacerbate the situation. 'Oh Jesus Christ!' said Finlay. 'It's Granny Fartalot, come to stink us all out!' And then, mocking cruelly, said directly to the old lady, 'OK, I give in, you disgusting old hag! I'll tell you everything. I just can't stand anymore!'

Though Finlay was sure she had not understood a word he had said, he was fairly certain that she had understood the tone. Her mouth fell open with surprise as he almost spat words at her. She turned and left the room, breaking wind loudly just before slamming the door behind her.

The comedy of the situation did not escape Finlay, who burst into laughter. Daria appeared at the bathroom door, clad in the scanty cotton underwear which Russian women wore both in summer and winter. Finlay's mood changed swiftly to bitter sarcasm. 'Oh do come in, Miss Daria! After all, you're quite safe, I've been gelded …!'

It was at this point he could see that she had been crying, no doubt from the previous hurt he had inflicted on her. He left his bed, went to her and held her gently. 'I'm sorry, Daria. I don't suppose any of this is of your making.'

She pushed her face into his shoulder and began to cry again. Finlay, exasperated, frustrated and remembering always that his life was in the balance, began to swear to himself about the ludicrous situation that had developed around him. He stroked the girl's head as she sobbed on his shoulder. The fresh scent of her hair permeated his nostrils and somewhere deep down inside him, something stirred. They were standing thus when the old lady returned, this time seemingly determined to do her duty. Finlay released the girl, who, blushing furiously, dressed and quickly left the room.

Finlay climbed wearily back onto his bed, ignoring the old lady cleaning around him. The last thing he wanted was to feel anything for Daria, for he feared it might weaken his resolve and he was sure that was precisely the reason his captors had placed her there. He was sure that they had not been in any way fooled by his apparent change of heart, just as he was also sure that, once he was well again, they would take her from him and subject him to the same treatment he had previously undergone.

The marked contrasts in treatment were undoubtedly designed to break him the more easily. He was thinking thus when he received a fairly sharp poke from the old lady, who thrust something into his hand and swept out of the room. Having unfolded the note, what he read started his heart knocking against his ribs. It read: 'Are you Finney? What is your state?'

Finlay snatched up his pencil from the bedside table and wrote 'Yes' beside the first question and corrected the name to Finlay. Against the second question he wrote: 'Unfit for anything other than mild exertion. Two weeks.'

Looking around wildly, he thought, 'How the hell do I get this back?' Then he understood. The old lady had left a duster beside him on the table and he quickly put the note within its folds. Within two or three minutes the old lady crashed back into the room, swearing, Finlay thought, and without even looking at him, swept up the duster and left again, still cursing.

Finlay's mind raced. Was it a trap, to test his alleged change of heart? He thought it out logically. The mistake in the way his name was spelt could easily be a decode mistake, but it was the question 'your state' which assured him.

He had answered it automatically in the same cryptic style as the question; the same question that appeared at the bottom of the debrief forms in the MOD. When returning from a mission, all field operatives had to report in writing if they had in any way been injured during the mission, and the question was relayed, 'your state'.

Did it mean now that help was at hand? Finlay had never doubted that the tentacles of the security services stretched to all parts of the world. Some of the information they received could only have been first hand and he had seen messages concerning information from deep within the heartlands of both Russia and China.

That such information should come out of Russia had never really surprised him. After all, the revolution was within living memory and not all of Russia, or Russians, had welcomed it. There were obviously a few who continued to be on the side of the angels.

He was still too ill to get so excited and he began to sweat and shake. The thought that somebody outside knew he was there, and alive, was hard to imagine. Daria returned to find him flushed and sweating badly. She took it as a relapse or that he had been overdoing things too soon and insisted that he return to bed.

A doctor was called in and left some pills. Daria, worried lest Finlay did not understand, showed him the two words 'mild' and 'fever' in the dictionary.

He had to force himself to eat at lunchtime. He was still trembling with shock. It was not until mid-afternoon that he was calm enough to think properly again. Questions raced through his mind: Would someone come to help? Would they admit that Finlay was an agent of the British Government and try to arrange a swap?

It was then that a horrible doubt crept into his mind. Would his own Service think that he had 'gone over' and, knowing the wealth of information Finlay possessed, would they try to enact their own way of silencing him?

He had known this to have happened in the past, for it was a fact that no barrier or obstacle was too great to protect all of the secret services of England. The thought he tried to dismiss was that in the hope of saving him more suffering, London might send someone to kill him. 'That would be the biggest irony of all,' he thought.

That night was sleepless. Finlay lay awake, watching the silhouette of the guard outside their room, and began to think about the possibility of making a break himself.

He looked across at the sleeping girl, tired no doubt because of so many disturbed nights. She had gone to sleep almost as soon as she lay down. Finlay had felt her eyes upon him and, on turning, had seen the flash of her white teeth as she smiled drowsily.

Finlay dozed fitfully before dawn, but when the girl had woken and gone to shower at the start of the day, he began to wonder what would happen to her if he escaped. He had no doubt that she would be severely punished, maybe even shot for so badly misjudging a situation. She may even be suspected of complicity.

But Finlay was certain too that it was his duty to try to escape. He was aware that he knew enough about his own and some of the other services to pose a threat to the security of his own country.

Throughout the following day his appetite again failed him. He was far too tense to eat. Daria put this down to the relapse from which he appeared to be suffering and began to fuss over him. The day passed slowly and Finlay was glad when the shadows gradually lengthened and the evening became night.

Despite his exhaustion, his sleep was again wracked with nightmares, nightmares so vivid he awoke shaking violently and had to stumble to the bathroom to be violently sick. He cursed them quietly in his hatred and frustration, these people who held his life in their hands.

'This is a slow death,' he thought bitterly. 'To have been killed with Pat would have been a better end.'

Previously, in one of the bush fire skirmishes of South East Asia, he had witnessed something he had never really understood. He had seen a marine officer take out his pistol, push it into his own mouth and blow the back of his skull away. The marine had just been told the wounds he had received had removed both of his testicles.

Eighteen

ADMIRAL JOHN WINTER arrived at precisely 12.30 in the foyer of White's and proceeded through into the anteroom, where he settled into one of the commodious leather armchairs. Other members nodded briefly or carried on sleeping and he grunted as the steward brought him a large pink gin.

Earlier in the day, a telephone call from Mr Smith requested they meet for lunch there. Smith had sounded elated and informed the Admiral, 'Lunch on you today, John!'

Winter heard the younger man arrive, his positive footsteps ringing sharply on the parquet flooring. Other members tsked and shook their newspapers in disapproval at his noisy entrance, but moved away discreetly when he sat down next to Winter. Both had been long-time members and, though other members were not privy to their exact positions within the establishment, they could all hazard a rough guess. The form was to move away from them and let them discuss the State's secrets in peace.

Smith looked around him and remarked, 'This place gets worse, John. You feel like getting a second opinion from some of the members, just to check whether they are in fact alive!'

Winter grunted and swallowed his gin. 'Hope I'm not included in that, Rupert! Just remember, thirty years ago, at this moment, I was standing on a Normandy beach, spotting for the guns of the Warspite. What were you doing? Train spotting?'

'Actually, I was in Paris, celebrating the landings. I arrived six months before,' Smith jibed.

'That's where you should have been, making it all possible. Anyway, what have you got for me?'

Smith leant across the space between their sitting positions. 'It's Finlay, John. We've made contact.'

Winter jerked upright, his gin glass skidding across the polished parquet in tiny pieces. 'How the devil... made contact! For God's sake man how... so soon? Are you quite sure? I mean, I'm going to his memorial service tomorrow!'

'Well, you'll be going to a memorial service for someone who is very much alive!' Smith drew from his pocket book a tattered piece of paper and held it up in front of Winter. 'Is that Finlay's writing?'

The Admiral looked and nodded. 'That's him all right! What's he doing? What's his state?'

'Claims he wants two weeks to be fit to move. Last we heard he was still in the hospital on the Aral Sea. He is only under light guard and my people think they can lift him from there and into Kabul by the year's end, if not sooner. One of the people with him is a KGB woman officer who, by the way, my people say he is bedding on a regular basis by the look of things!'

The Admiral laughed loudly. 'Two weeks more, indeed! If he's fit enough for exercises between the sheets, then he's fit enough to move!' He took out a large white handkerchief and blew his nose.

'Are you all right, John?' Smith asked.

The older man smiled, a little embarrassed. 'Yes, of course. Just a bit of a shock, his coming back like this. His aunt would never believe he was dead.'

'Well,' continued Smith. 'We haven't got him back yet, but what we have worked out so far stands a fair chance of success. It will depend largely on what sort of state Finlay is in, just how fit he is.'

The Admiral interjected. 'Never one to look after himself properly, smoking, reading all night, that sort of thing. Always fancied himself as somewhat indestructible. Always lucky, though – if he fell from twenty storeys he'd land in soft shit and come up smelling sweet!'

Smith took some folded foolscap sheets from his pocket. 'Well, he's going to need his luck this time!' He smoothed the paper flat. 'Now this is how we see it, John, and even though he's your man, with your permission, I'd like to run the show and get him out.'

The Admiral waved his arm airily. 'You have the men on the ground and the contact outside of Europe. I'm sure I'll agree to your demands. Just make quite certain that he is not taken alive again - as far as you possibly can, that is.'

'Right!' began Smith. 'Roughly, the plan is as follows. The break itself we are going to leave to Shoe - he knows the ground. He is confident he can get Finlay to Tashkent, keep him there for as long as it takes to get him fit to travel – then from there by a trading caravan into Afghanistan, where we can get him picked up by a Pakistani Army unit who will be exercising in the area-'

'Pakistani?' queried the Admiral.

'Yes, leave that side to me, John. I have promised their government something special for their help. As I was saying, the army unit will meet the caravan and remove Finlay to Kabul – to the American Peace Corps Hospital. From there he will be flown to Karachi. You lay on a ship there to get him away quickly, over to Salalah, I suggest, and from there to Cyprus or Gib and then back to Lyneham.'

'Is there anything we can do to help with the breakout?' asked Winter.

'Nothing, nor should we! If we interfere locally, with no knowledge of the area at all, I think it would be disastrous. Do you know, Finlay will be the first Englishman in decades to have actually been in Tashkent. It's all very restricted, even to their own nationals!'

The Admiral was worried about the number of people involved. 'This caravan idea, how can you be sure that they won't talk, either before or after? They could endanger your sleeper.'

Smith started folding the foolscap with an air of finality. 'They are being paid gold bullion after they return to Shoe in Russia. The way I have it planned they will remain silent.'

He paused to give his next statement added emphasis. 'We plan to break him out one week from today - 13 June to be precise.'

Winter started. 'Christ, so soon!'

'Yes,' replied Smith. 'I'd like to do it tomorrow. The sooner we can get him the better. Once the Reds think he is fit, they will move him again and we may never find him. It was only luck this time. Leave it to me, John. It's one I owe you. Just lay on a flag-waving visit to Karachi at short notice. Have something lying about in the Indian Ocean over the next three or four months.'

The Admiral rose. 'I shan't be able to face his people easily at his memorial service tomorrow, Rupert! I shall feel very uncomfortable!'

'Well, if it doesn't come off properly, it won't have been a complete waste of time, but do go, John. It adds weight to the conviction we think he is dead - just in case your movements are reported to Moscow!'

They headed off to the dining room.

WINTER FOUND THE next day at Finlay's home more difficult than he could ever have imagined, knowing what he did. There was also a distinct coolness directed at him. Finlay's family and friends gathered around the tree that had been planted by Finlay's great-grandfather at the top of the estate. Finlay's grandfather spoke to say how proud he was that Finlay had done his duty, but nothing could make up for his loss. Winter himself spoke briefly about how important Finlay's work had been, and how he had approached it with light-heartedness and a sense of humour.

Tables had been set up with food and drink in the hall. Janet Ward and her sister Cassy pressed Winter for more information about how Finlay had died, but got nowhere.

'Where is Mrs Terry, Sir James?' Winter asked Finlay's grandfather, as they stood by the front door with their pipes.

'Niney went to the beach early. She still says that Keith is alive, so she refused to be here. She wouldn't even think about doing the food. Hengistbury was always very special to her and Keith. Maybe one day she will come to terms with it all. Niney was much closer to him than his mother, you know.'

'How did his mother take it?'

'Admiral, she has not been told...' Finlay's grandfather sighed, and took a long draw on his pipe. 'Niney wouldn't have it, any more than telling Jenny. She said that telling them meant she agreed that he would never be coming back, and that she has yet to accept. His mother is due home at the end of the year. She will have to be told then, and as far as Jenny goes, I really don't know. Maybe when Niney accepts he's gone I can get her to go to Toronto and tell her. At the moment she's adamant that she should not be told.'

'And what do you think, Sir James?' Winter asked.

'I don't want to think about it. She keeps his room as it was left and the door locked. Sometimes I wonder if she's going over the edge. I hear her talking to him some days and Christ help anyone who speaks of him in the past tense. Will we ever know what happened to him, do you think?' The old man fixed the Admiral with his piercing blue eyes.

'One day maybe ... I will just say this to you, Sir James. What he did was beyond any evaluation. I sent him because he was the best we had; it was that important to the country, else I should never have risked him. If I got him a posthumous VC do you suppose it might help Mrs Terry?' Winter asked.

'Don't even think about it, Admiral! She would have your guts, and I don't suppose Kee would have wanted such a thing. Remember, as a youngster, when he saved that girl in the river? He refused an award then.'

The Admiral nodded slowly and the two men sucked thoughtfully on their pipes, remembering.

Nineteen

FINLAY FELT HIS strength returning as he paced the room each night, driving his sluggish bloodstream back to maximum effort. It came slowly at first and his muscles ached and quivered with his exertions. His left thigh muscle, badly pulped by the machine gun bullet, was taut and unyielding and occasionally locked up solid, causing him to gasp with the pain of cramp.

Throughout the daylight hours he slept or remained morose and uncommunicative towards Daria. She, seeing him become stronger, managed to obtain more and better food for him, which he wolfed down as though trying to extract every particle of goodness from it. She did everything she could to help him back to the fitness for which he strove, but, because he was somewhat embarrassed by her concern for him, he ignored her shy displays of affection and pushed her away, ashamed of his incapacity.

In the early dawn, just after Finlay had finished his pacing and violent exercise and had returned to his bed, she came and lay down beside him. He felt her crying quietly and softly. He began to comfort her. Her tears ran warmly over his naked chest and again Finlay felt so dreadfully sorry for her. Then, to his great surprise, she whispered through her sobs, 'Forgive me, please, for what they have done to you.'

At last she spoke to him in English. All vestiges of her professionalism had disappeared and with that one sentence she had laid herself bare to him. From within came an instant surge of compassion for the girl, so caught up in something beyond her control. Against his own wishes now, something stirred within Finlay and, with infinite care, he gently loved her.

Afterwards, as she lay sleeping, he cursed himself for his lack of resolve, but the cynical side of his nature mocked him for this.

Finlay had very little doubt that Daria had told all during her morning debriefing. To her seniors it would have been a large step forward, showing them that Finlay had begun to feel something for the girl. No doubt they would now look forward to the flow of information increasing.

Finlay cursed himself again in the cold light of day for the weakness he had shown, putting himself in the position of being that close to someone who was technically the enemy.

The rest of the day was spent as usual, walking around the grounds and chatting in their room. To make the charade seem more real, Finlay talked about the ships on which he had served, keeping up the pretence of trying to make Daria understand English. He said at one point, 'I wish you could understand me. Perhaps I should try harder with Russian.' And, reverting to the dictionary and phrase book, Finlay ploughed on with the deceit. Daria became attentive, happy that he seemed so very relaxed with her now, and he was sure her debrief the following day would bring her praise.

Finlay wondered for how long he would have to maintain the charade of being ill, how long it would be before the Russians moved him away from the contact he had made with the outside world.

By nightfall, Finlay was very tired and he slept fitfully for some two hours. Afterwards he lay awake watching the guard, obviously dozing at his post. He must have fallen asleep again then, for some time later he suddenly awoke, knowing something was wrong.

In the moment between sleep and wakefulness, he thought he had heard the guard's dog whine and was about to dismiss it when the French windows were dragged open and the room seemed full of people.

Finlay's first instinct was to protect the girl and, moving as fast as his badly used body would allow, he made to jump from his bed. Strong arms gripped him and held him fast as Daria, shocked from deep sleep, sat up in bed, snapping on her bedside light as she did so.

For just a second she sat there blinking against the brightness, then, as Finlay watched in horrified fascination, one of the intruders fired at her twice with a silenced weapon. A cherry-red hole appeared above the arch of her right eyebrow, another beneath the line of her jaw as the bullet snapped her head backwards on to the pillow, which at once burst under the impact of the bullet and filled the room with tiny white feathers. Daria was dead.

It had all been over in a matter of ten seconds, but Finlay's befuddled brain saw it in slow motion as he was propelled quickly through the windows out on to the lawn. As though in a dream, Finlay heard the roar of an outboard motor as he was half carried and half pulled down towards the sound of the engine.

Instead of clambering into the boat with the rest of the party, Finlay was dragged off to the left by just two of the men, exhorting him to move faster by tugging at his arms. No sooner had they made the cover of some scrub then the guards at the hospital came running across the lawn.

They immediately opened fire on the boat, now retreating

northwards and bucketing about as the men within it struggled to maintain control during the initial acceleration.

Within seconds, another outboard roared into life somewhere to Finlay's right and he was dragged away by the two men as the Russians took up pursuit in their own vessel, firing incessantly over the water.

They ran for perhaps half a mile before Finlay was totally exhausted, his bare feet cut to ribbons. They were in the low hills above the hospital complex now, and below them they saw the whole area illuminated and shadowy figures running about like scurrying beetles. Vehicles left the complex and drove down both sides of the narrow sea, obviously intent on joining in the chase of the fleeing boat.

Finlay, who had had neither time nor breath to speak, could only appreciate the professional way in which it had all been done. He had been broken out, freed and pitched into a situation over which he had no control.

He looked at his two companions. 'Did you bloody well have to kill the girl?' he rasped, realising immediately that it was a stupid question.

Both men looked at him in amazement. A guttural 'Yes' was the only reply given before they started running again. They had barely made another quarter of a mile before they stopped again, Finlay now dropping. This was as far as Finlay's two companions intended to come. They sheltered in the rocks and Finlay's breath was audible as short gasps.

'Put on!' cried one of the men, handing Finlay some evil-smelling clothing. 'We stay here now.' The clothes were of rough wool: a coverall smock, some baggy white trousers, rough sandals and a flat turban completed the garb.

'You animal man now,' said the man who had not previously spoken and they both laughed at the apparent joke.

Finlay understood the plan. The boat was the decoy, the

obvious escape route, but he and the two other men would remain quite openly as shepherds on the hill above the hospital where Finlay had seen them daily. 'Who are you?' he asked the man who had done most of the talking.

'Yuri Shellmov,' he replied, pointing to his own chest. 'My fadder, he love Englis and talk me Englis.' And that, evidently, explained it all. 'We stay night and two three day, look to animals and when Reds not find you, then you Tashkent, then you Englis.'

Finlay sat down, head in hands. This was his rescue and he had begun the journey home!

'Red cow, she good fuck, yes?' asked Shellmov, laughing. 'She not fuck more now!'

'No,' Finlay replied, choking on the words as he said them. 'She not fuck more now.'

Yuri began getting into his stride. 'Good Englis, fucking bloody mothers!'

Finlay felt that whoever had taught English to this man's father had much to answer for.

'You drink, then close eyes. Morning,' said Shellmov, waving his arms to indicate sunrise. 'Morning, plenty men here, plenty bloody bear-shaggers,' Shellmov announced using CIA slang for Russians. He handed Finlay a skin bottle from which to drink. Finlay gratefully took two huge swallows then staggered upright coughing and choking. The liquid, whatever it was, was icy, but burned a passage right down to his sandals.

'Jesus Christ, what's that?' he gasped.

'Jesus Christ, real vodka,' repeated Shellmov, who roared with laughter.

Finlay sat down again, his head spinning with the influence of the drink. He reached out for the skin flask. 'Give me another please, Yuri!'

Shellmov handed him the flask. 'Jesus Christ, good, yes?'

'Very good, Yuri,' replied Finlay, drinking the fiery liquid. 'Just the thing if you've got a lot of forgetting to do.'

'Not drink all,' protested Shellmov. But Finlay was asleep.

Twenty

THE NEXT MORNING, as Shellmov had predicted, the whole area was swarming with troops, and helicopters clattered noisily over the sheep, scattering them across the hill.

Finlay and the other two shepherds gathered them up time and time again and when a small lorry loaded with troops arrived, Shellmov, with the aplomb of a Shakespearian actor, stormed across to them. Finlay watched the arm-waving and foot-stamping display from about two hundred yards away, and their companion, standing next to Finlay, shouted the occasional curse in their direction. Finlay, for good measure, shook both his fists at them.

Whatever Shellmov said to the troops worked, for the lorry drove off with the Russian in the back shouting and gesticulating at Shellmov.

He, in turn, looked away from them and bent over, pulling his baggy trousers down as he did so. This brought peals of laughter from the departing vehicle and Shellmov, with great dignity, recovered himself and walked back to where Finlay and the other shepherd were standing.

Once the lorry was out of sight, they could contain themselves no longer and the two shepherds clung to each other laughing, until the tears ran down their cheeks. Finlay joined them in their laughter, but his was more from relief than anything else.

The Russians concentrated the main area of their search to the north of them and as the day wore on Shellmov started moving the sheep south. For three more days, they grazed the flock southward, during which time they saw only a few more military vehicles, at which they either waved or shook their fists, depending upon how close they came.

During the daytime the sun shone down on them, the heat hitting Finlay in hammer strokes and burning his skin the colour of mahogany. The nights were warm and balmy. They sat around, quietly eating their meagre rations of bread and cold mutton or cheese, washed down with vodka or water from the river. On the fourth evening, Shellmov told Finlay that later that night they would be leaving for Tashkent.

'How are we going to get there, Yuri?' Finlay asked.

'We walk, the river. One week fadder find us, then ride,' the shepherd answered. 'Day you sleep, night you walk.'

Finlay wondered if, in fact, he could manage to walk all night, but this very resourceful shepherd saw the look of doubt in his face. 'We go on water sometime,' he continued, laughing.

Later that night their small camp was approached by two men dressed in similar clothes. After effusive greetings between them, they began talking among themselves, pointing and nodding at Finlay. Shellmov broke from the group and, taking Finlay by both shoulders, said, 'One week fadder come for animals.' He made a charade of driving a lorry, with lots of gear changing and engine revving.

'We go,' he said simply. 'Now.'

Finlay shook hands with the other shepherd with whom he had spent the last few days and left with Shellmov, walking in a southerly direction, keeping the river to their right. As they walked, clouds of mosquitoes followed them, feasting on their blood, and Finlay prayed for the morning when the heat would drive them away. The Russian shepherd seemed utterly indefatigable, always cheerful, and for his size he seemed to exist on practically nothing.

Next morning, before the sun was properly up, they breakfasted on bread and cheese and drank from the river. They found a place to hide in the reed-fringed bank and slept while the sun passed overhead. The mosquitoes hovered around them in droves while they shaded from the direct rays of the sun. They made a meal of Finlay, raising lumps on any exposed skin. Finlay, though cursing them, had real hope now that he might yet be able to leave this accursed country.

During the day a few military vehicles passed by on the road on the other side of the river. Night found them marching again after another meal of bread and cheese. 'Save meat. Later you not strong,' said Shellmov.

'OK, Yuri, as long as this leg holds out, I can keep going.' Finlay said it, but he was not really very confident. His leg did hold out though, and for five nights they walked beside the river and just before dawn on the sixth morning they swam across and hid in the reeds near the road.

As the sun came up, Finlay saw they were quite near what could have been termed a lay-by on the rough road before them. Throughout the day, several lorries carrying goods southward stopped there, their drivers getting out to stretch their legs and answer nature's call.

About mid-afternoon they heard motorcycles approaching and Yuri hissed him a warning. Two mounted policemen passed them then pulled up just further from the lay-by and stood talking and laughing together. A moment later, a large yellow lorry, made by Seddon, pulled up behind the policeman. Painted across the canvas of the trailer, Finlay read 'N.J.Crisp Limited, Birmingham. International Transporters.'

Finlay couldn't help but smile when he saw it. He knew it was the way with the Russians: every foreign lorry that entered their borders was escorted by the police. They had good reason to be suspicious. MI6 had once tried to smuggle some equipment in a tanker into Russia; the equipment had been found, with the consequent embarrassment to the British. It occured to Finlay that such a lorry may have provided a possible means of escape, had he been on his own. He was glad he was not and quickly dismissed the idea - it would have been far too risky.

The lorry parked for about twenty minutes and then, following a wave from one of the motorcycle police, the convoy pulled away again to the south.

'Him going Tashkent. You see Tashkent tomorrow.' Shellmov was very nonchalant about it.

Later that night another lorry stopped in the lay-by, this time heading north. The driver climbed down and, after urinating in the reeds, walked towards them.

'Yuri,' he called. Shellmov whistled back and, motioning to Finlay to follow, walked up on to the road. The lorry driver was Shellmov senior and, after clasping his son's hand, he hugged Finlay to him. He smelt of sheep, pickled cucumber and tobacco.

'Hello, Englis. By fuck you make great trouble! Last night you seen in Ryazan. Soldiers turn whole bloody fucking town inside out!' He roared a great belly laugh. 'Tomorrow you in my home Tashkent. You wait until my uncle come with camels, take you to where the bloody Afghans live, then you go home.'

'Thank you, Mr Shellmov,' said Finlay, quite overcome.

'You not thank! Winston Churchill my good friend!' Again

the Russian laughed. 'Tomorrow you hide with sheep in lorry, then you safe my home.' He grasped Finlay's hand and left, walking back with his son to the lorry.

He could hear them talking for about five minutes and when the lorry had pulled away, Yuri returned. He carried with him a rucksack, tightly packed. That night they ate well on cold meat, bread and tea from a bottle, and smoked cigarettes of harsh Russian tobacco.

Just before they made ready to sleep, Yuri came to Finlay and showed him a large Webley pistol. 'My fadder say you not take alive, OK?'

Finlay grinned. 'Why, does that cannon still work, Yuri?'

The next morning Finlay felt very ill and was running a high fever, and although he slept fitfully throughout the day, by evening he felt drained. They ate some more bread and meat and drank from the river, Finlay having to force the food down.

The waiting seemed interminable and it was very dark before the Shellmov lorry came roaring towards them. When it stopped, the elder Shellmov stepped down and ushered Finlay up through a side door into the back. It was full of sheep.

'They still look for you, Englis, but still in wrong place! Tonight you have bed.' He slammed the side door shut, then a minute later Finlay heard the cab door close and thus they left for Tashkent.

The sheep in the back gazed at their new companion with their yellow eyes and then ignored him. Finlay slept, the fever still on him, and had to be shaken awake when they reached their destination. Staggering weakly, he was ushered from the lorry into a square-built house and up some open steps from which he saw briefly below him a family having a meal. They all stared at him, amazed.

Yuri Shellmov pushed him into a small attic room and showed him the bed. 'You sleep, Englis. You bloody sick with weakness.'

And Finlay slept. He slept for thirty-six hours, even the nightmares failing to wake him fully. The Shellmovs gazed at him thrashing about on the pallet bed, shook their heads, and leaving one of their number to watch him, the rest trooped out.

Over the next three weeks, the family nursed Finlay back to something approaching health. Below, Finlay could hear them going about their normal family routine. He was aware of the risk they were running by sheltering him there, but whenever he could the father joined him in the attic and regaled him with tales of where he had last been seen. He found the whole thing highly amusing and laughed his great belly laugh and belched pickled cucumber.

One day Finlay had a special visitor whom he recognised immediately. She came into the attic. It was the cleaning lady from the hospital. She greeted Finlay and spread her awful smell around him.

'My mother sister,' said Shellmov proudly. 'She tell me all hospital.'

Finlay nodded to her and blew a loud raspberry, causing the old lady, with her nephew, to fall into fits of laughter.

When she had left, Shellmov told Finlay about what had happened at the hospital and how the men who played decoy – some of his nephews – had all escaped safely and were back in the hills with their sheep. Finlay was relieved he had not cost Shellmov any grief, but felt profoundly depressed when told of Daria's body being taken back to Moscow for a hero's funeral.

Shellmov, sensing his mood, said, 'She no bloody good, Englis. Fadder bigwig in Moscow. Bloody shit Commie, all them bastards.'

'I wonder,' thought Finlay. 'You're likely right, Yuri,' he said.

Another three weeks passed. The hunt for him had switched to the north-west and the Finnish borders were heavily guarded.

He was fretting to leave and when Yuri told him another week's waiting was all that was required of him he began pacing up and down endlessly. The week dragged by slowly. Finlay read some children's Russian school books, played chess and was soundly thrashed by the younger Shellmov until, at last, one day Yuri Shellmov came into the attic and announced, 'Tomorrow the Englis leave for home. We ask him to take our love to England and to Winston Churchill!'

Finlay did not have the heart to tell him that Sir Winston Churchill was now a very old man with a very weak heart. Instead, he just drank his toast with them with the liquid fire-ice they called vodka and wished Canavan were with him to see the finish.

Twenty-One

THE FOLLOWING MORNING Finlay, who had barely slept, was given fresh clothing - folds of unmanageable white coarse cotton which the Shellmov daughters showed him how to wear - and then came the goodbyes.

Yuri Shellmov the elder wept openly, while his son kept kissing Finlay on both cheeks. Mrs Shellmov gave him loaves and salt wrapped in a white cloth and kissed him on the forehead. She said something in Russian to him and sharply told her husband to translate: 'My old bitch say to go with the God of your country.' She smiled through her tears and went back into the house as the two Shellmov men climbed into the lorry cab, pushing Finlay up before them.

Shellmov the elder said, 'We go meet my uncle. Him bloody Afghan. Crazy mad bastard!'

As they drove through Tashkent, Finlay gazed about him. 'I must remember all this,' he thought, looking at the old and new buildings jumbled together. The ancient minarets winked in the sun next to the non-reflective glass of the office blocks. 'I hope I never pass this way again!'

What lay in front of him he could only guess. His geography of the area was fairly sketchy. He had, during his initial training as a naval officer, studied the area closely, in preparation for the time when the Cold War might become a Hot War. But that now seemed so many years ago, and his tired mind could not return there. What he did know was that he was going to be left with strangers to make a journey over some of the most inhospitable places on earth. Under normal circumstances this would not have bothered him, but in his weakened condition he would have to rely on them and he wasn't happy about that.

After they had left the bounds of the city they drove on for perhaps another five miles to meet the beginning of the sandy steppes that ran away to the north-west. A camel caravan, in swirls of dust, was making ready to leave. The grunts and roars of the protesting beasts, the shouts of the drovers in their baggy, unkempt clothing, made Finlay feel he had been transported back a thousand years.

The Shellmovs found their relative and spoke but briefly to him, pushing Finlay forward as they spoke. He was tall and gaunt, a deeply swarthy man with shifting dark eyes and a long moustache.

'This is my uncle, Englis. He take you to his own land, many weeks away. You will be all right with him. He is honest and a smuggler of opium.'

Finlay was again hugged by father and son before they walked back to their lorry and were gone.

Finlay felt very alone among these darkly suspicious strangers, in a land where he was hunted and his blue eyes marked him out as the stranger.

The camels were already on the move and Shellmov's uncle, the camel master, led him quickly to one and motioned Finlay to hold the girth of its pack saddle before disappearing into the clouds of dust and flies. For about six hours, Finlay walked beside the animal, adjusting his headgear so that only his eyes were showing. He kept them half closed because of the sun and dust, but even so, within the first hour they burned and ached with tiredness.

After about four hours, Finlay had to resort to leaning heavily on the camel, such was his weariness. The camel objected to this and kept turning its head and snapping at him. A drover from somewhere behind him saw what was happening, ran forward and gave him a light cane to strike the camel with as it turned to him. Finlay decided that he did not like baggage camels very much and used the cane with as much alacrity as his fast diminishing strength would allow.

At the first halt, he was shown how to couch his camel and release the girths, then he was led away to the campfire where he sat down thankfully on the ground, tired beyond belief. He was handed a cup filled with the strongest coffee he had ever tasted and as he drank from it he was aware of many pairs of dark eyes watching him.

Finlay knew very little about the modern Afghans. His only knowledge was historical – their long-running battles with the British and their almost fanatical defence of the mountain passes along the North-West Frontier. Judging now by the glances in his direction, he was sure that some of these Afghans considered the issue not to be over.

Suddenly, directed by a shout from Shellmov's uncle, the camp was broken, the loads were readjusted and the camels rose as one, roaring in protest. Again the dust swirled about them as Finlay resumed the march towards the south-west.

They walked on for another eight hours, well past dusk, the camels' feet swishing softly over the sandy earth. Finlay began to experience real thirst. It was evident that he was not going to be any kind of passenger on the journey and he determined that no matter what was expected of him, he would do it, and more.

It was almost dark before the camels were halted. Finlay was shown how to unload and hobble the beast to which he had attached himself and, as he watched it meander away to graze with its fellows, he could not help but think what an evil-tempered bastard that animal was!

The night camp was something of a more social affair than the short stop they had had during the day. Shellmov's uncle had come back down from the front of the train to find Finlay and led him to the cooking fire, where he sat on the rapidly cooling earth and immediately began to doze, only to be woken by a sharp nudge as food was presented to him.

He watched the others eating with their fingers, forcing the rice dish into balls and pushing it into their mouths. Finlay could not make out what the meat was. It was rubbery in texture and required a great deal of chewing, but it tasted good for all that. Coffee was again served strong, black and very sweet, cloying stickily to the roof of his mouth.

The men lay back after drinking their coffee and smoked thick cigarettes. One of the drovers gave Finlay a leather pouch filled with about a pound of rough-cut tobacco and some rolling papers. Finlay thanked him. 'When in Rome,' he thought, and proceeded to roll himself a smoke. He handed the pouch back but the drover motioned him to keep it.

Shellmov's uncle indicated to Finlay to follow him out of the circle of firelight and into a small tent. He gave Finlay some more sandals, a blanket and a skin bag of water. Then, pointing at the bag and back at Finlay, he held up five fingers.

Finlay nodded in understanding. 'Five days,' he said, holding up his hand, and the Afghan almost smiled.

The skin held about a gallon, Finlay judged - not a lot for five days, but if the others managed on it, so would he.

The Afghan called back over his shoulder into the blackness of the tent and a tiny child trotted out of the shadows, a boy dressed in only a striped shirt, which hung like a nightshirt below his knees. The camel master looked at the boy fondly and said something to him, pointing at

Finlay. The child visibly swelled with pride at what was said to him. Then the Afghan pointed at his son and said something like 'yackaholdoo'.

Finlay tried to repeat it but his Western tongue could not circumnavigate the extraordinary string of vowels. Finlay pointed at himself and said, 'Englis', which the child repeated with ease.

And so it was arranged. Finlay, known as 'Englis', would be looked after by a child of not more than five years of age whom Finlay named 'Abdul'. The child could not understand that Finlay did not speak his language - he was probably the first foreigner he'd ever met - and it perplexed him that when he said something to Finlay, even something quite simple, it was beyond the adult's comprehension.

He withdrew back into the shadows of the tent, motioning Finlay to remain where he was. The proud father looked at Finlay and shrugged. When the boy came forward again, he was leading a lanky Saluki bitch, as yellow as the sandy earth over which they had travelled that day.

Finlay knelt and fondled the bitch's silky ears. He then looked at the boy and said, 'Saluki.' The boy registered nothing. Finlay tried the Arabic 'el hor', which the boy jumped up and repeated and nodded frantically. The bond had been forged.

Walking back to his makeshift bed among his camel's baggage, Finlay looked up at the stars, which seemed almost within reach, and thanked God for his luck. He had seen sights already that were rare for Westerners and he determined that, despite the obvious discomfitures of the journey that lay ahead, he was going to remember everything about his trip across this part of Asia, barred to outsiders. 'I wonder when the last Englishman passed this way,' he conjectured.

The day had tired him enormously, but the caravan's progress was at a rate he considered to be typical of a Sunday afternoon walk. If this was normal, and the ache in his left thigh became no worse, he was confident he would make it.

The next day followed the same pattern – breakfast, loading and the slow march until past dusk. They were crossing arid land bordering onto the steppes away to the north. The only covering over the stony sand was a wiry, tough and bluish grass which clung grimly to what life it could forge in the dry earth.

One long day led to another. They saw nothing but the distant horizons all around them and the silence of the steppes was oppressive. Finlay rapidly became accustomed to the midday heat and the few parts of his skin exposed to its almost vertical rays turned from its mahogany colour to a dirty blue-black and the hairs on his arms bleached white.

At first, the monotonous marching left him exhausted and he slept deeply, untroubled by nightmares or fear of being recaptured. He soon lost what little weight he had gained during his stay with the Shellmovs and he became as spare and gaunt-looking as the other drovers. Only his blue eyes made a mockery of his disguise, and the blond beard, which he had to keep trimmed as best he could with a knife. He also tried to darken it with the remains of the coffee pot each night.

On about the fifteenth day of their march they passed a caravan going in the opposite direction. It had appeared above the mirage early in the morning, bobbing and weaving in ethereal shapes.

Guns suddenly appeared among Finlay's companions, and for a while it looked as though a firefight would develop. However, as the approaching caravan came within easy sight, recognition followed and there was much shouting and banter between the two sets of drovers as they passed. They remained in view for nearly an hour, swaying in the liquid mirage.

Abdul, now Finlay's firm friend, walked part of the day beside him, chattering to him in his guttural language. Then, as he tired, he would run forward and clamber on to a camel, swinging up on its girth and hauling himself hand over hand until he won the top of the load. Here he would sit, dozing and swaying in time with the animal beneath him until, batteries recharged, he would leap down and scamper, imp-like, to another part of the column.

On the twenty-fifth day, the roofs of a city showed briefly in the early morning sun before the heat haze rose and hid it from sight. They marched all day towards it and not until the sun was almost down did the buildings show themselves again.

Finlay stopped his march, his camel walking on, doubtless glad to be rid of him. He just stood and gaped. There, about five miles away, was this most mysterious of cities, Samarkand. From this distance it was like something from *The Arabian Nights*, green, white and gold. The gateway between Asia and India, once the hub of the spice and drug trade of slavers and warriors, it had stood there for more than a thousand years and had provided a stopping place in all that time for the caravans of many races.

Finlay wanted to go into the city that evening when they finally halted about a mile outside, but Shellmov's uncle refused and motioned him to stay away from the firelight, as traders would be coming from the city to buy and sell. He pointed at Finlay's blue eyes, sharply contrasting with his brown skin, and made a mime of shooting him with a pistol, reminding Finlay of his still very precarious position.

The caravan rested all the next day and Finlay kept himself

hidden among some of the baggage at the bequest of the camel master. Then, the following day, at sunrise, they broke camp and again marched towards the south-west, moving more quickly than usual to make up the time of their halt. Before midday, the heat haze had hidden the city, and by nightfall it had disappeared to Finlay for ever.

About a week after leaving Samarkand, the land around them began to change. The earth was richer and the grass became greener and more lush. The camels fed well at night, with the consequent effect on their bowels. Their hindquarters became green, plastered with dung, and the flies became more troublesome than ever.

There were compensations in the form of animal and bird life. Larks and pippet-like birds abounded, their songs a joy to Finlay. If he closed his eyes as he marched along, he could almost imagine he was back in England.

Also, there was now variety in the food. Hare became part of their diet, and on one occasion a goat was killed, a stray from some nearby settlement.

There was great rejoicing about ten days out of Samarkand when the Saluki bitch ran down a huge bustard and young Abdul carried it proudly into the camp. It was a bird almost as big as himself. At the night camp that evening a feast was prepared with meats of wild donkey and hare, but the centrepiece was the child's bustard.

The change in climate brought on Finlay's malaria every few days and he gradually became weaker. Blood appeared in his urine and he had doubts about whether he would now be able to hold out much longer.

It took them three weeks to get from Samarkand to a town the camel master pronounced 'Kershye', which Finlay judged to be Karshi. Again they stopped to trade and Finlay, glad of the rest, remained hidden for twenty-four hours.

Shellmov's uncle, aware of Finlay's failing health, produced from his trading some aspirin tablets, which he gave to Finlay. Though of some help, they could do but little towards fending off his illness. Finlay began to doubt his body's ability to withstand much more punishment. 'And even if I do survive,' he thought, 'will I ever fully recover?'

When alone with the camel master, Finlay drew a map in the dust, marking in the towns of Kushka and Tersney in Turkmenistan and Mayar-i-Sharif in Afghanistan and held up four fingers to indicate four days.

The Afghan shook his head and indicated that their route would turn east and they would cross into Afghanistan south of Kulzal. With much gesticulation he made Finlay understand that there would be fewer soldiers and helicopters there. He drew his own map and, running his finger along the border, he turned it dramatically south-east across the Hindu Kush area and held up both hands, signifying ten days. Then he held up two fingers and began to drive an imaginary car.

Finlay nodded. 'Twelve days more,' he said out loud. 'I'll make that. I'll not die in this bloody land!'

The march continued, swinging to the south-east. They watered the camels and themselves at a well somewhere outside of Dushanbe and pushed on to the hills and mountains leading to the Afghanistan border.

On the sixth day they dropped down into a pass. The ground here was rockier and the going in places became harder. Several times one or other of the camels foundered and they were delayed for hours. The air became colder and damper, the camel drovers more tense, as though sensing danger.

Camel caravans had used the route for centuries with scant regard for borders or customs, but the modern world demanded such formalities. With Finlay as an added danger to them, the Afghans were viewing the coming crossing with more circumspection than usual.

Advanced scouts were detached and sent ahead, guns appeared and were cleaned, oiled and made ready. Finlay showed an interest in them, but they would not let him look closely. He could see that some of the older men carried Lee Enfield rifles of indeterminate age, but most of the younger ones carried American weapons of more modern manufacture – Remingtons mainly.

Two days into the pass the routine changed. The camels remained couched all day. They waited patiently, their long necks stretched out, resting on the ground and, when night fell, they were reloaded and the caravan moved out south-east into the darkness.

Twenty-Two

Rupert Smith stepped off the small executive jet which had taxied to a quiet corner of Charles de Gaulle Airport, walked briskly to the waiting embassy Daimler and swept out into the French traffic.

He hated the French. He could think of nothing good about them, his opinion being that the only thing you could rely on them for was their treachery. And today he was going to do just that.

He had managed to wangle himself an invitation to an official banquet and he knew a certain French Foreign Service attaché would be present. He also knew the attaché was in the pay of the East Germans. By the time he was back on his jet later that day, he would, by innuendo and the dropping of certain information (his tongue supposedly loosened by wine), set the seal on the last of Operation Kingstone.

Meanwhile, the frigate HMS Aurora, on patrol in the Arabian Sea, completed a turn to the north-east and headed for Karachi, her mission being ostensibly a courtesy call on Pakistan. Her crew had been told they were picking up a British national who would return home with them and at the same time they were reminded of their obligations with regard to the Official Secrets Act. A stoker summed up the situation with his mess section: 'In other words we are picking up some glamour pants poofter spy who's somehow got his bum in the custard!'

At London Heathrow, Admiral Winter settled himself into the first-class cabin of a British Airways flight to Karachi and ordered a pink gin.

In Kabul, a Pakistani Army Captain climbed into the passenger seat of a Land Rover and, checking he had his full complement of troopers in the back, ordered the driver to move off.

Also in Kabul, the American Peace Corps Hospital welcomed a new doctor into their midst. He apparently knew very little about medicine and kept himself to himself, spending all day reading, pacing his room or chain-smoking.

Twenty-Three

THE CAMELS WERE pushed as briskly through the rocky pass as the light from the stars would allow and they made surprisingly good time. By morning they had covered some half of the journey and, as the camels were being unloaded and couched for the day, Shellmov's uncle walked with Finlay to the top of the crag flanking the pass. The Afghan pointed away to the south to a distant range of hills and through the clear air Finlay felt he could almost reach out and touch them.

'Afghanistan?' asked Finlay. The camel master nodded, smiling. They were almost there.

Finlay could not rest that day. He had no idea of the date or of what lay ahead in Afghanistan, but provided that they were not checked at the border, tomorrow he would be out of Russia. He tried to imagine the moment when he would step from one side of the border to the other and wondered what his feelings would be. He was so weak now from malaria that the rarefied air of the mountains could barely produce from him a rational thought.

The day passed slowly. It was another cold, damp day with no fires and movement restricted to a minimum. Towards evening they heard a helicopter somewhere to the north. The darkness closed in around them and once again the camels were loaded and they struck off southward.

Everybody seemed tense; nerves twitched if a camel roared and when a small fall of rocks hurtled from the crag above everyone dived for cover, waiting for the bullets to start singing around them.

The first light of dawn found them clear of the pass and on to the beginning of a plateau. The helicopter was airborne again, but the camel drovers seemed relaxed and happy and completely ignored it.

Finlay left his camel and ran forward past the line of swaying animals. He was looking for the camel master. He found him walking beside a beast, his young son Abdul riding piggy-back style across his shoulders, fast asleep. Finlay stopped him and pointed to the ground.

'Afghanistan?' he asked. Shellmov's uncle nodded and marched on, smiling at the elation evident on this strange Englishman's face. Finlay stood rooted to the spot and watched the camels swing past, tired after their night's exertions. Away to the north, the helicopter still clattered back and forth. 'You're too bloody late, Ivans, I'm out!'

He waited until his own camel drew level and began walking by her side, hanging on to her girth. She had long since given up trying to snap at Finlay. He, for his part, had a deep affection for her now, this bad-tempered beast which had half dragged him from Tashkent, across Turkmenistan and over the Hindu Kush. The relief was enormous.

They marched on for another two hours, the sun swinging in the sky with them, through a small gorge and up on to a hilly plain dotted with scrub. By now the camels had had enough and were beginning to complain. Hungry and tired, they were couched and their packs unloaded. The camel master came back down the line and, finding Finlay, motioned him to return to the head of the column with him.

The Afghan made motions of driving a car, bade Finlay sit

and produced the coffee pot. They had been sitting drinking and smoking for about an hour when, to Finlay's great joy, he heard the unmistakable roar of a Land Rover engine and suddenly, there it was, breasting a ridge and heading straight for them.

Finlay stood up, waiting as the Land Rover approached and stopped in front of him. A man dressed in the uniform of a Pakistani Army Captain climbed out, looked about him for a moment, then, seeing Finlay's blue eyes, said, 'Welcome to Afghanistan, Englishman. I've come to return you to Kabul.'

He spoke briefly to the camel master, shaking his hand, and turning to Finlay said, 'Come, Englishman, we must get you out of here quickly. You are still in great danger this close to the border.'

'Captain, please thank the Afghan for me and for all he has done. Can you tell him I will never forget him or the journey?'

The Pakistani translated the message and Shellmov's uncle smiled. Finlay bent and ruffled Abdul's hair.

'Come!' ordered the Pakistani. 'Come, Englishman. We must move!'

Finlay climbed in the front of the Land Rover, his appearance causing some guffaws from the troopers in the back. The Captain barked something at them and they lapsed into silence.

The vehicle gathered speed quickly, but instead of carrying on it drew to a halt under some scrub about a quarter of a mile from the caravan.

'What's happening, Captain?' Finlay asked. They had climbed down from the Land Rover and the Captain remained looking at the couched camels. He handed Finlay a cigarette and lit one himself but still said nothing.

Finlay looked at the Afghans on the other side of the

valley. 'Those are some bloody tough people, Captain ...' he began.

Suddenly there was a flash of something in the sky which Finlay recognised as a fast-approaching aircraft on an attacking run. He realised at once what was happening and, shouting a warning, he started to run back towards the caravan. But he was too late.

Three strike bombers, line astern, swept in over the caravan and napalmed it.

Finlay stopped, horror-struck and dumbfounded. He began to run again, only to be brought down by a Pakistani trooper. He held Finlay to the ground. 'Stay down, Englishman. Wait!'

A fourth aircraft swept in about a minute after the others, lower and slower, and the crump, crump of cannon fire echoed from the near valley wall. The aircraft banked sharply and came in from another angle, firing into the flames and smoke where the caravan had been. Then it climbed away, its passing creating a smoky, swirling vortex as it headed north, its work done.

Finlay broke free from the trooper and ran down to the burning camp. The heat singed the hairs from his arms as he raced around the perimeter of the devastation. The stink of napalm and burning flesh made him retch and when he saw a child's arm torn off between shoulder and elbow he was finally very sick.

The Captain arrived. 'Anyone left alive?' he asked coolly.

Finlay looked up. 'Not one! Not one, not even the child! Forty-three people! Why, for Christ's sake? Did they know I was with them?'

'Yes, we let them know you were there. Your own people-'
Before he had finished, Finlay attacked. He bludgeoned the Captain to the ground and, having no weapon, picked up a rock to kill him. Before he could do so, the Corporal of the

Company kicked Finlay squarely in the face, whereupon he collapsed sideways, unconscious.

How long the state of oblivion lasted, Finlay had no way of telling. He began to recover consciousness slowly and was dimly aware of being driven somewhere. In fact, he was lying in the rear of the Land Rover, hands securely tied behind his back. His already aching head was banging on the bare metal of the floor and the only thing in his line of vision was the bottom of an army boot, with its V patterns of synthetic rubber, and, stamped in the heel recess, he read: 'Made in Great Britain'.

Trying to collect his thoughts, he felt, by moving his face, the extent of the damage. His lips felt thick and puffy and his nose full of caked blood. He tried to sit up.

One of the soldiers said something to the Captain, who turned around from the front of the vehicle and looked down at Finlay.

'Ah, we are awake again, English. What a nasty piece of work you are! If you promise to behave, we can untie you and perhaps you will be more comfortable.'

In assent, Finlay struggled upright and offered his back to the nearest soldier. As he started to untie his hands, the Captain placed the muzzle of his Walther against Finlay's mouth.

'Just to make sure you understand me, stay quiet or I will kill you. I've no love for your sort or what you stand for. I've been ordered to get you back alive to Kabul, if possible. You make it possible or you'll be found in a roadside ditch!'

'OK, Paki, bring me back alive. But you'd better give me something to drink or I won't make it.'

Water from an army issue bottle was provided and Finlay moved to the back of the Land Rover and drank, splashing some over his face with his free hand. He looked at the

Captain and asked, 'What was all that about, back there? Why did those poor sods have to die?'

'As I tried to explain, your own people requested it so the Ivans would think they had killed you. By the way, we left a half-burned body of a European with the others – a drug addict seeking meditation with a needle. We are hoping Ivan is at least fooled for a while. We need some time to get you out of Afghanistan and into Pakistan, then you will be on your way back to England.'

Finlay understood. While not enjoying it, these people from Pakistan were concerned for his safety. 'What is your government getting in exchange for me, unlimited immigration to Bradford or Sea Cat?'

The Captain seemed unconcerned by Finlay's jibe. 'Chobham armour actually. London must want you very badly, English. Why? We do not know who you are or what you were doing in Russia, only that we, while working closely with Afghan friends, had to get you out and back to Kabul. From then on, you will be on your own as far as we are concerned.'

'Do the Russians come and go over the Afghan border as they like, then? What happens about the air strike on the caravan?'

'One day, English, the Russians will walk into Afghanistan and occupy - then Pakistan, then India, always on a pretext. The Afghans will fight, but you have seen them. They have no answer to today's warfare.'

Finlay thought about the Afghans in the caravan. 'Oh, yes,' he thought. 'They'll fight all right. Let's hope the CIA gives them something with which to fight.'

'Where are you taking me, Captain?' he asked. At least some of the venom had now gone from his manner. After all, they were on the same side, or nearly.

'Kabul. To the American Peace Corps. In the back door. That's where my orders end. For this we get better armoured tanks. We have to take you to the outskirts of the city, where they will pick you up.'

The drive seemed interminable, the other soldiers murmuring among themselves. The Captain dozed for some of the time, occasionally waking and asking the driver how much further it was. Then it was evening and the cold made Finlay shiver. The Captain woke and spoke quietly to the driver, then to the rest of his party. Finlay could not understand but, from the tone, he knew the journey's end was near.

'Lie down and cover yourself with the tarp, English. We are nearly at the rendezvous. We must be careful. There are a lot of pro-Ivan chaps in the Afghan regulars and they have their eyes everywhere. We do not want to lose you now!'

Finlay did as he was bid, making a mental note of the angle between him and the automatic rifles in the racks. If something went wrong at this stage he had no intention of being taken alive. One spell in Russian hands had taught him that he could never stand another.

The Land Rover whined on for another half hour or so and by the amount of gear changing and corner turning, Finlay knew that they had entered the city.

Eventually, the vehicle came to a halt and only quiet murmurings were heard. The tarpaulin was hauled back and the Captain whispered, 'Out you get, English, and best of luck.'

Finlay climbed stiffly out and a hand caught his arm, ushering him into the back of a large station wagon.

'Don't talk! Get in and lie down!' The order came from a woman whom Finlay could only just make out in the gloom. The Land Rover jerked away down a back alley without using its lights and suddenly he found himself riding quietly towards the city centre.

Shortly, they pulled up in some sort of compound, backed up to a loading ramp and stopped. 'Stay down, mister. I'll go and open up some doors.'

Finally the woman returned with a couple of orderlies, one of whom was pushing a wheelchair. The tailgate swung open and a middle-aged man looked in and said, 'Don't talk! Get in the wheelchair, but don't talk!'

Finlay got out and lowered himself into the chair. The orderlies covered his legs, shoulders and head with blankets. They smelt of camphor and shielded his face from the light. With the woman's hand upon his shoulder and one orderly pushing behind, they propelled Finlay along a series of well-lit corridors. Looking out from under the cowl of blankets, Finlay could only see the floor and his sandalled feet. He thought, 'I really must have a bath. Look at the state of my feet. They're black.'

At last they arrived in a small room. Finlay realised he was in a modern hospital and the smell of hygiene made him giddy. 'Sit here and wait! Don't speak!' the woman said as she left with the orderlies. A wave of exhaustion suddenly overwhelmed Finlay. It had been a long time since he had slept ... too long.

He began to relax, but as soon as he did so the door swung open quietly. He sprang to his feet and dived towards an alcove, rolling twice as he hit the floor. Coming upright again, he was confronted by the entrant, a tall Western man of about thirty, dressed in Peace Corps uniform. The man smiled and held out his hand.

'My name is Bob and you are Keith. Welcome back. You've had one hell of a journey, young man, and by the look of you you need at least six months in hospital. Christ, you're a mess but you did it, Keith. By Christ you did it! I've been waiting here two weeks as a Peace Corps doctor and all the while your people in London never gave up. They said you'd make it out. Let's get you cleaned up, fed and into a bed. Anything you want right now?'

Just at that moment Finlay knew that it was all over. It had been, as the American had said, one hell of a journey.

Finlay looked at the American, grinned and asked, 'Have you any decent cigarettes with you?'

'Surely,' replied the American. 'But aren't they bad for your health?'

Twenty-Four

FINLAY'S STAY IN the Peace Corps Hospital was noticeably short, for they were anxious to be rid of a charge who might prove to be an embarrassment to them. After a bath and food he slept the rest of the night, exhausted, and when Bob came to pick him up in the morning he felt strangely detached.

'We've a plane leaving for Karachi now, Keith. We'll get you on it and back to a degree of civilisation. You look a bit cleaner than when you arrived last night, but, by Christ, you do look ill,' the American said.

'I don't feel too good either,' replied Finlay. 'Maybe the shock of being here. Any idea what happens in Karachi?'

'Yes, Keith. There's one of your frigates waiting there for you, doing a bit of flag-showing to the old empire!' the American joked.

Finlay was laid on an ambulance stretcher. 'We're sending you out as an emergency case we can't deal with here, so keep your head down and your eyes closed. I'll be coming on the plane with you to see you through the formalities at Karachi,' Bob added, closing the back doors of the ambulance.

At the airport Finlay was loaded on to a small jet showing large red crosses on its side. Once inside, Finlay climbed off the stretcher and strapped himself on to the seat beside it.

'Do you know, Bob, I don't feel a bit excited over this. I just feel worn out and numb.'

The American smiled. 'Have you looked at yourself in a mirror, Keith? I should avoid it as long as possible. You look like somebody from Belsen!'

The little jet whistled down the runway and climbed steeply towards the mountains. The pressure pushed on their ears as the aeroplane levelled out and headed for Karachi.

The journey seemed to Finlay to last an eternity, the mountains below causing the aircraft to bump heavily on the air pockets. Finlay, who hated flying, did what he always tended to do when airborne: he slept.

When he awoke, the American asked, 'Feel any better?'

'Yes thanks, Bob, I think so.'

'Would it help to talk about it?'

'I don't think so. I doubt if I ever will, thanks all the same.' Finlay's mind went back over the past nine months. 'It was so bloody awful,' he said simply.

When they landed in Karachi, there were no problems with the customs or immigration. They walked through the airport buildings and out onto the street. Bob opened a waiting taxi door. 'In you get, Keith,' he said.

'This is all so easy,' thought Finlay. He remembered how the ordinary people of the Soviet Block lived with daily restrictions placed on their movements, even having to get permission to move from one area to another, controlled by the whims of politicians and bureaucrats. He himself had been whisked through an international airport, with no hindrance or questions. He thanked God he was born in the West, with all its freedoms.

Bob ordered the taxi driver to take them to the British frigate in the docks. Standing at the bottom of the gangplank,

Finlay looked up at the ship's pale grey sides. 'Jesus, am I glad to see you!' he said aloud.

They walked up the gangplank, an incongruous-looking pair, the American in the almost regulation pale suit, the Englishman in an ill-fitting Peace Corps uniform.

At the top, a young sub-lieutenant approached them. 'Good afternoon, gentlemen. Can I help you?'

Finlay looked at him and thought, 'I was like that once.' He answered, 'I'm Lieutenant Finlay and this is Bob ... I believe you are expecting us. Permission to come aboard, please.'

'We weren't expecting you until later tonight, sir,' he replied. 'I'll call the Captain down.'

He moved to a telephone attached to the bulkhead. 'Captain, sir, Lieutenant Finlay has arrived ... Yes, sir, with me now.' He turned, smiling at Finlay. 'The old man's on his way.'

A tall, thin officer came clattering down the companionway from the bridge and walked up to Finlay with his hand outstretched. 'Finlay, Finlay,' he beamed. 'You look bloody terrible. What the devil have you been up to?'

'What a way to welcome me, Tom. When did you get the other half?' Finlay said, pointing at the gold braid on his sleeve. 'Oh, this is Bob, American Peace Corps,' he added. Then, turning to Bob, 'Tom Wright, an old friend of mine.'

They shook hands, Wright looking at Bob with a doubtful smile. 'Peace Corps will do!' he joked.

'Right, down to the sickbay for you, Keith. Wardroom for you, Bob. I'll be just a while on the bridge.' He motioned to the sub-lieutenant. 'Take Keith down to the sick bay. I'll send the doc down and bring down a large pink one for you, Keith, later!'

Finlay lay on top of one of the sickbay bunks. The familiar noises of the ship around him, the quiet hum of the generators, the feet moving overhead, all allowed him to drift in and out of sleep, with a strange unease about him. 'I'll be all right when we get underway,' he thought.

Next time he woke he could feel the ship moving through the water and the gurgle of the sea as it passed over the ship's sides.

There was a light tap at the door and Admiral Winter entered. Finlay started. 'What are you doing here, Sir?' he asked, rising into a sitting position.

'I flew out to come home with you, Keith,' the old man answered. 'By God, it's good to see you, lad.' He came over and hugged Finlay.

'Have you told Niney I'm all right?' asked Finlay.

'No, I'm afraid I flunked that one, Keith. Had a Wren detailed for the job as soon as we left Karachi. Hope you don't mind my doing it that way. I didn't want to let her know until we had you safe!'

'Sir, that was bloody awful in Russia. Thanks for coming!'

Tears started in the old man's eyes. 'Least I could do, old chap. Wish it had been the Ark Royal.' He looked pointedly away from Finlay and walked to the cabin door. 'I'll let you rest now, Keith,' he said, his voice breaking.

Much later, the Admiral found Finlay leaning over the stern rails, watching the frigate's churning wake.

'How did Hampshire do this year, Sir?' Finlay asked, without looking at him.

'Not very well. About eighth, I think.'

'And the salmon, what were they like?'

'Not very good,' replied Winter. 'The sea trout were wonderful, though,' he added.

'Yes,' replied Finlay. 'I expect they were.'

LIFE HAD BECOME almost automatic for Niney. She'd grown thinner and her blue eyes looked mournful. She did her work silently and efficiently, but no longer sang or even smiled much. It was all done without thinking; one day just drifted into the next. The bills were paid, the cattle food ordered, the fertiliser bought and stored, but the banter and bargaining on the phone had gone from her.

When she was alone, she would creep away to Finlay's room, tidying things that didn't need it, washing his shirts, clean and ironed already from the last time she had done it. During these times she would speak to Finlay as though he were in the room, chiding him or laughing over some things they had spoken about in the past.

Only once had Niney's resolve almost left her. It was as she had been unpacking the family's guns, just back from their annual service, putting Finlay's gun in the rack. A sudden, smothering wave of grief had swept over her, making her shudder. She had grabbed the table for support, her breathing coming in short gasps.

'Hurry home, Kee,' she had moaned.

She rose on this particular morning at 6.30 as usual, bathed and dressed and gave her hair a perfunctory brush, barely looking at herself in the mirror. She made herself some tea and toast, and began preparing breakfast for Finlay's grandfather and Jack.

Janet Ward came bouncing in at around 7.30. Since Finlay had been pronounced dead, she had taken it upon herself to have tea and toast with Niney in the mornings. At first Niney had found her constant chatter irksome, but of late, if she didn't turn up, Niney missed her presence.

'Will you come and choose some clothes with me, please, Niney?' she asked. 'No hurry, but I could certainly do with some.'

'If you wish, Janet, next week perhaps ... anyway, young lady, you could choose your own. You don't need an old bat like me helping you,' she said easily.

'Yes I do,' she answered.

'I know why you do this, Janet, and I thank you for it ... Let's all see if we can get Niney out of herself - that's it, isn't it?' She smiled softly at the younger woman.

'Well, in part, Niney. But you know what I mean - you're too young to just go into a decline. He wouldn't want that, you know,' Janet said, wondering if she had gone a bit too far.

'I shall be all right when he gets home,' Niney said firmly. 'I know you all think I'm going around the bend ...'

'No, we don't, Niney, we just worry about you,' Janet replied.

'Well don't, my dear. You will see the old Niney the day he walks back through that door,' she said, suddenly remembering what Jenny had said once. 'I used to scoff at Jenny when she would go into mourning when he was away. I wouldn't now!'

Janet laughed shortly. 'He was such a bugger, wasn't he? Nobody could say no to him.'

Niney didn't answer; she began cooking the bacon.

'I'm sorry, Niney, I shouldn't have said that,' Janet said softly.

'Yes, Janet, he is a bugger, and it is difficult to deny him anything... Do you know, miss, I might take up riding again? It's years since I was on a horse. Yes, dear, I might well come and shop with you. I'll get some riding gear; my bum is still good enough for joddies.' Niney's face brightened. 'Come along, young lady, get your work done, then come in at coffee time and we'll choose a time.'

'Good!' Janet smiled. 'Shall we do London?'

'Yes, you baggage! Now bugger off and let me get on,' Niney said, ushering her out of the door.

Around eleven, Niney was preparing coffee for herself and Janet when she saw a strange car pull into the yard. A chill gripped her when she saw a Wren officer get out and walk towards the house. Niney went to the front door. 'Have you news for me, young lady? I'm Mrs Terry.'

'Yes, ma'am. Shall we go indoors?' the Wren suggested.

Janet, seeing the Wren and fearing the worst, ran across the yard and crashed into the house in time to see Niney sag and grasp the table top.

'Oh Jesus, Niney … have they found out what happened to him?' She pushed very unceremoniously past the Wren to get to Niney.

'We have Lieutenant Finlay on board *HMS Aurora*, which has just left Karachi. He is alive and fairly well and should be home within the week,' the Wren smiled.

Niney wanted to say something but her voice failed to work. Janet reached for the telephone. 'Carl, this is Janet. Get James and Jack quickly. Tell them Finlay is alive and is on his way home. Niney is in shock.' She put down the telephone and went to Niney. 'I'll get you a brandy, Niney. I know I bloody well need one!'

Janet poured some brandy down Niney's throat. She was shaking badly and coughed it up immediately.

'Make her some weak, sweet tea, miss,' the Wren said. 'I think she was expecting bad news.'

Niney came around in a couple of minutes. 'Give me the brandy bottle Jan,' she croaked. 'The hiding I give that little sod will be worse than anything I ever gave him in the past! He won't sit down for a week!' She swallowed more brandy.

'He is something of a hero, Mrs Terry,' the Wren said. 'And maybe a little too old for a good spanking.'

Janet, her green eyes already glassy and bright with the effects of the brandy, slurred 'And when you've finished giving him what for, Niney, I'll start on him, the bugger.' She sank slowly into the chair. 'Oh sod it, I'm pissed!' Janet hiccoughed loudly. 'Then I'm going to roger him into a coma.'

The Wren smiled at their joy.

'Are you quite sure it's him?' Niney asked, still disbelieving.

'Quite certain, ma'am. I cannot tell you much more than that. Only that he did walk on board unaided. Do you think I could have a cup of coffee?' the Wren asked shyly.

'Sorry, my dear,' Niney said, trying to stand. 'I don't know what I was thinking.' She tried to rise, but shock and the brandy gripped her tightly and kept her sitting.

'Do you know him?' Janet asked the Wren.

'No miss. My name is Miranda by the way. Shall I make the coffee?' she asked Janet, who was struggling to stay coherent.

'You all thought I'd gone batty, didn't you?' Niney slurred. She wagged a long finger at Janet. 'Thought Niney had slipped off her perch. Well, she hadn't, had she?'

'Is it true?' Finlay's grandfather asked, walking into the kitchen, hardly daring to believe the garbled message given to him by Carl. Niney, sitting at the kitchen table, nodded. 'Yes, James. He's coming home.'

'Sir,' Miranda interrupted. 'He left Karachi some six hours ago on a frigate, which he walked on board. He is alive and mobile - beyond that I know nothing more, except that he will be home within the week.'

'Well, thank God for that ...' Finlay's grandfather sat down next to Niney and reached for her hand. 'You were right, Niney. I should have known.'

'Sorry, Niney,' Janet mumbled.

'I must make a Dundee cake,' Niney said happily. She started to cry, great wracking sobs of relief. 'Excuse me,' she said and walked through into the hall.

When Jack arrived, he received the news gratefully before going through to Niney. Within half an hour the kitchen was full as the news spread and friends came to check that it was true and share their joy with the family.

SURGEON COMMANDER MARKLAND looked down at Finlay's wasted frame. 'The things you have wrong with you physically we can put right fairly quickly,' he said. 'Mentally, that might be another story. I'm not much at the shrink part, old man.'

'Please don't call me that,' interjected Finlay.

'Call you what?' The Commander looked surprised.

'Old man,' answered Finlay. 'I think for the rest of my life anyone calling me old man might well get a severe rap in the mouth. It reminds me of someone I want to forget.'

'This is just the problem, Finlay. You cannot hold it in yourself. It has to be spoken about. Not to do so will, I'm sure, precipitate a mental breakdown. For instance, tell me how you're feeling right now? What are you thinking about?'

'I feel I ought to be elated, sir. After all, I got away with it. But right now I'm utterly drained, thoroughly pissed off, in fact. I'm not even excited about seeing England, when I feel I should be dancing on the ceiling.'

'Classic symptoms, Finlay,' said Markland. 'It's a bit like post-natal depression – all that excitement for nine months, then suddenly it's all over. There is no doubt in my mind you'll overcome it. Get you physically back in shape and the rest will follow. Admiral Winter wants to go through your debriefing as soon as possible. Talk about it, Keith, then the bogeymen will go away.'

Finlay managed a smile. He knew the only way would be to write Winter a full report, as the Admiral didn't stop talking long enough for anyone to get a word in edgeways.

But this time Winter did listen. That afternoon, halfway across the Indian Ocean, Finlay began his debriefing. The old man made notes as Finlay spoke into a tape recorder, recounting every incident in such detail that the Admiral found it difficult to cope.

For four days during the afternoons Finlay poured out his story. The sweat ran down his ribs and dripped from his nose as he struggled to remember and to recount.

When he was finished he turned to Winter. 'What about the Pakistani Army Captain? Who was he?'

'He belonged to anyone who would pay him enough,' replied Winter. 'The Russians were paying him as well as us. We just paid him more.'

'And the bullet. Was it what we thought it was? I mean, did it work?' There was some urgency in Finlay's voice; he wanted to believe that the mission had been worthwhile and that Canavan had not died in vain.

'Yes, indeed. We had to modify the armour again. But the boffins have come up with a better way of stopping tanks being penetrated by small projectiles. They have some idea about blowing them up as they hit the tank. Kingstone was not a waste of time and lives though, Keith. It is only through strength that we can negotiate with the bastards.'

'I doubt Pat Canavan's parents see it like that, Sir,' Finlay replied. 'I wish he could have been here now.'

AURORA MADE BEST speed towards Simonstown, her wake stretching arrow-straight behind her, churning the water into white cauldrons, the long ocean swell making the ship rise and fall in a gentle rhythm. During the nights, Finlay watched the dark passing seas, the glow of phospherence fleeing along the ship's sides. He spent hours drinking in the freshness of the air, enjoying the spray when *Aurora's* slim beauty sliced through a larger wave, challenging her power.

A day out from Simonstown, after the evening meal, Winter joined him, standing with him under the foredeck gun-mounting. They were very easy together now, informal, just friends.

'Are you coming all the way with me, Sir?' Finlay asked.

'No, Keith, sorry. Protocol demands that I at least show myself at Simonstown, stay for two or three days. You'll be flown up to Bahrain, from there to Cyprus, then Lyneham,' Winter said. 'Just think, in a couple of days you'll be back in England.' Winter rested his hand on Finlay's shoulder. 'There will be hospital, of course, but not for too long. You'll be catching grayling by bonfire night; I've detailed Robert Keith to see you right.'

Winter walked across to the starboard rail, watching the wash creaming along the ship's sides. 'I'm going to turn in, Keith,' he announced. 'I'll see you off in the morning. Good night.'

'Good night, Sir,' Finlay answered. He watched Winter walk back towards the stern, and felt a huge wave of love for him.

BECAUSE OF THE ongoing need for secrecy, Finlay's homecoming was low key, but Niney had had her way over what the Admiralty wanted. Captain Keith, Commander-In-Chief, Portsmouth, had borne the main fury of her verbal assault. He had insisted that Finlay be transported to Haslar Hospital immediately upon his arrival at Lyneham, but she was having none of it. Finlay was coming home to Nursling. If there was any medical check to be done at once, it would be done there or not at all. He could go to Haslar later, she argued. The Keiths were long-time friends of Finlay's family. They spent holidays together, enjoyed the same lifestyle of field sports and agriculture, and shared the same bloodlines of pedigree pigs. Strong bonds indeed, and so Robert Keith understood Niney's passion, forgave her and acquiesced.

So it was that Finlay's grandfather, Uncle Jack and Niney found themselves in the VIP suite at Lyneham, waiting for the aeroplane bringing Finlay home. Niney had dressed herself in a way she knew would please her nephew: a dark blue dress in heavy silk, black stockings with seams and decorated with tiny black swallows, her hair in a French pleat and a row of pearls around her throat. She stood gazing into the distance, waiting for the first sight of the aircraft. A flash in the sky at some distance caught her eye, as the plane banked on its final turn.

'There!' she said, pointing. She gathered up her small handbag and moved towards the exit.

'Could you wait here please, ma'am,' an RAF officer asked.

Niney looked down at him coolly. 'I could, young man ... but I won't,' and she left the suite. Captain Keith, waiting with the others, motioned to the young officer to let her go. She appeared below them on the tarmac, where she stood watching the aircraft touch down. As it came to a stop in front of her and the side door swung open, she watched intently as various service people walked down the steps and went into the building. Then she saw him and for just a moment her composure almost fled. She moved to the bottom of the steps, and waited as a medic helped him down. Then he was there in front of her.

'Hello, my beautiful auntie,' Finlay said.

'Hello my love,' Niney said, taking him gently to herself.

'What are you doing here? I thought I wouldn't see you until I got to Haslar,' Finlay said, holding her closely.

'No, my darling boy, I'm taking you home,' she said, her voice beginning to shake.

'Well, Jack,' Finlay's grandfather said, watching from the VIP suite. 'She's got him back. She'll be all right now. I expect you've had a pretty thin time these past months.'

'Like sleeping with a log, James. Look at that smile now though,' Jack answered. 'The boy looks bloody ill. He won't be fishing for a while.'

'You want to put money on that, Jack?' Finlay's grandfather laughed.

Niney walked Finlay back into the VIP suite, holding his arm tightly. 'There now, you two,' she said to Finlay's grandfather and Jack. 'Say your hellos and then we must get him home. And Captain Keith, there will be some late lunch for you as and when, so can we go please?'

Finlay was deeply asleep long before they reached Devizes, comfortable in the rear seats of the Armstrong. He remained asleep until his grandfather had to brake sharply at Plaitford to avoid a cyclist.

'Not far now, Kee,' Niney said. 'Once Captain Keith has finished with you, you can go to bed and sleep properly. Are you OK? ... I mean, you don't hurt anywhere?'

'No, not now ... It's all a bit strange, that's all. I keep thinking I'll wake up in a bit and find I'm still in Russia. That's the end of it now. I'm home,' he said.

As they came down the hill into Romsey, he said, 'Go slowly over the bridge, Grandfather. I want to see the river.'

'Do you want me to go down to Sadlers Mill?' his grandfather asked.

'Do you think you could go straight to the hatch pool and leave me there for a bit? I need to collect myself up together before I go home.'

His grandfather slowed the car and waved Captain Keith to stop. 'Take him home, Jack, I'll drop Kee and Niney and come back to the house ... Don't rush him, Niney. I expect Kee needs to straighten his thoughts.'

Finlay and Niney left the car at the mill and walked down to the hatch pool and on to the wooden fishing stand. Finlay gazed at the river, drinking in the smell of the water. 'Why don't I feel elated, Auntie?' he asked.

'Too much to take in, darling ... and you must be so tired,' she answered. 'You're in a bit of a mess, I expect, not just your skinny little body either. It will come home to you soon.'

'It's been a bit of a queer time, this year. I don't think I ever want to go away again.' He sat down on the platform and dropped his hand into the water, feeling the current rushing through his fingers. 'So many people died ...'

Niney bent to him. 'Hush now, pet. Come on ... let's get you home. The deal was the doctor would see you while Robert Keith was here. I knew you had to come home before going to hospital.'

They walked back towards the house together, arm in arm. The few remaining swallows chittered at them from the telegraph wires and from somewhere in the willow beds a moorhen fussed and clucked about her life to something unseen. Over towards Rownhams, Finlay could hear a tractor working.

'I'm so sorry I caused you worry, Auntie,' he said quietly.

'To which I should say, don't be silly, but I'm going to say, never let it happen again. They told us you were dead, but I knew you were not. There was a memorial for you a few weeks ago, up by your great-grandfather's oak tree. But I couldn't do that, so I went to Hengistbury. Just to show them I knew best,' Niney answered. 'I've told everyone to stay away today. Except Janet, of course, who flatly refused. Let's go up through the kitchen garden and you can see how good it looks.'

'Don't say anything about my resigning yet,' Finlay said.

'You are going to, though. You promised!' Niney said quickly.

'Yes, I am - but I'm going to need some fairly extensive stays in hospital. If the MOD thinks for one moment I'm not staying in, I shall be shifted onto the NHS lists, and you know what that could mean.' There was resignation in Finlay's voice.

'They couldn't do that, surely. Your injuries were got doing your duty,' she protested.

'Auntie, they stopped my salary the day I was captured! They're soulless bastards. Admiral Winter is on the case, though, so just for the moment keep mum,' he said.

'That is wholly iniquitous, darling,' she said sharply, stopping in her tracks.

'Quite frankly I'm amazed they didn't send somebody to pick up my car. It must have slipped through the system somehow; it doesn't belong to me, does it?' This time Finlay almost managed a wry smile. 'From the MOD's point of view, I'm just a number on a computer printout. To stop my pay would probably have meant no more effort than pressing a computer key. They don't pay dead people: that would be the attitude. Getting the back pay will be more difficult - I shall probably have to prove that I'm alive!'

They carried on walking again, stopping sometimes just so that Niney could look at him.

'I knew you weren't dead, my love,' she said quietly. 'I could feel you were in trouble though. Still, you're back home now, thank God. Make sure you get your money's worth out of them. I know you don't need it... but it's the principle that counts.'

'FEEL BETTER FOR that?' Finlay's grandfather asked as Niney and Finlay walked into the kitchen.

'Yes thanks,' Finlay answered. 'Hello Janet. How are you?'

Janet Ward looked at him, her eyes brimming with tears. 'Hello Finlay ... you look like shit!'

'Thanks!' he smiled. 'You could have said I look very trim and spry.' He bent to where she was sitting and kissed her cheek.

Captain Keith coughed to get attention. 'I have your

medical report here, Finlay, from the surgeon on *Aurora*, which I have to give to your doctor when he gets here. Your stay at home can only be short, very short. You've been ordered to Haslar in two days. You have to be there, Finlay. No arguments.'

'Understood, sir,' Finlay answered. 'But my aunt was right. This is the best tonic ... just being here for the moment.'

'We needed him here as well, Captain,' Jack added. 'Just to know he was all right in our estimation.'

'Of course,' the Captain said.

'Can you talk about it, Finlay?' Janet asked. 'Where the hell have you been, and how did you get in this state?'

'No ... I can't, Jan ... I don't want to ... not ever ...' Finlay began.

'Help me get the table laid, Janet,' Niney ordered. 'No questions, let's eat! And when the doctor's been, Kee's having a bath and going to bed, and you can get on with your work.'

'I only asked!' Janet said.

'Well, don't! Just be glad we've got him back,' Niney said very sharply.

Finlay winked at her and made her smile. 'Sorry, Niney,' Janet said quietly.

Lunch was Irish stew, which had been baking in the bottom oven from early that day. Niney watched how and what Finlay ate, and was satisfied with what she saw.

'Well, Robert Keith. Will they feed him properly in hospital?' Niney asked. 'If not I'll fetch him home again. Be aware of that!'

'Yes, Mrs Terry, I'm sure you would.' The Captain smiled, already aware of who was in charge of the household.

Later, when Doctor McQuitty arrived, Finlay's grandfather said, 'Come on, Jack. We'll leave this part to Niney. I'll see you this evening, Kee.'

Janet got up from the table and deliberately brushed the back of Finlay's head with her breast in passing. Jack saw and smiled quietly. 'See you later, nipper ... Glad to have you home. Get some rest, else you ain't never going to cope.'

Later again, the doctor and Captain Keith gone, Niney said, 'I'll run your bath, darling, then get off to bed ... you look shattered.'

She stayed and watched him bathe, almost flinching when she saw his scars and injuries, and later sat on his bed until sleep came to him.

Three days later she took him to Gosport and left him at the hospital, and Finlay began the long haul back.

Twenty-Five

HOSPITALS, BY THEIR very nature, are places of routine. Finlay slotted into this regimen easily, knowing that the sooner all the tests were completed, the sooner he would be released and back home. Over the first week of his stay, seemingly every system of his body was checked. He was young and mended easily; only the weeping hole in his left side refused to heal. The medics seemed to think the most likely long-term damage, though, would be psychological, a sort of shell shock, and to this end he was told he would be transferred to G Block the following week for another battery of tests. G Block was where brain- and mind-damaged patients were housed. This was not really what Finlay wanted to hear, and when he found out he was not going to be allowed the weekend at home, his outlook became more peevish.

The only break in a weekend of total boredom was when Niney and Janet Ward arrived. Niney, not convinced that he was being properly cared for, brought some steak pies, home-made bread, a great slab of butter fresh from the churn and, most important of all, a large, a very large, jar of chutney. Janet brought her effervescence and had the doctors in something of a spin. Her jodhpurs, which she wore everywhere, were so tight that they seemed to show even the stitching on her brief knickers under them. The young medics homed in on Finlay's room like bees around an open honey pot, as they all set about eating one of the steak pies. An impromptu indoor picnic soon developed, which carried on noisily until the arrival of a very senior nurse, who had the doctors scuttling away like startled rabbits. There was a brief but very fierce altercation between Niney and this senior nurse about diet. Poached eggs and spinach were not on Niney's list of nourishing foods; meat, meat pies, meat puddings and unlimited milk stout was the way to get a man back to rights, the nurse was informed, and she had best get to it or blood would flow. The senior nurse soon fled.

'I think you must come home, darling,' Niney said to Finlay. 'They don't know how to feed you properly. I certainly don't think staying here is doing you any good at all.'

Finlay could only agree, but explained to Niney that he still had to do as ordered, hospital or not. Unconvinced, Niney gathered up her handbag and announced she was 'going to find somebody and make a fuss'.

'Oh dear,' Janet sighed as Niney left them. 'Somebody's for it, Finlay. She can be bloody impossible ... When you were missing she got to be a proper bloody madam.'

'Why don't you slide in here, Jan? Be nice to have you alongside again,' Finlay said.

'That's better – more what I wanted to hear. Can't be too much wrong with you if your thoughts are on what's in my jods ... You just rest easy though. One of your nurses might wander in,' she replied.

They could in fact hear approaching footsteps and voices, one of them Niney's, obviously telling somebody something she thought they should know.

As Niney swept into the room, the severe-looking four ringer trailing in her wake, she said, 'They are more concerned with the insurance implications than your health, Kee darling. I think you should give them their marching orders!'

The Surgeon Captain looked somewhat harassed. 'I do wish I could get your aunt to understand, Finlay, that the Navy has a way of doing things.' He turned to Niney. 'I promise you, madam, he is having the best that medical science can provide.'

Finlay cringed; he knew what was coming next.

'Huh!' Niney answered, as dismissive a statement as was ever uttered.

'One more week, then you can take him home again. How does that sound?' the Captain suggested.

'One week and that's your lot, sailor blue, else you will be dealing with the CDS himself!' Niney said softly to him; softly showed she meant it.

Niney and Janet stayed for a couple of hours, certainly longer than visiting hours strictly allowed, but news of this modern Valkerie had flown around the hospital, and as a consequence they were left alone.

On Monday Finlay was transferred to G Block. It was not really a place to engender anything but sadness and pity. Some of the patients Finlay found in the dayroom were so far destroyed mentally it was obvious they were never coming back to the world of normality. There were men there, ordinary men, who had been taken from their jobs in civilian life, sent to the war at sea, from banks, factories and offices, to fight the Germans, some having never seen the sea before. They had spent months on convoy duty, witnessed things nobody should see: ships being sunk, men burnt to death, blown to pieces; they had heard them screaming their last screams of anguish, struggling and drowning in the cold salt water. For men like these, the war would go on for ever.

The unit was run by a very severe Surgeon Captain. Doctor

L. Williams was the civilian in charge. Finlay had met him before: once before joining up, at his primary medical assessment for the Admiralty Interview Board; the second time, after being involved in some very brutal fighting in the Middle East. Williams had concluded his written assessment on their first meeting with the words: 'This is a very strange, intelligent child.' On the second, he had written: 'I do not understand this person.' This pleased and amused Finlay; he thought Doctor Williams to be something of a 'quack'. For all his qualifications and training, he lacked understanding in the world in which he worked, having had no experience of the things his patients had endured.

At their first meeting of the week, Finlay was not the least combative, as had been his way with Williams in the past. He was sweetness and light, answering the psychiatrist's questions thoughtfully, helpfully, even truthfully sometimes. Whether or not Williams saw through this charade, Finlay could only guess; what he wanted was a clean bill of health on his mental state, though he himself knew it to be fragile.

During one of their sessions, Williams asked him directly, 'What do you feel about your Russian case officer now, sitting here with me, home in England?'

'He did his job, I did mine. I don't think I apply any more thought to it than that now,' Finlay answered.

'What would you say to him if you met him?' Williams asked, scribbling quickly on a pad.

Finlay thought for just a moment. 'I won, you lost! By about an innings.'

'So it was like a game of cricket? Why not tennis?' Williams asked. 'After all, it was a one-on-one contest.'

'I don't play tennis, therefore it didn't occur to me,' Finlay answered, wondering about this line of questioning.

'You wouldn't want to kill him, then?'

'No. There was enough killing, one way and another.'

In the following session, Williams picked up where he had left off. 'What did you feel when Canavan was killed?'

'That's a bloody stupid question,' Finlay said, not at all sharply.

'You might think so, perhaps. It is one I would like an answer to, nonetheless.'

'I was saddened, angry.' Finlay paused and thought back. 'I felt crushed.'

'Describe that feeling for me, please,' Williams carried on. 'Do you feel responsible for his death?'

'No. It was a consequence of what we were doing. I have thought about it, of course. I started the shooting on the border because we had to get the bullet to the West. That was the important thing. Both Canavan and myself were largely expendable compared with that.'

'That's what you thought?' Williams asked.

'That is what I did indeed think,' Finlay answered quietly.

IT WAS THURSDAY evening; Finlay lay dozing on his bed waiting for dinner, only half awake, when there came a tentative knock and the door opened gently. 'Arnold, sir,' a handsome young man announced. 'Flags to Captain Keith. Could you come to the dayroom, please?'

Finlay rose and washed his face to wakefulness in the hand basin. 'I'll be along, Flags; just let me come to a little.'

Captain Keith was effusive in his greetings, warmly shaking Finlay's hand. 'Your Admiral has come to your rescue and I'm engaged in effecting your release.' Quieter, he said, 'Got to get you out of here, Finlay. With your record, in ten years time someone may look and see a sojourn in G Block and hold up promotion ... Doctor Williams is objecting, but it has been arranged that you get off home and your own family doctor will be paid to oversee your convalescence.'

'Thank God for that!' Finlay said with feeling. 'Another week in here and I should need certifying. Shall I make arrangements for somebody to come from home and pick me up? I mean, is my discharge definite, sir?'

'No, Finlay. I'm on my way to Portland; I can drop you at home – give me the chance to see your beautiful auntie and maybe have an invite to catch some grayling.'

'You can do that at anytime, sir,' Finlay said. 'Get me out of here and home tonight and I'm certain Niney will give you several days' salmon fishing next season!'

'I'll hold you to that, Finlay. Go and get packed up and ready to leave. Sir John was adamant you were out of here today.'

Finlay needed no second bidding; he didn't feel unwell, not hospital unwell anyway, and wanted to be home. In the event it was a good two hours before they were ready to leave. 'Finlay,' the Captain said. 'At the risk of seeming very rude, can I drop you near your home? I have to be in Weymouth by eleven and at this rate of progress I'm going to be hard-pressed to make it.'

'Drop me by the lodge, sir. I can hoof it from there. I shall, of course, not say a word to my aunt about not wishing to avail yourself of her company and hospitality,' Finlay answered, smiling.

'Bastard!' Keith said evenly.

Around nine o'clock, Finlay was dropped at the entrance to Lee. He watched the tail lights of Captain Keith's Humber pulling away from him, before turning to walk the couple of miles to his home. It was dark but clear, and the air smelt heavily of autumn and the coming winter, the earthy smell of fresh-drilled fields mingled with the dank smell of wet, rotting leaves.

Finlay picked up his holdall; it felt heavy in his still weakened state. Rather than overtax himself with it, he pushed it into the lane-side hedge, thinking to drive back in the morning to pick it up. Free of any encumbrance, he was able to wander slowly along the lane, listening to the night, scenting the air of his home.

The ash trees lining part of the lane had long since dropped their foliage, their summer glory gone, and the tracery of their topmost branches showed black against the stars. The oaks still clung tenaciously to their drying, dead leaves, as though in denial that summer had passed, but the first frosts and winter winds would soon strip them clean. Finlay reflected that less than one month ago he had been walking through a dark and foreign land, where there were no proper trees as he saw it, where his life had been bargained for with money. That was behind him now and he was home.

When he reached the small humpback bridge on the top lane he stopped and looked toward the house, surprised but unworried that it seemed to be in darkness. Only the softer glow of the stable-yard lights seemed to be on. Knowing the routine, he thought Janet may yet be doing evening stables, so he headed through the kitchen garden and into the yard the back way, determined at least to make free with her pert breasts. As he reached the concrete apron which surrounded the stables, he heard a female voice talking small talk to a horse. A girl was backing out of one of the loose boxes and, turning, caught sight of him. She gave a yelp of shock and visibly began to buckle at the knees, whimpering, 'Please don't hurt me.'

Finlay realised his sudden appearance from the dark garden had frightened her. He was dressed in his normal black trousers and blue pullover, so she would not have seen him coming. She clung to the stable door, her eyes staring and terrified.

'Hey, young lady, nobody is going to hurt you ... I live here,' Finlay said softly, moving past her into the tack room. He switched on the large overhead yard lights. Suddenly it was as bright as day, the white light flooding the yard up to the house.

'Look at me, girl,' he said softly. 'I'm Niney's nephew. Where is Janet?' He was giving her familiar names to calm her; she was shuddering as though frozen through.

Taking her arm gently, he led her to the tack room and sat her down.

'What's your name?' he asked her quietly. 'I'm not going to hurt you.'

He squatted down on his haunches, so that she looked down at him. She was very pretty, cascades of brown hair, green grey eyes and long legs. 'I'm sorry. My name's Lesley. I can see now you are the man in the photographs. Well, like him, a little.'

'Good. Now we've established who I am, you sit there. I'll finish the horses, then take you home. Where are you living?' Finlay said, getting up.

'At the vicarage,' she answered, a little more composed now. She was avoiding looking at him though.

As Finlay walked through into the stables, he was overtaken by a feeling of complete calmness. The sweet smell of that year's meadow hay, the biscuity scent of thrashed wheat straw, mingled with the faint aroma of molasses; this had always been part of his life, his home. There was very little left to do. He walked along the front of the boxes, looking in at the occupants, speaking to those he knew.

He stopped by one at the far end and said, 'Hello Bee. Do you remember me?' He entered the box and spoke again. 'Hello Bee, it's me. Come and say hello.'

The mare eyed him curiously, her ears twitching towards him. He squatted again for the second time that evening, making himself smaller, less threatening. The mare took a tentative step forward, stretching her neck down to sniff Finlay's hair.

'Hello baby,' Finlay murmured. She took his breath gently with her wide quivering nostrils, and blew her caramel-smelling breath back on him, remembering. He stood up. The mare took his breath again, then began to push her face into his. Finlay kissed the soft, silky side of her mouth. 'My little angel, my dove. I've missed you.' He buried his face into her sleek neck, fondling her ears. 'My darling girl,' he said, his throat suddenly choking, tears falling down his face.

'I've never seen that stroppy bitch behaving like that,' he heard Lesley say from behind him.

Trying hard to hide the emotion he felt, Finlay forced himself to laugh softly. 'We're lovers, aren't we, Bee?' The words came out choked. He wiped his eyes on the cuff of his pullover, his back still turned to Lesley. The mare rubbed her face on his chest and began nibbling his pullover.

'You're a man's horse, aren't you, darling girl?' Finlay said, stroking the mare.

'Obviously!' Lesley commented.

'I'll come and see you in the morning, Bee,' Finlay said, and he turned to the stable girl. 'I had better get you home, Miss Lesley. First though, I need a cup of tea.'

They walked up to the house, Lesley following Finlay a few paces behind, silent. Finlay went through the complicated ritual of unlocking the front door, then dived through and shut off the alarm.

'Come on in,' he ordered the stable girl, and switched on the lights in the kitchen and the hall. 'Come in,' he ordered again. 'Do buck up, girl!'

She started to laugh quietly, still shy of him. 'Your auntie orders everyone around too.'

'It's good to see you can smile,' he said, laughing himself. 'Now, let's have some tea.' He shifted the kettle to the hot side of the Aga and, taking some ham from the refrigerator, started to make some hefty sandwiches.

'Would you like one?' he asked, not looking up from his task.

'Please,' she answered timidly, standing awkwardly by the door.

'Mustard?' Finlay asked, the butter knife hovering above the ham, laden with the fiery condiment.

'A little, please,' she said, beginning to relax and edging towards him. Finlay spread a thin smear on the ham, sliced the sandwich across and scooped it on to a plate. 'There you are – try that,' he said.

Lesley started to giggle. 'You're just like Janet said … just like your auntie. You even look like her.'

Finlay picked up the framed photograph of Niney and himself that lived on top of the refrigerator. The photograph showed them sitting together at some outside function, Niney obviously laughing at something he had said. 'Hello, beautiful Auntie Niney,' he murmured, gazing at the picture. He kissed the image of her gently.

'Niney does that as well … on your side of the picture,' Lesley said.

'Do you know where she's gone?' Finlay asked.

'Niney and Janet went off together earlier in the day to buy some clothes. Then they were going to a show. Bournemouth, I think they said,' Lesley answered. She paused, wanting to say something else. 'I'm so sorry about earlier, but I really was very frightened. You've changed a lot since that photograph. Have you been very ill?'

Finlay laughed easily. 'Something like that,' he replied. He got up and went to the mirror. 'Yes, I see what you mean. I do look pretty grim – probably enough to frighten dogs and children.' He was making light of the subject deliberately. 'Does Janet ride Bee much? I've tried to buy her from Jan a dozen times, but she would never let her go to me.'

'She does seem special to you,' Lesley answered. 'I'm sure if you offered enough money, she would sell her.'

Having veered the conversation safely back on to horses, they stayed chatting together and eating the food Finlay had prepared. Lesley was from Horsham and studying for some obscure horsey exam. She was twenty-three and had the same fanatical dedication to the equine race as the other young women who gathered around Janet. Finlay delivered her back to the vicarage around 11.30. She briefly touched his hand on leaving the pick-up and said a quiet and grateful, 'Thank you.'

Back at the house, Finlay cleared the crockery into the sink and left a note saying hello and that he had gone to bed. He climbed the stairs, savouring the smell and warmth of the house, and went into his bedroom. It never occurred to him to wonder if his bed would be made up, it just would be. There was a framework under the blankets and a cable leading out. The cable powered a piano heater which kept his bed aired and warm, always.

'Thank you, my love,' he said, thinking of his aunt as he removed the small frame and heater. Naked, he climbed into his bed and was asleep almost immediately.

Niney crept into his room about an hour later and gently touched his face and rearranged the bedclothes, but he didn't stir.

In the morning he awoke, as he had always done at home, to the sound of the birds. The sparrows in the chimney sent debris into the hearth below; the blackbirds, almost silent at this time of the year, were replaced by robins, singing their songs of autumn. He could hear the moorhens on the feeder that ran through the top of the garden, and the bellowing of one of the dairy cows away in the distance. 'Home,' he thought. A small warm tear escaped from the corner of his eye. He remembered his journey here, walking what had seemed all the way across Asia, and his joy at seeing the frigate that had been sent to collect him and bring him away from that living nightmare. He slept again until voices and the sound of horses woke him. It was properly light now and the world around him was awake.

He rose and went to the half-open window, where a chilly draught made it necessary for him to dive across the corridor and into the loo opposite his bedroom. Below, Niney, who had had her ear cocked for any movement upstairs, wiped her hands on a kitchen cloth and went to find him.

'Hello you,' she said, sitting on the side of his bed. 'How did you work this then?' She kissed him gently and tut-tutted at his pronounced ribs.

'Captain Keith rescued me,' Finlay laughed. 'He was concerned how a lengthy stay in the psycho ward would look on my service record. He brought me home, as he was on his way to Portland.' He suddenly remembered. 'I've left my luggage bag in the hedge by the lodge. I'll drive up later and pick it up – don't let me forget.'

'What! He couldn't bring you back to the house?' Niney asked, scandalised by the thought.

'He was in a rush. He had to be in Portland to catch the tide,' Finlay answered. 'I scared the hell out of one of the stable girls, just appearing out of the dark behind her,' he smiled. 'She was properly shaken up. I calmed her down, then fed her and got her back to the vicarage.' He could tell by the look on Niney's face that she was curious. 'Her name was Lesley. I was quite taken with her, rather ducky.'

'Well!' Niney snorted. 'You can forget about her for the moment. That sort is not for you, young man!'

'Oh, I don't know ...' he began, teasing.

'Well, she's not! Lesley likes other girls! I'll say no more than that! Now let me look at your wounds,' Niney ordered, removing the bedclothes in one movement.

'Honestly, Auntie ... I'm not a child, you know!' Finlay half objected, laughing.

'Shut up, fool! You're no different now than when I scrubbed you in a water trough.' She examined the deep burn scar that still refused to heal, then the exit wound of a bullet on his left leg. 'It's only because your systems are so low, darling, that they aren't healing properly,' she said sadly. She brushed her hand over his manhood. 'Does that still work?' she asked lightly.

Finlay shouted his laughter. 'Jesus, Auntie Niney! I've only been home five minutes!' Used as he was to his aunt's somewhat robust approach to matters sexual, she had never gone quite so far before.

Niney drew the covers back over him. 'Your physical health I can deal with; what goes on in your head is different, and a man's potency is as good a guide as any to his mental well being ... so keep me informed, please,' she ordered softly. 'What happened to you should not happen to anyone ... and I am serious when I say I want to know that you are still able.'

Finlay looked up into his aunt's blue eyes. This wonderfully complete woman, who always knew his deepest thoughts, had realised his worries. 'Well, I think I'm all right. There was a girl in Russia ...' he said, then looked away again. 'She was killed – I don't want to talk about it. That was before the hookworm and malaria. Still, I was all right then, and a lot less well ... Anyway, don't go on about it, please.' He laughed lightly. 'I'm not a bloody stud horse, you know!'

Niney giggled in turn. 'Well, there are more than a few young ladies who would give you a good argument about that! So let me know when you do know.'

'I will,' he said quietly.

'Thank you, my love,' she said, kissing his forehead. 'Get a dressing gown on and come and have some breakfast ... How many eggs do you want?'

'Three please,' Finlay said, getting up.

For the dozen years that Finlay had lived at Lee, he had come to love the kitchen as the best and most favourite room in the house. Sometime back in the 1920s, it had been 'modernised', and had hardly changed since then. The walls were painted ivory, with panels and cupboard doors picked out in pale blue. The cupboards themselves were made from inch boarding, heavy and substantial, and ran along virtually the entire wall length. Under the windows, which looked out on to the yards, were long white sinks and huge draining boards. Sitting like a huge throne on the left was the Aga, white and regal, exuding warmth and almost love. In the right wall was the door to the dairy, a place of coolness, redolent with smells of decades of butter and cheese making; the sweet sourness had seemingly seeped into the very fabric of the walls. Old-fashioned earthenware dishes, at least a yard across, leant in heavy racks, pink and white and now redundant, only one still in use to raise enough cream for the family. In the summer, when the Aga warmed the kitchen a little too much, then the windows and the dairy door would be opened and propped back, and the smell of sweet new milk would then pervade the lower storey of the house. It was a smell that Finlay loved and, walking into the kitchen that morning, the smell of the fresh milk, butter and the earthy smell from outside blowing through the open window almost made him giddy with the love of it.

'There, my love,' Niney said, putting a huge plate of bacon, eggs and mushrooms down in front of him. 'I shall have you back to rights in short order ... The stable girls will be in for breakfast soon. That job sort of crept up on me. One minute I was feeding just Janet, now there's four or five of them.'

'Every day?' Finlay asked surprised.

'Most days certainly. They were going back to the vicarage after morning stables to get their own breakfast, but they spent far too much time doing it. By the time they got back here, two hours was lost from the day. Janet asked if I would feed them breakfast, then get them back to work again. I don't mind. It can be quite fun. They're certainly a lively bunch and Janet pays up at the end of the week for their food.' Niney busied herself by the Aga, putting the finishing touches to a row of plates.

'How on earth does Janet afford their wages?' Finlay gasped, knowing the costs of such things.

'*They* pay *her*,' Niney laughed. 'Or their parents do. They're students, studying for some British Horse Society examination!'

Finlay started to laugh loudly. 'Trust Jan to have it that way around! They pay her: I like that.'

'She's become quite famous in the horsey world, always being quoted in the *Horse and Hound*, that sort of thing.' Niney looked out of the window, across to the stable yard. 'We'd better change the subject, Kee. They're on their way in. Just be a little careful with Charlotte. She's very shy and the others tend to pick on her a bit.'

'Yes, of course,' Finlay answered. 'I can't manage all of this, Auntie. Eyes bigger than my belly.'

Niney, not put out at all, scooped up his half-eaten breakfast and redistributed the untouched portions on the other plates.

They heard the front door open with a crash. The sound of female voices, along with the smell of horses, drifted into the kitchen. There was a brief interlude of screams and giggles coming from the downstairs loo as the girls got cleaned up, ready to eat, then they trooped into the kitchen. Lesley smiled at him shyly; the others viewed him with curiosity, before seating themselves one side of the table. Lesley sat beside him, again with the same shy smile.

'This is my nephew Keith,' Niney said. 'You had better introduce yourselves.'

'I'm Ronnie, she's Charlie and this is George,' Ronnie announced. 'You've already met Lesley, so we've been told.'

Lesley blushed pink and the girls began to giggle, giving each other significant looks.

Finlay ran a quick eye over them. They were all dressed in the unofficial uniform of stable girls – figure-hugging jodhpurs, tight woollen pullovers, with check shirts showing at the throat – all but Charlotte, that is; he had noticed her torn-at-the-knee cord jeans when she walked in. Her pullover was of some indeterminate grey colour, studded with hay seeds, one elbow badly darned with orange baler twine. Her hair, red gold and in the almost regulation long single plait, reached down to her waist. She glanced at him and, embarrassed by his look, turned quickly away.

'Good morning, ladies,' Finlay said. 'What's the weather doing today?'

'Mild,' Lesley replied beside him. She smiled at him again, more boldly this time. The others started digging into their breakfasts.

'Well, I know Lesley comes from Horsham, but where do the rest of you hail from – Charlotte?' he asked quietly, turning to the redhead.

'Oh, don't bother with her, Keith!' Georgina interrupted. 'She barely speaks. She's so quiet we call her "mouse".' Georgina gave Charlotte a scathing look.

Finlay turned his attention to Georgina: overweight, coarse featured, the type of girl who perhaps shouldn't be wearing such tight clothes. He smiled. 'Well, Georgina. You look like a young lady who enjoys her food – what's your nickname?'

'Ow!' Lesley whispered. 'That hurt.'

Georgina turned pale and stopped chewing, as though she had suddenly lost her appetite. Charlotte gazed up at Finlay from under her lashes and flashed him a mischievous smile, her eyes sparkling.

'Charlotte has a champion!' Ronnie laughed.

'And who might that be?' Janet asked, walking in.

'Mr Finlay,' Ronnie squealed with delight. '*Charlie is my darling, my darling ...*' she began to sing.

'Oh, do stop it, Ronnie,' Charlotte murmured. 'You're just being silly!'

'He squashed George flat in one sentence,' Ronnie told Janet. 'She hasn't said a word since, shot her right up the bum!'

Janet picked up her breakfast from the top of the Aga and walked back to where Lesley was sitting. 'You're in my place,' she announced.

'Since when?' Lesley answered sharply.

'Since now!' Janet said, equally sharply, giving her a hefty shove out of the way.

'Cow!' Lesley said, getting up, moving down the table.

'I think I shall go and get on with something,' Niney said brightly, 'before you little cats start fighting.' Niney ran her hand over Finlay's shoulders as she left the room. 'Have fun, darling,' she chuckled.

Janet looked at Finlay, her green eyes holding him fast.

'Now then, Finlay. Would you like to wish me good morning with a great big wet sloppy kiss?'

Finlay obliged. She tasted wonderful and any concerns he had about his potency momentarily dissolved.

'How come, Finlay ... how come, you bugger ... this bloody creature here,' Janet said between kisses, giving Lesley a fairly sharp poke with her finger, 'this bloody creature ...' A pause for breath. 'How come Lesley thinks you are wonderful?' She kissed him again, then imitating Lesley's voice said, '*He's got lovely manners and eyes.*'

'Would you believe the one about the damsel in distress, Janet?' Finlay said, making certain he was holding her firmly.

'Not really! Lesley is hardly a damsel, is she? And she claims not to like men.' Janet giggled, still holding his face close to hers. 'It's lovely to have you back home, you sod of a bloke, and you, Lesley Jarrett, can keep off the grass!'

'Sorry, I'm sure!' Lesley answered, now thoroughly vexed. 'I'm not interested ... you can be sure of that!'

'Liar, liar, pants on fire!' Ronnie squealed, determined to embarrass Lesley more. 'When you got back last night, you were in a proper state!'

'I was not!' Lesley snapped.

'*He was wonderful! You should have seen him with Bee. It was so emotional! So lovely!*' Ronnie yelled through her giggles. 'I've never known you to be so soppy.'

'It wasn't like that!' Lesley objected.

Ronnie stood for effect, and placing both hands on her heart she almost wailed, '*He was so wonderful!*'

Finlay started to laugh quietly, which got them all going. Even Lesley had to surrender to the giggles. When she had recovered her composure, she wiped the tears of laughter away with her cuff. 'I was very badly frightened, Finlay. You looked like somebody who had died and didn't know it!'

'What happened to you?' Charlotte asked quietly.

'I was in the wrong place at the wrong time, Charlotte,' he answered, looking at her lovely face, the splash of freckles across the bridge of her nose capturing his interest. He realised he was embarrassing her with his stare again. 'I got into a bit of a scrap, then it was bad food, bad water and a lot of hard travelling to get home again.'

'Oh,' she answered quietly.

'Darling, I forgot to say,' Niney said, suddenly arriving back in the kitchen. 'The doctor is coming around midday. Now, you girls, if you've finished breakfast, out and do your work. Keith is meant to be having bed rest and convalescence, not taxing his brain on who has the prettiest bum.'

Twenty-Six

ADMIRAL WINTER ARRIVED back in England two weeks later than Finlay. After flying up to Cyprus, and then on to Gibraltar, he had accepted an invitation from Captain D of the destroyer flotilla there to complete his journey by sea. The flotilla was coming off deployment and going back to their home port of Portland. *HMS Duchess* was booked on a sudden courtesy call to London. The MOD accountants would doubtless have something to say about such an expensive detour, but since Admiral Winter had been instrumental in saving the Army's blushes over Chobham armour, he was sure he would weather their unimaginative complaints. In fact, Winter was feeling wholly ebullient. The voyage had been very rough around Biscay, but he found that he still had his sea legs and had enjoyed the trip immensely. As Captain D piped the Admiral away to the banks of the Thames, the boat's crew from *Duchess*, under the command of a midshipman, gave the watching onlookers on the embankment a superb demonstration of boathandling. It was all very impressive and Nelsonian. A ripple of spontaneous applause gave the Admiral the excuse to stop briefly, salute them, before folding himself into the waiting car. *Duchess*, having executed the Navy's equivalent of a three-point turn in the river, picked up her boat and crew, then majestically moved off downriver.

Winter was driven back to Horse Guards. As far as he was concerned Operation Kingstone was over: the tank armour had been upgraded to cope with the projectile which Finlay and Canavan had secured, and the long arm of the intelligence services had rescued Finlay from under the Russians' noses. It was all very satisfactory.

Back in his office, Winter felt a little out of touch, having been away for the better part of a month. He drank a large sweet coffee that Miss Grant had brought in, and that he himself had dosed liberally with his best Napoleon brandy. Skimming through the correspondence that was piled upon his desk, he discovered there had been no breakthroughs on the search for the leak that had blown Kingstone from the start. He had requested MI5 help in this matter some months ago, but they had found nothing. Winter sat back in his chair with a sigh. That being the case, the leak must still be there, still in place, feeding information to their enemies. The offices had been swept for bugs, the telephones checked right back to the exchanges at regular but random intervals: nothing had come to light. Convinced it was a wholly human agency passing on information, Winter had decided on his journey home from the Far East on a more drastic course of action, and the wheels were already in motion. It had come to him as he'd been musing on something Finlay had said before he'd left for Berlin: 'When we started out, this was Navy. Now we have a general and the FO involved, and I, for one, do not like it ...'

A light tap on his door broke his chain of thought. 'Come in,' he called.

It was Rupert Smith. Winter left his desk and met Smith in the middle of the room. 'Rupert, how lovely to see you. Good of you to come so soon.' They shook hands warmly.

'After such a wonderfully dramatic return, I thought I

would bathe in some reflected glory. The capital is agog with the pure theatre. You'll be all over the evening papers. Quite the Nelson touch!' Smith enthused.

'A splendid way to let the public know the Navy is still out there, looking after their interests.' Winter smiled. 'Probably have a welcome surge of recruitment after such a display.'

'Well, you do look well on it all. You've caught the sun, a regular bronzed hero, John. The ladies in the city will be beating a path to your door, their hearts a-flutter.'

Winter guffawed. 'Well, a latter-day Lady Hamilton wouldn't come amiss! A final fling before old age. Can I get you a drink, Rupert?'

'Later, perhaps,' Smith answered, sitting down. 'How did your trip go?'

Winter went back to his desk and lit his pipe, suddenly serious. 'The first part was fairly harrowing, seeing the state of Finlay, but against that the short time up from Gibraltar was good. Lovely to catch up on things ... you know, the weapon systems on board these days; probably a little complex for me now.'

'And what of Finlay's health? I've read your reports, of course, but would still like to hear it from you. Is he sane?' Smith asked.

Winter laughed. 'That would have been a difficult question to answer before Kingstone! Seriously though, he seemed OK when I was with him: lucid, coherent, but very chastened. He volunteered that he couldn't be sure what he had told the Russians, but said he had always had control of his inner mind, whatever that might mean. From what he said, there didn't seem to be too much that the Russians didn't know about Kingstone before it got underway. Very disturbing, that!' Winter looked squarely at Smith.

'Does that look mean you think the leak came from my department?' Smith asked, very matter of fact.

'That would be my judgement, Rupert,' Winter answered. 'As you know, we've had a very thorough search here and found nothing, but we still have a weakness.'

'What would that be, John?' Smith asked, a little affronted.

'Civilians,' Winter replied evenly. 'I intend to effect a very harsh "cleansing of the temple", so to speak. I am taking Lady Masham, Assistant Director of Naval Intel, and installing her here. In charge. I'm outing the civilian staff entirely, then bringing in what I need from the Navy. This place will be an entirely naval unit, HMS Narvic, from the second week in January.'

'Good Lord!' Smith breathed.

'You will be the only civilian allowed in; that much has to stay the same,' Winter announced.

'And Miss Grant?' Smith asked, still taken aback.

'Early retirement, with the right terms, of course. The CDS is behind me in this, Rupert. It will happen. We ask our men to go out and risk their lives; I have to make quite certain they have the very best chance of reaching their retirement age.'

'But will you get the funding for this change?' Smith looked doubtful.

'Already in place!' Winter beamed triumphantly.

'So where did this idea come from? It's a little radical, wouldn't you say?' Smith said sourly, seeing part of what he considered to be his empire slipping away.

'An aside ... from Finlay, would you believe?' Winter laughed.

'*That* I would believe!' Smith snorted. 'You be very careful, John. Just mind that young bugger doesn't bite your ass!'

Winter roared with laughter. 'He would never bite me,

Rupert. But your ass will always be in some danger ... Want that drink now?'

Smith nodded, giving the Admiral a wry but friendly smile. Winter kept chatting as he went to pour them a couple of gins. 'Mind you, I don't suppose Finlay will be up to biting anyone's ass for some time. Doctor Williams said he was surprised by his demeanour: calm, not so dismissive as he used to be. Williams was also sure that at some stage, within weeks even, that Finlay would suffer from what he called "slow shock", which might lead to a complete breakdown.'

'Where is he now?' Smith asked, taking the glass Winter offered him. 'Still down at Haslar?'

'No, he's back at his home. I left Robert Keith in charge of his case. We took it upon ourselves to have Finlay discharged from hospital and put under the care of his own doctor, who sees him on alternate days.' Winter picked up a batch of letters. 'These are his reports to me. I've not had chance to read them yet. I have a feeling that Finlay's aunt had a hand in them. The Keiths and Finlay's family go back many years. Mrs Terry is a formidable woman, Rupert, used to having her own way, and some!'

Smith raised an eyebrow. 'Something of a looker, I'm told though.'

'Absolutely stunning, very, very competent, also damned determined and downright autocratic on occasion.' Winter paused, thinking, smiling to himself. He snapped back to the moment. 'Every man's dream, Rupert.'

'The question is, John, what do we do with this paragon's nephew?' Smith asked.

'Too early to say. Certainly we look after him, get him back to rights, keep a fairly tight eye on his progress, then see where we go from there,' Winter said, draining his glass and reaching for his pipe. 'We're a fairly tight community in our valley. One of my gamekeepers, for example, is a long-time friend of Finlay. Perhaps he can keep me informed of Finlay's well being. It's all very incestuous in the country, you know, Rupert.'

Smith seemed to want something more concrete. 'Now we've got him back, we don't want to lose him, John. Finlay is a real pain to deal with sometimes, but he does have that special perception of things.'

'I don't think that will happen, Rupert,' Winter said through a fog of pipe smoke. 'Finlay is a crusader, remember? Duty first.'

'I do hope you are right,' Smith observed. 'There are some busy times coming. Perhaps we should flatter him with a bar to his DSO.'

'Rupert, my friend, do you honestly think Finlay wouldn't see through that? I'll offer him a half ring: Lieutenant Commander Finlay. Has a nice ring to it, don't you think?'

Twenty-Seven

FINLAY'S FIRST FULL day back set the pattern for the next week: up at around seven for a quick bath, breakfast with the stable girls then some gentle walking and fishing.

The doctor came every other day. Finlay felt more than well physically, but was sometimes overtaken with a mild melancholy, which he put down to tiredness – a diagnosis the doctor was inclined to agree with. He was sleeping well enough and untroubled by nightmares. The doctor was happy with his progress.

As daily Finlay got stronger, he wandered further on his walks. On one particular day he went as far as the estate's northern boundary. Crossing the river, he had walked back down the trout stream, a construction project of his own years before. On other days he would sit by the hatch pool, watching that year's late run of salmon as they pushed upstream. Somehow, it was hard to make the reconnection with agriculture. It would come, he knew. He was content for the moment to bond with the entity he had always loved most: the river.

Sunday breakfast was a quiet affair. The stable girls had time off so Finlay and Niney ate alone.

'The place seems so quiet now, Auntie. No people. It all seems so sterile,' Finlay said.

'Ghastly, isn't it? Farming used to be such wonderful fun; now it's all crash bang, get it done. The land is bashed into submission. Everything that is not producing is sprayed out of existence, and then we sit and twiddle our thumbs.' She began to refill Finlay's teacup, the tea splashing angrily into the saucer. 'We no longer have the welfare of our people to think about and the new ones resent it if we try to help them. Patronising, we're called, and there's no Christmas do this year. Such things are frowned upon – they take it as lording it over the peasants.'

'The middle classes are on the march, Auntie. Grandfather always said this would happen. There will be those who hate us and our way of life. Look at the way some are already going on about hare coursing. I shall live to see hunting and coursing done away with ... and I really can't bear the thought,' Finlay sighed.

'Come on, darling, don't let's think about that now. Let's go out somewhere together. We can work towards lunch in Leckford and look over every bridge on our beautiful river. That, at least, hasn't changed.'

They left around ten and drove to Ashe, parked by the church and went to the farm, where they were welcomed with open arms and fed tea and biscuits. Afterwards they walked to a small muddy pool, which was the source of the River Test. 'Hardly what you would think, is it?' Finlay said.

But later, just downstream a little, they parked the car on Christmas Cake Bridge and gazed down into a crystal stream. Finlay went back to the car and found the flask he kept there for Admiral Winter. He emptied the port on the ground and climbed down to the stream and washed the flask out carefully before filling it with the river water. He had just returned from the car again with a small bottle of gin when a little grey Ferguson pulled up.

'Well, bugger me, if it ain't Niney! What you doing all up here?' It was Bert Holmes from Lower Ashe.

'Have a drink, Bert,' Niney said, smiling at him. 'We've come to pay homage to our Lady.'

Bert took the proffered small metal cup and drank the mixture of river water and Gordon's gin. Smacking his lips, he said, 'Here's to better times, the pair of you. I don't think us will see too much more coursing across these downs.'

'For Christ's sake, Bert. We left home this morning to cheer ourselves up. We ain't beaten yet!' Finlay laughed.

'Ah, but these buggers be nasty vicious bastards,' Bert said glumly. 'They don't like our sort.'

'Well, I cannot gainsay that, Bert,' Niney said, her eyes flashing, 'and by the way the new vicar speaks in Romsey, there ain't any hunting or coursing in heaven, so I suggest we all have a bloody good time down here, get on with some serious sinning and we can all go to hell where there will be gin and greyhounds a plenty.' She offered him the cup again. 'Have another one, Bert.'

'No, and you 'ad better work out which one of you is driving, cos if you stop on every bridge between here and Redbridge, you're going to be well puggled,' Bert said, but then he took the proffered drink and downed it as an afterthought.

Niney and Finlay drove on downstream and spent an hour walking along the trackways of Chilbolton Down. The wind was blowing hard from the west, throwing down an occasional scuddy handful of raindrops, still not cold to the touch. The air was clear but not sharp.

They had lunch at the Seven Stars at Leckford: beef sliced generously from the bone, with everything that was available locally. For company at this time of the year there were fellow farmers, keepers and others who loved the river. Then it was on to Mottisfont, where they stopped on Main Bridge and watched the river gliding beneath them, the grayling rising and falling in the current and the few dabchicks and moorhens fussing along the sedges on the banks.

As he watched the fish slip past below him, Finlay's thoughts turned once more to Canavan, to the promise they had made to each other to head to the rivers of Ireland after Operation Kingstone. His mind drifted along with the current: how fast and suddenly life could slip away from you, he thought, making a mockery of one's plans and dreams. Perhaps it was better to keep one's head down and go with the flow, than leap about at the thin edge where the air could be suffocating. He felt that sinking feeling in his stomach at the memories of his friend, and a constriction in his throat that made him cough.

'Come on,' Niney said suddenly, as if sensing Finlay's depression. 'Let's go home. I need a proper cup of tea and the warmth of the Aga.'

JANET CAME BOUNCING over from the stable block as Finlay parked the car.

'Hello, you two, have you had a good day? Where did you go? Down to the beach?' she asked.

'Don't be such a nosey little baggage ... I've been out for lunch with my nephew. And now, I suppose, you want tea?' Niney said, pretending to be very fierce.

'When I've finished,' Janet replied, unabashed by Niney's manner. 'I'll see you in a few minutes.' She skipped down the steps from the front door. From behind she looked like a child of fourteen, slim to the point of thinness, and no discernable hips.

Niney caught the look on Finlay's face. 'I don't know that it would be wise to breed from that one,' she said absently.

'Eh?' Finlay asked.

'You heard!' Niney said softly.

Indoors, Finlay moved the kettle to the hot side of the Aga; it was a ritual, a conditioned reflex. When anybody walked into the kitchen, the kettle, if not there already, was moved over to make it boil.

'Thank you for your company, Auntie,' Finlay said. 'It's been a lovely day, just the two of us.'

'Thank you, darling boy. What a lovely thing to say,' Niney said.

'I could be upset by it, though,' Janet said, kicking off her boots in the passageway. 'You went off early so I couldn't come with you.'

Niney ignored what she said. 'Are you doing evening stables here or back at your yard?' It sounded almost peevish.

'Here. The doctor chap is treating the others to a "cultural evening" at the vicarage, so he volunteered to take the two girls on duty over to my stables in his car, then pick them up later. I thought perhaps, while I had the chance, I would spend a little time with Finlay, without the others being present,' she wheedled.

'Well, you can stay to dinner then,' Niney said: not an offer but an order.

'Hoped you'd say that,' Janet said, kissing Niney's cheek. 'Thank you.'

'Get off, you silly bitch! I'm a bit worried about you, Janet. I mean to say, Ronnie, Les, George and Charlie, do you all want to be men?' Niney had always been tricky about same-sex kissing.

'Are you going to bother to cook tonight, Auntie?' Finlay asked.

'Did it yesterday, Kee! Steak and kidney pie ... got to build you up,' Niney smiled triumphantly, showing Janet how well organised she was. Turning to her, she wrinkled her nose. 'Now, Jan, my angel, not to put too fine a point on it, darling, but you stink! Your clothes reek of horse pee. Before dinner go and have a bath and put some of Kee's clothes on ... I'll run the ones you're wearing through the washing machine.'

'But –' Janet began to object.

'*Now*, Janet. You're making the kitchen smell. Go and show her where your gear is, Kee!' Niney ordered. 'I'm quite sure she can manage to bath on her own.' This last statement was made with the same inflections Niney would have used to state the table needed laying.

'Blimey, Finlay – sent upstairs together with Niney's blessing! We must make the most of this,' Janet laughed.

Niney looked at her watch. 'You have five minutes, Kee, then I shall be up if you're not down. You are not up to wrestling with girls yet!' She half smiled as she shooed them from the room. She waited in the kitchen until she heard them crashing along the top landing, then she removed her shoes and quickly went to the bottom of the stairs, and listened. She could hear muffled conversation and movement, and then Janet hissed urgently, 'No, Finlay. Niney will come up!' She turned back to the kitchen, her face wreathed with smiles. 'My boy is home and back to what he should be.' She looked upwards. 'Thank you,' she said quietly.

Finlay almost followed her into the kitchen. Niney, effecting to be busy in the sink, said over her shoulder, 'Lay up, darling. I doubt Janet will be long. I hope she wasn't offended by what I said.'

'I doubt it, Auntie. She was a little bit smelly,' Finlay laughed.

Janet rejoined them wearing a check shirt and a pair of Finlay's shorts, bare-footed and sweet smelling.

'Honestly, Janet, if you did yourself up a bit, you could be really beautiful.' Niney adjusted the collar on the shirt. 'You must take more care of your looks. See how you've cleaned up ...' She thrust Janet in front of a mirror.

Janet wriggled free of Niney and slumped down at the table. 'Don't you think I know that!' she said almost angrily. 'How long is it since you looked at me like you just did, Finlay? That look you gave me when you first saw me ... that look that says I'm going to screw the ass off of you. My jods smell because I haven't any clean ones, and I've had no time to do any washing.'

'Well, what's your mother up to?' Niney snapped.

'My mother is in The Park at Bursledon and has been these past six weeks.' Janet began to sniffle. 'And I can't cope with everything. I'm bloody well exhausted.'

Niney grabbed her up in her arms. 'You silly little cat, why didn't you tell me?'

Janet again looked like a child. 'You had enough to think about, and you do too much for me now. And anyway, it isn't very easy to admit your mother is shut in a loony bin!' she sobbed.

'My love,' Finlay said, getting up and taking her from Niney. 'I was in a loony bin, as you choose to call it, last week. Your mother ain't crazy, girl, just a bit highly strung.'

'You belong in a loony bin!' She tried to laugh through her tears and runny nose.

Niney handed her her hanky. 'You stay here tonight. We can sort your clothes out tomorrow. Telephone Lesley – she seems the most sensible – and let her know where you are. We'll do the stables with you tonight.' She paused. 'What do they say is wrong with your mother?'

'Just gone over the edge, sort of. Cassy lives in London with three other women, all from deepest Lesbania; where Jo is, God alone knows – haven't heard from her in years; and me,

I'm stuck with my love of horses. My father sends Mum money but wants nothing to do with any of us. She feels worthless.' Janet tried to sound nonchalant. 'The last time we were together here – do you remember? – when Granny Fortune spoke to us all about false tits and false diamonds, well, that was the last time I remember my mum being anything like her normal self.'

'For Christ's sake, Jan, why didn't you say? I knew the house had become a tip, but I didn't put two and two together.' Finlay felt consumed with guilt.

'I think my mother just somehow gave up,' Janet said wistfully.

'Come ... let's eat, and then we can decide how best to cope with the situation. Janet, telephone and let the others know where you are. Kee can drive over to your home after dinner and check all is well, while we deal with things here,' Niney said, happy to be directing operations.

The meal looked wonderful: beef steak and kidney in a gooey sherry-filled gravy, with broad beans, carrots and roast potatoes.

'Eat up now, both of you,' Niney ordered. 'I was looking at you earlier, miss, and thought how skinny you have become.'

They ate in silence, a sure sign of good food. Janet was the first to speak again. 'Are you going to get another horse, Finlay?' she asked.

'Probably. At the moment my Admiral is telling me to take a year off, and who am I to argue with that? I shall have to do something to get back fit,' Finlay answered.

'Niney told me you said you were going to change your job, come home and live –' Janet said.

'No, Jan,' Niney interrupted her. 'He did not *say*; he *promised* me.'

'What I have in mind, both of you, is this,' Finlay said.

'Now that somebody else does the farming, I thought perhaps Carl and I could do up vintage cars and sell them. I did talk to him about it before I got hung up in Russia and he seemed quite keen. He wants to stay with us, and, as you know, Jan, the amount of machinery we now have is nothing as to what it was, so that's my first idea,' Finlay said.

'Well, there's a long time before we have to make any decisions about you, Kee,' Niney said. 'Now, if nobody wants any more to eat, you pop out to Janet's house to see that all's secure and we'll clear up here and then do the stables.'

WHEN FINLAY GOT home later that evening, he assured both women that everything was in order. The horses there had been fed and settled, the house was locked, with just a light on upstairs to deter burglars.

Niney looked at him sadly. 'I think you should get to bed, Kee. You're as white as a ghost and your eyes look like saucers. Janet, I've put you in down the corridor; I would be grateful if you stayed there tonight.' She gave Janet a stern look. 'OK?'

'Oh yes ... sure, Niney. I wasn't with you,' Janet said, feigning innocence. Finlay had made the observation before that green eyes cannot convey innocence as well as blue eyes can.

He went to his bed, tired, his head now muzzy with sleep. It had been a fairly long day. He lay listening to his aunt bathing in the next room, singing quietly. Janet seemed to be making the right bathing noises in his own bathroom opposite ... Sleep overtook him suddenly.

Niney crept into his bedroom a little later and listened to his breathing and looked at his sleeping face. Satisfied, she left for her own room, leaving his door slightly ajar and the passage light burning.

Around two in the morning Janet eased herself into Finlay's bed beside him. Struggling a little, she removed the check shirt she had been wearing to sleep in and lay naked and warm beside him. Finlay was still sleeping deeply, unaware of her presence and urgency. She kissed the end of his nose and licked his face. Finlay slept on, his breathing regular and deep.

'Bugger you, Finlay,' Janet hissed. 'Are you going to wake up?' It was apparent that he wasn't. She snuggled herself into him and, throwing caution to the wind, slept. She wasn't sure what Niney's reaction would be if she found her in her nephew's bed, so blatant after being told to stay in her own.

Finlay's mental and physical exhaustion was profound and deep-seated. For the best part of a year, he had lived minute by minute, aware that each day might well be his last. But each day survived on his way out of Russia was a day nearer to England. Now, at home, when he slept it was the sleep of black oblivion, a state of almost complete unconsciousness. Somewhere deep in his sleeping mind, he felt his left arm was trapped; it was trapped beneath something heavy. His instinct to survive dragged him back to something close to wakefulness. His sleep-befuddled mind refused to tell him where he was and who was there with him. He lay still trying to get his brain working, and eventually it was the sweet smell of Janet's light perspiration that made him remember. He eased his arm from beneath her sleeping form and flexed the aching stiffness from it.

'Are you awake at last, Finlay?' he heard her whisper. 'Christ, how can you sleep? A girl could be offended.' She turned to face him fully, pushing her small pert breasts into his chest. In the spare yellow illumination that came from the passage light outside of the bedroom door, all Finlay could see was the whiteness of her face, skin so pale and fine it had almost an opaque glow in the dimness. She leant forward and pushed her tongue into his mouth, her breathing quickening as she felt for his tongue. He held her gently, stroking the softness of her skin, squeezing the firmness of her bottom and pulling it into him. She began breathing in short gasps as Finlay stroked and touched her. Then suddenly she stopped and stiffened. 'Finlay!' she breathed. 'You've been gone bloody near a year; now will you stop playing pat-a-cake with my bum and bloody well buck up and do your bloody duty!'

She wriggled beneath him, the wetness between her legs warm on his stomach. There was a moment of farce as like two people in a narrow corridor who dodge from side to side to avoid each other, they each went side to side to find each other. 'Keep still!' she ordered sharply and Janet completed the manoeuvre. As he entered her she exhaled one long breath, her head almost hanging over the side of the bed. 'You sod of a bloke,' she whispered. For Finlay there was a sudden and uncontrollable maelstrom in the pit of his stomach, almost a pain, such was the whirling, sharp sweetness of the erupting reawakening of his male sexuality. It seemed to explode around them. All his strength suddenly left him and entered her, leaving him limp and stunned, and her shocked by the sudden intensity of the physical pleasure she felt.

'Now you can sleep,' she whispered to an already sleeping Finlay. She lay beneath him, dozing, until the first hint of dawn appeared above the ash trees at the top of the garden and a wren sang briefly and thinly at the new day. With some difficulty, she wriggled out from beneath Finlay. She could not comprehend the depth of his sleep and wondered briefly if he was ill, but his steady deep breathing allowed her to dismiss the thought.

Finlay woke again well after eight. He felt distinctly odd, light and very stiff. His joints ached desperately and his ears were full with house and yard sounds, horses and laughter.

He felt marginally better after having a bath. His aunt came into the bathroom and scrubbed another helping of the black dust from the Hindu Kush that daily seeped from the skin of his back.

'Your skin is getting better by the day, darling. I cannot bear to see those ingrained dirt marks in it ... Don't forget the doctor is coming today, so I shouldn't bother getting dressed.' When she had cleaned his back to her own satisfaction she said, 'Stand up ... I want to see the burn scar in your side.'

'Auntie ...' Finlay began to object; he did not mind in the least about her seeing him naked, just that she still treated him like a child.

'Do-as-you're-told!' she ordered. The words had always come out as one, as long as Finlay could remember. 'Anything you want to tell me?' she asked in an exaggerated conversational way, studying the weeping hole in his side.

'What about?' Finlay asked, not getting on to her wavelength.

'What we were talking about the other day,' she said more firmly and looking at him squarely in the eyes.

'Ah yes ... um, yes, I see,' Finlay replied. 'It all works ... Yes, it all works.'

'Good ... very good. Janet did seem rather full of herself this morning.' Niney stopped and thought. 'I could have put that better perhaps ... Now, this year off, young man, I want you to take serious account of your life. It's no use just drifting on with Janet, else you'll finish up with no wife, no children and nothing. I know that Janet doesn't want children or to get married, though she adores you well enough and likes the bed bit with you, so cast your bread on the water a little ... I've just met a very nice girl who lives up the river –'

'No, you don't, you bugger,' Finlay laughed. 'She's out there somewhere and will turn up. Don't go pushing it.'

'Only thinking ahead, darling ... I want to see you settled,' Niney continued. 'This young lady – I would like her to come to tea.'

'Auntie, will you give it up, please?' Finlay said, laughing. 'I have a year's leave and I don't intend wasting it playing petty fingers with what you think are suitable young ladies. I'm going to buy another horse. Maybe Janet will let me buy Bee. You see, Auntie, you don't need to marry me off to get me stay. I really don't want to go back to the Service. These past few days have shown me where I ought to be, and that's home.'

As Finlay said this, he really meant it. Inside of him, though, the mindset that drove him, the thing that demanded he serve his country, mocked him vilely. Not only was he lying to his beloved auntie, he was lying to himself.